Mile Forty

By Craig Colboth

I0654174

Chapter 1

Sam White looked down to his watch to see it was just past eight and well past the seven o'clock he told his mother he would be home by. He was two miles from home if he stuck to the highway but only three quarters of a mile if he went through the woods. The moon was rising in the north-east casting an eerie glow over the forest of dense trees and brush. He knew of a trail his friends told him about and with little trouble was swiftly moving on it.

As he went down the trail he could hear the sounds of crickets, the hooting of a distant owl and what sounded like a large animal walking parallel to him just past the tree line. The trail would take him to the railroad tracks that would then lead him into the small hamlet of Riley Wisconsin.

As Sam followed the trail, it took a sharp decrease in elevation when it came along a large swamp. The buzzing of the mosquitoes drowned out any other noises as he made his way toward the tracks. He walked up a slight hill only to go back down to a semi-muddied area. His shoes sunk in causing him to lose his balance a few times. As he climbed another hill, the tracks came into view shining like steel ribbons in the moonlight.

Sam knew he was about to be home free and free of the mosquitoes. As a trail took a sharp right toward the railroad embankment, Sam saw something that caused him to stop dead. His small frame started to shake as his eyes focused on a figure of a young woman. She glowed, but not by the moonlight. Sam was so frightened he could barely breathe. The woman appeared to float on the trail in front of him. He could make out her figure, but not so much her face with her eyes as nothing more than dark holes in the blank glowing face. Her glowing lips were thin, but could easily be made out from the rest of her face. Pulled back into a tight braid that laid across her left shoulder was her glowing white hair. Sam squinted his eyes as the glow from the figure made them hurt as if he was looking directly into the midday sun.

In an instant, the sound of the crickets stopped and the owl could no longer be heard. Even when Sam managed to take a breath, it was silent. Sam was so scared that while his mind was telling him to run, his legs stayed still. The figure moved closer to the frightened boy with not a sound. As she came within five feet, maybe just a little closer... she held out her right hand to him. Sam could feel his heart racing. As almost with no knowledge he started to raise his left hand as if to touch hers. He could see her fingers, her white glowing fingers that appeared to be more bone than skin. Just as his fingers were about to touch hers, a loud blast of a locomotive's horn dumped the boy onto his side.

Sam looked up to see the woman was gone. The sounds of the woods were now alive again as the sound of the approaching train got louder. He quickly got to his feet and ran toward where he had first seen her. She was not there. He ran to the tracks just as the locomotives were passing. He could not see her as he looked toward the direction the train was coming from. He turned his head the other way only to see the locomotives lighting their way through the countryside. A distant searchlight signal turned from green to red as the lead locomotive past it. Sam was shaking both from fright and from the rumbling of the passing freight train.

Sam turned back to the trail, but it was only dimly lit by the moon. The woman was gone. Quickly a pain came over his left arm; he looked at it to see it scraped up by pebbles and mud. He wiped off the debris just as the bay-windowed caboose passed. Sam walked up onto the closest of the two tracks and followed the flashing red light of the caboose. Within a few minutes he was coming back to the highway and only a few blocks away was his home.

Sam walked up the stairs of the porch to see his mother sitting in an Adirondack chair waiting for him. "Sam… what time is it?" his mother asked perturbed. Sam raised his arm to look at his watch, it read nine-thirty. Sam looked at his mother in horror, "Nine-thirty!?" She shook her head in disbelief, "You were supposed to be home by seven… and here it is nine-thirty!" Sam searched around wondering where the time had gone.

"What do you have to say for yourself?" his mother asked. "But mom, I left at eight and I took the shortcut through the woods," Sam stated pleading his case, "I should have been here over fifty... maybe sixty minutes ago!" Before his mother could say another word, the slam of the wooden screen door caused the teen boy to jump as if it was a crack of thunder.

Sam looked to the door to see his sister, Danielle, walking out with can of cola in her hand. "Look whose home," Danielle said with a touch of humor. "I was about to send your sister out to look for you," his mother said as he turned to face her.

"Danielle? No, she can't drive! I don't know who gave her a license," Sam stated. "I can drive just fine you little pimple," his sister said as she sat in the chair next to her mother. "Mom, she's hit so many garbage cans, the car permanently smells like a garbage truck," Sam said with a straight face. "I have not!" Danielle rebutted. "Last week she hit the fire hydrant in front of school," Sam said with a louder tone. "The brakes didn't work!" Danielle yelled back. "They would if you had only pushed the petal!" Sam yelled while holding his hands up as if holding steering wheel only then to jump around as if to crash into a wall.

Before Danielle could get her next barb in, their mother said, "Sam, what is all over you? That's mud! What have you been doing?" Sam looked to his dirty arm with small spots of dried blood, "I fell… when I was on the trail… you won't believe what I saw!" His mother grabbed his wrist, "You even broke the skin. Fell on the trail… you were rough housing. I know I should never let you hang with the Jones boys… rejects just like their parents." Sam shook his head in disagreement, "No, we just played videogames. I fell on the trail, oh, you should have seen it."

His mother stopped him, "What trail were you on?" Sam pointed to the south, "The trail through the woods. I took it to get home faster… I swore it had to be faster." His mother shook her head, "How many times have I told you not to go into those woods? There is a homeless camp back there… who knows what could have happened to you!"

Danielle piped up, "They may have made him a man… of course it would be with another man…" Her mother looked at her, "Shut up, now. Go inside so I can deal with your brother." Danielle got up with a smile, "Hope you will still be able to sit after dad finds out." Sam stuck his tongue out to the young woman as she giggled while walking back into the house.

"Mom, you should have seen her! She glowed!" Sam said with excitement. "What? Who glowed? What the heck are you talking about?" his mother asked. "The woman on the trail, she glowed. She kind of floated toward me." Sam said his eyes big and his skin getting flush. His mother placed her right hand on his forehead, "You must be running a fever, heard the flu is going around…." Sam pulled her hand away, "I don't have the flu… she was… she was beautiful, but I really couldn't see her face." From inside the house came a large laugh, "Sounds like they raided the Jones' liquor cabinet."

Their mother turned toward the open window, "Go to your room, Danielle… Sam, let me smell your breath." Sam gave his mother a queer look, "What?" She moved forward toward him, "Exhale, now." Sam did as he was told and blasted his mother with the breath only a teenage boy could have. "What where you guys eating?" his mother asked with disgust. "Their mom made chili for dinner and we also had potato chips with dip… and later a few corn dogs." His mother placed her head down while shaking it slowly, "Well if you had been drinking you would have surely puked all that up by now."

"Mom I wasn't drinking… she was on the trail just before the tracks. Her hair was braided like an Indian in one of those old movies dad watches on Sunday morning." Sam said again pleading his case. "Just stop right there. I don't want your excuses. Go upstairs, get cleaned up then go to bed. I don't care if it's Friday night, go to bed," his mother said with a cross tone, "Your father is working a double shift so you will be fast asleep by the time he comes home. I am sure he will want to talk with you in the morning."

Sam looked down to the porch floor knowing he was in trouble and starting to seriously doubt what he had just seen in the woods. "Good night, mom," Sam said in a sad tone. As he walked to the screen door his mother said, "Sam, we can keep this between us, but you know your sister will tell your father as soon as he walks in that door tonight. I'll do what I can to make sure he doesn't get upset." Sam looked back to his mother, "Thank you." He was just inside the door when his mom said, "Sam, let's also keep what you saw in the woods between us too." Sam shook his head in agreement then went into the house.

As the late September sun rose slowly in the morning sky, a bright streak of sunlight came through the curtains and landed right on Sam's face. This caused him to open one eye then quickly close it and recoil into his blankets. He moved around to get more comfortable; his underwear tight like it has been every morning for the past two years. The vision he had on the trail less than twelve hours before was replaced by images of Cindy Stewart. The thought of her deep blue eyes like that of the depth of a deep lake and her long blonde hair shining in the summer's sun, caused him to get a warm feeling all over. He could feel his hand slowly going down his side toward his crotch. Just as his hand came close, a large bang came on his bedroom door.

"Get up you little turd, mom made breakfast!" came Danielle's voice through the door. The images of Cindy quickly left his mind only to be filled with hatred toward his older sister. Sam lumbered out of bed, pulled on a pair of sweatpants and an old faded t-shirt. He went downstairs to the kitchen to find his mother flipping pancakes on an electric skillet and his father hiding behind a newspaper. Before Sam could say good morning, his father said with a gruff voice, "Danielle said you were late again last night. Didn't I tell you to be home when I have to work late?" Sam looked at his mother who just rolled her eyes then turned her attention back to the pancakes. "Yes, sir," Sam said with a humble tone.

Elizabeth, Sam's mother, placed a plate of pancakes in front of him. As he reached for the bottle of syrup, his father said, "What do you say?" Sam looked to his mother, "Thank you." Danielle reached for the bottle but was quickly stopped by Sam who pulled it from her reach. She gave him a dirty face as a knock came at the front door. "Go see who that is, Danielle," Michael said. Danielle gave a soft huff then did as she was told.

"It's the brother's Grim," came a yell from the front of the house. "Good God, what are they doing here so early? I don't have enough to feed those three," Elizabeth stated. Michael put his head back in his paper doing his best to avoid the situation. "Sam, go tell them to come back later," Elizabeth said. Before Sam could get up Danielle returned, "I told them to keep their grimy selves out on the porch. And tell that Tommy to quit staring at my boobs!" Sam went past his sister then jogged to the front door.

"Hey guys," Sam said, "My mom asked if you could come back later." Staring back at him were three boys; triples to be exact and they are exactly the same in most ways. Tommy, Johnnie and Donnie Jones were well known throughout Riley. There was no bigger news than when the three were born at the stroke of midnight on Christmas Day. They were also news because the Jones family was known as the types to stay away from. The father knew the inside of a jailcell better than his own bathroom and the mother was just as feisty. Elizabeth and Michael White didn't like Sam hanging with the boys, but he has a hard time making friends so they tolerate them as much as they can.

"Mama gave us money for candy and cokes, we're headed down to the drugstore," Tommy said. "I'm about to have breakfast and I know I won't be allowed to leave until I'm done," Sam said with a sad tone. "Fuck, that's what the candy is for!" Donnie said with sincerity. "Shh!" Sam said, "Don't swear around here. My mom will go ape shit if she hears it. What are you going to do afterwards?" The boys looked at one another then Tommy piped up, "Maybe go to the bar afterwards. Pa knows the owner. He lets us come in and shoot pool or play with the arcade games. He just got Pacman!"

Sam looked back toward the door as he heard his father calling his name. "I'll come down there if they let me," Sam said then walked toward the screen door. "Okay, we'll be there or around," Tommy said, "Say hi to Danielle for me… God she has great tits!" Sam gave a look of displeasure, "Yeah… see you in a bit."

Sam walked back into the house to see his father almost at the door, "So where are they going?" Sam shrugged his shoulders, "Just around I guess." His father placed his right hand on Sam's back and guided him toward the kitchen, "Don't let those boys get you into trouble. They are not on a good path in life. It's not their fault, just look at their jailbird father." Sam walked into the kitchen, sat on his chair and took a bite of his pancakes then said, "These are good."

Elizabeth sat in her chair and as she went to cut her first piece said calmly, "Sam, your father and I would like to have a talk about the Jones boys." She was stopped mid-sentence by Michael, "I talked with him. He'll be more careful around them. They are going to go hang out around town when he's done with breakfast." Sam looked toward his father not knowing why his father was being so nice. "Mike, I thought…," she stopped talking when her husband raised his eyebrow.

"I'll be fine mom, they are not that bad," Sam said between bites. "Ugh, you eat like a pig," Danielle said with disgust. "Tommy said hi by the way," Sam said then winked to his older sister. "Can I be excused?" Danielle asked. "Sure, go get ready. I have some shopping to do downtown. You can come with," Elizabeth said.

Sam finished his plate, drank his glass of milk with one gulp then took his dishes to the sink. "When will you be back?" Sam's mother asked with a slightly stern tone. "Dinner... What time?" Sam asked. "Five o'clock and no later," Elizabeth said. "Okay, I'll be back by five," Sam said and before another word could be muttered, he was flying through the house toward the front door.

"Michael, I though you said you were going to talk with him about those boys?" Elizabeth asked. "You were never a teenage boy. He needs to get out and have some fun. Teenage boys have a lot of energy to expel... physical exercise and cold showers usually did it for me," Michael said with a chuckle. "I'm so afraid they will get him into trouble. They are just no good. What if the police bring him some day or God forbid the hospital calls us?" Elizabeth asked. Michael took a sip of coffee then said, "They are not as bad as their father was at that age. He had already stolen his first car, went to juvie and made it with a girl. Those boys are... well... geeks."

Sam made his way down to the drugstore to find the triplets sitting out on the curb drinking soda. "Hey your old man let you come out into the sunshine," Donnie said as Sam sat on the curb next to him. "Yeah, they pretty much let me do as I want," Sam said, "Hey, you guys ever go through the woods at night?" Tommy, who was the more dominate brother took a swig of cola then said, "Sometimes, why?"

Sam was trying to decide if he was about to say something he would be made fun of for, "Last night I took that trail… well, I saw a woman." Donnie turned toward Sam with giant eyes, "Was she naked?" Sam rolled his eyes, "No dumbass, let me finish. She was, well, I think she was…" Tommy looked over, "She was what?" Sam looked down to a trail of ants crawling through the gutter, "A ghost." The triplets stayed quiet for a second then burst into laughter. "A ghost, what the fuck are you talking about, man?" Johnnie asked.

Sam stood up to walk away. "Come on, sit back down. Tell us what happened," Tommy said. Sam sat back down on the curb as he was asked, "Well she was near the tracks. All white and glowing, it's like she was floating toward me. She reached out to touch my hand… her hand was boney like a skeleton, but had some skin on it. Very white, white skin. Well I reached for her hand but a train came and she was gone." Tommy looked at Sam, "Gone? Like she disappeared?" Sam shook his head in agreement. "Too bad that train came,"

14

Jonnie said, "Maybe she would have screwed your brains out." Sam just shook his head as the boys started to giggle once again.

"Well this is what was really weird, "I didn't get home until nine-thirty," Sam said. Johnnie piped up, "So?" Tommy shook his head, "You really are dumb when it comes to math. He left our house at like eight, unless he walked on his hands he should have been home in twenty minutes taking the trail, stupid. You really think you saw something out there?" Sam shook his head slightly, "Yeah, just don't know what or why I came home so late."

"I have an idea. How much money you have, Sam?" Donnie asked. Sam shrugged his shoulders, "I've been cutting lawns again… four, maybe five dollars I guess." Donnie stood up, "Okay, say you did see a ghost. Maybe there is a way to talk to her." Tommy looked up, "Talk to a ghost… what is Sammy going to do, pay her to speak?" Donnie shook his head, "No dipshit, the psychic out on route two. He could talk to her!" Johnnie chuckled, "You mean that rag head that mom goes to every week asking what the winning lotto numbers will be?"

Donnie shook his head, "Yeah, him!" Tommy hit his forehead with the open palm of his right hand, "How many times has mom won the lotto since going to that fool?" Donnie shrugged his shoulders, "I don't know, but she did buy us that Atari. That thing cost real dough." Tommy shook his head, "Dad got us that Atari the same place he got the VCR and that big screen TV. Somewhere an insurance company had to payout big time." Sam laughed as Donnie gave a naive, blank stare. "Face it, mom is blowing money on horseshit," Tommy said, "That, or he is nailing her." Sam looked to Tommy with horror, "You really think that?" Tommy smiled, "Anything is possible with our mom."

"Come on, what would it hurt?" Johnnie asked. Sam shrugged his shoulders, "I have no problem with it if you guys are up for it." Tommy looked to Sam, "The man is a con, I'm sure of it." Sam looked out onto the dusty street, "What else is there to do today?"

Chapter 2

Past the outskirts of Riley on the route two bypass was a small house understated by a gigantic billboard in its front yard. The sign read in large red lettering 'Sir Francis Abraham – Psychic'. The majority of the town did not pay much attention to the town physic, but he did get good business from those passing through. On occasion one of the locals would pay a visit if they thought a loved one was cheating or to talk with someone who just passed on. In any case, they typically left a little poorer and without the results they hoped to have found.

The boys followed the tracks through town then walked the highway until they reached the house. Sitting under the billboard was a dirty yellow Pinto and a small red British sports car. "You think he's in yet?" Johnnie asked. "Only one way to find out," Sam said then proceeded to lead the group up the broken concrete sidewalk. The front porch was just a slab of sandstone worn from years of foot traffic. They walked inside the open door to find a beautiful woman sitting at a small wooden desk. She was looking at a magazine lying flat on the desk while brushing her long auburn hair.

"We're here to see Sir Francis," Tommy said with his best fake deep voice. "Hold on... I have to see if he is here or not. This is my first day, you know," the woman said with a rough, whisky type of voice while chewing a wad of gum. She got up from the chair revealing her tight jean shorts and white belly shirt. Through a red curtain that hid a back room from view, she went to find the physic.

"Holy crap, did get a look at her?" Tommy whispered to the group. "Man, is she hot. That's the type of woman I need!" Johnnie said with a not so quiet voice. "Shut up! She'll hear you... besides you don't have a chance with a broad like that," Tommy whispered back.

"There is a bunch of kids to see you," the woman said to two men sitting at a table playing cards. Sir Francis was an older gentleman; bald with a rotund structure and a snow-white beard. Next to him was his biological brother, Randy, who was a confidence man in its true definition. "Kids?" Randy asked. "Yeah... a group of kids. Hormone driven boys to be exact," the woman said, then blew a bubble with her gum. "Tell them Sir Francis will be ready in a few moments," Randy said. The woman with a nod of the head and a roll of her eyes left to do as she was told then disappeared behind the red curtain.

"Where the hell did you get her?" Francis asked with disbelief. "Met her at the bar last night. She did things to me that don't even have names for yet," Randy said with a touch of humor. "So, you gave her a job? You know we're not running a cash rich business here," Francis said while trying to keep his voice down. Randy stood up and walked to the curtain. He carefully opened the curtains just enough to get a look at the boys sitting side by side on a beat-up leather couch.

"Jesus Christ, come look at this," Randy whispered. Francis walked over then carefully looked through, "What, is Radio Shack closed today?" Randy did his best to quiet his laughter. "Those kids have no money, get rid of them," Francis said. "Come on; let's have a little fun with them. I'll get the stuff ready. Let's give them a good show," Randy said while handing a white turban to Francis.

Randy walked through a white painted door into another room. Francis sat back down at the table then picked up the playing cards. "I'm ready for my guests... um... what the fuck is her name?" Francis whispered to the door. "Sarah... no Sasha... I think, Sasha," Randy whispered back. "I'm ready for my guests, Sasha," Francis said with a fake Middle Eastern accent.

The curtain opened with the assistance of the woman allowing the boys to walk in. "Ah boys, you have come to ask my services? I am Sir Francis Abraham; medium, physic and teller of fortunes," Francis said, "I am sorry I do not have enough chairs for all of you." Tommy stepped toward Sam and placed his hand on his shoulder, "Sam here is the one to see you."

"Sam, yes, Sam. Please come sit on the chair," Francis said while gauging the boy up, "Now, I must ask for an offering for the Gods... do you have money?" Donnie exhaled loudly, "Shouldn't you know if he has money or not?" Francis swallowed quietly trying to hold back some anger, "Oh no... I do not see things like that. That would be like looking at a woman and seeing through her clothes." Johnnie elbowed Donnie, "That would be awesome!"

"I have five dollars," Sam said then placed the five singles on the table. "The God's, they are happy, all be it, humbly. Now, Sam, what have you come to see Sir Francis about?" Sam looked to Tommy who nodded back. "Well I think I saw a ghost," Sam said bluntly. "A ghost? You saw a ghost? Where did you see this ghost?" Francis asked with skepticism. "Last night on the way home. I was taking a short cut through the woods," Sam said but was quickly interrupted by Francis.

"Yes!! I see... trees. Yes, trees and, um, bushes, yes bushes," Francis said. "She was floating above the ground. I could not make out much about her but she had long braided hair down over her one shoulder," Sam said, "She went to touch me, but the train scared her away." Francis stayed silent waiting for the show Randy was going to put on, but nothing was happening. "The spirit you saw, she

20

was… floating? Yes, yes, floating on air," Francis said waiting for Randy to do something.

"Yeah, she was floating. Can you contact her?" Tommy asked bluntly. "I am sorry boys, the God's; they do not show her to me. I cannot communicate unless they allow me," Francis said stalling. He looked up to see a small red light flashing three times above the door. It went blank then flashed three times again.

"I am very sorry boys, the God's, they are not letting her come through…," Francis said but was quickly shouted down by Tommy. "I told you this was all horseshit," Tommy said angrily. Francis grew irritated, "You leave my house, you little unbeliever. Boys, if you do not have a trusting heart the Gods, they will not talk. This one, he has anger in his heart! He drove the Gods away!" Francis noticed that the light was now flashing in a pattern of one short flash then one long followed by one short.

Francis recovered quickly, "Please, I am sorry for the outburst. Sam, perhaps you could tell me where you had seen this ghost or spirit as they like to be called. I can try to contact her without the God's help." Sam stood up from the chair in anticipation to leave, "West of town, along the tracks. There was a small sign that said forty-one. Right there is the trail and not far down it I saw her."

"Thank you, Sam. Tell you what, return tomorrow with twenty dollars. I should know by then who the spirit is, yes?" Francis said with a reassuring tone. "Twenty dollars? I don't have that kind of dough," Sam said. "Ask you parents; tell them it is for one of those new videogames. Now, I have an appointment in a few minutes. Sarah! Please escort the boys out," Francis said. He waited but the woman never appeared. "Sarah!?" Francis yelled. "I think its Sasha," Donnie said. "Oh yes… Sarah was my old receptionist. Sasha?" Francis yelled with a boiling anger, "Come show our young guests out."

The curtain opened with the woman's assistance. The boys walked out except for Tommy. "Pure horseshit. Nothing but pure horseshit," Tommy said then walked out through the curtain. The painted door slowly opened, "Are they gone?" Francis took his turban off, "Yes they are gone… What the hell were all of the signals for? I thought we were going to have fun with them?" Randy sat down on one of the chairs, "That story… you know, I think the kid really thinks he saw something." Francis shook his head, "I think he did, after too much candy and pizza I'm sure."

"Remember when we were kids and dad told us about Indian burial mounds in those woods?" Randy asked. "Dad told us anything to creep us out," Francis said bluntly. "Yeah, but he even showed me a newspaper article about them. I remember they said they found all sorts of artifacts out there… I bet that stuff is worth money," Randy

22

said with wide eyes. "Is that why you wanted me to ask where he saw his ghost?" Francis asked.

"Yes… come on, go grab that collapsible shovel from the basement and meet me at the car," Randy said with an excited tone. "I'm not going out to the woods on a hot day. You do remember we are cons, right? That kid saw right through me, he knew I am full of shit!" Francis said angrily.

"Dad also said he saw ghosts when he was young," Randy rebutted. "Dad said a lot of stuff…. Do you really think we were helping him plant oregano along the tracks when we were little too?" Francis asked. Randy gave his brother a blank look, "He was not the best man around, but he was our father. I believed in him until they buried him. Now you can either stay or come with me. All I know is, if I find something good and you're not there, you won't get your cut."

The boys were making their way back toward town when a Pinto went flying past them. "Look, that was the car in the parking lot," Sam said. The car slowed to go over the railroad tracks then made a left onto Orchard Street. "Yep, that's the so-called physic," Tommy said. "Wonder who the other guy is?" Johnnie asked. "Don't know. I would rather be with that woman. Man, I would love to motorboat her!" Sam said as the boys broke out into laughter.

"You don't think he's going out to the woods, do you?" Tommy asked. "Why?" Sam asked. "He wanted to know right where you saw her... he's up to something," Tommy said, "Come on, if we run down the tracks we can be there in twenty minutes or so."

"What for?" Sam asked. "Because maybe he knows something we don't. Maybe he was behind what you saw," Tommy said. "There's no way he caused what I saw. She was real, well as real as a ghost can get," Sam rebutted. "In any case, let's go see if they show up there," Tommy said then took off jogging down the tracks. "Come on guys," Sam said, "Hopefully he doesn't get us into trouble."

The pinto pulled on to a small gravel pad just down from the crossing. Randy turned the car off then looked toward the woods, "Those are the only real woods around here, so it must be down the tracks that way." Francis picked up a ratty old baseball hat from the back seat and placed it on his bald head, "I'm giving you a half hour. You find nothing by then, you can walk back home because I'm leaving."

The men got out of the car and walked to the crossing. "No trains at least, let's see if we can find the sign the kid was talking about," Randy said. As the men walked down the tracks they came to a set of block signals and a silver instrument cabinet.

"Hey Randy, look at that shed. It says forty-one point fifteen. You think that means anything?" Francis said slightly out of breath. "Yes. That is the milepost. So, he must have been near milepost forty-one. We don't have far to walk," Randy said with a childish excitement.

The men continued down the tracks until they saw a white sign on a rusty, bent post. It read, '41'. Randy looked around, "There! See though the weeds? The trail." Before Francis could react, Randy was jumping through the weeds onto the trail. "Come on, lard ass!" Randy yelled. Francis lumbered through the tall weeds onto the trail, "Okay, now what?" Randy looked around, "Look for a mound or something raised above the rest of the ground. The Indians buried the dead in a mound." Francis looked at the topography to see nothing but rolling hills along the tracks and into the woods, "Look, the whole ground is hilly. It's just how the ground is, nothing is buried here you idiot."

"Look around for anything that looks odd," Randy said with a touch of anger. "Well you're number one, what else can I find?" Francis said. The men looked around through the thick weeds and brush. The bugs were abundant in the cool shade of the forest and had no problem attacking the two men. Francis was accustomed to humoring his younger brother, but this time was just too much for him. He pretended to look, but for the most past he just kept looking at his watch. He took a step only to feel his foot sink into the ground.

"Randy. Come over here," Francis said with hesitation. Randy walked to his brother who was just off of the trail standing in waist high weeds. "Did you find a mound?" Randy asked. "Oh I found something, but it's not an Indian burial mound," Francis said while pointing to a plot of land that looked to have been dug up recently.

Randy unfolded the shovel and went to start digging. "What are you doing?" Francis cried, "Someone buried something out here and I think we shouldn't be dicking with it." Randy forced the spade into the soft earth then flung the dirt in his brother's direction. "There could be something valuable buried here," Randy said while taking another shovelful of earth. "Randy, stop! We don't know what is there. I think it's best to get out of here before we're seen and the cops are called," Francis said.

Randy turned his back to his brother and continued to dig. Francis stood watch over his brother but kept enough distance to run if someone was to come upon them. Randy was not careful as he flung dirt in all directions. The deeper he dug, the more reckless he became.

The boys, now tired from their running were walking down the tracks coming to the railroad crossing. "Look, there's the pinto," Sam said. "Okay, we need to go down the tracks as quietly as we can," Tommy said, "Sam and I will take the lead, you two hold back a bit and watch for my signals."

The brothers nodded in agreement. As Tommy and Sam walked down the tracks, they tried to be as quiet as they could. The reddish stone ballast was loose in spots and would make a crunching noise when stepped upon, the older wooden ties would creak and pop. With each noise, the boys would look at one another.

"I can hear someone digging," Sam whispered to Tommy. "Yeah, let's go over on that little hill, maybe we can see them from it," Tommy said. The boys carefully walked off of the roadbed and into the thick weeds. They knelt down and spread the weeds to see Randy digging into the earth. The boys remained quiet as they could, while Johnnie and Donnie were still on the tracks.

Randy was now about two feet into the soft earth when he saw something that caught his eye, "Francis." His brother walked into the weeds, but kept his vision on the trail, "What is it?" Randy stood up from the hole, "Bones. Fresh bones."

Sam was opening his mouth but Tommy quickly placed his right hand tightly onto Sam's face. "Come on, let's get out of here," Francis pleaded. "Maybe there is something of value… let me look a bit more," Randy said. "No, let's go!" Francis said with alarm. Johnnie and Donnie were frozen on the tracks as they too could see what was found. They were so froze with fright they did not hear a truck coming up the rails.

Randy bent down and pulled up a pair of jeans that were folded with care. "They look to be women's," Randy said quietly. He reached into the pockets, but nothing was found but dirt. "I don't see any flesh, but the earth smells," Randy said. "I'm begging of you. Put the jeans down and let's go!" Francis said. Randy bent down again and moved some of the soil with his right hand. He could feel something in the earth, it felt like rope. He pushed the dirt away to reveal blonde braided hair. "Oh my God, this is what the kid described." Randy said with shock, "You think that kid did this?" Francis looked down to the hair and few bones unearthed, "No, that kid didn't do this. We need to get out of here before someone thinks we did!" Randy pushed more of the soil away from the hair. He picked up the end in his hand and said with a somber tone, "This is hair, I can feel it."

A yellow hi-rail truck pulled up on the track next to the boys. "Hey, what are you kids doing on the tracks?" the man from the truck yelled. "Holy shit, let's get out of here!" Francis yelled to Randy as he grabbed his arm. Sam and Tommy jumped out of the weeds onto the track and started to run toward town. "Come on you two!" Tommy yelled to his brothers who were still frozen with fright.

Randy and Francis ran down the trail only to come to the marshland. "Where should we go?" Randy asked winded. "I… I don't know," Francis said, "Let's just follow the trail. We can't go back that way." As the men went their way, the boys ran as fast as they could to the crossing. Tommy turned and looked back, "Where did that truck go?" Sam turned, "I don't know, he must have kept going down the rails. Do you think he saw the bones?" Tommy shook his head in disagreement, "No. I think he just thought we were playing on the tracks."

"What about the other two?" Donnie asked, "You think they'll tell the cops about us?" Tommy looked over toward the old railroad station, "No. Those two want nothing to do with the cops. There might be a pay phone at the old station, maybe we should tell the cops." Sam piped up, "Tell them what? That I saw a ghost? They will laugh at you." Tommy shook his head, "No, we'll tell them we were digging in the woods and found some bones. I won't tell them who we are. No one will ever know."

The boys walked the roadbed to the old station. The building was a faded white with peeling brown trim. Near one of the boarded-up windows was a pay telephone. Tommy reached into his pocket and pulled out a dime, "Who wants to make the call?" Donnie shook his head, "Not me! It's your idea, you call them." Tommy rolled his eyes then placed the dime into the phone. He placed his finger at zero then spun the dial.

"This is the operator. How may I direct your call?"

"Riley police," Tommy said softly.

"Riley police. Is this an emergency?"

"Um, no I don't think so… we were digging along the tracks and found bones. Human bones."

"What? Wait, you saying you found a human body? Where?"

"On the tracks way south of the old station. Look for the sign that says forty-one and it will be off in the weeds." Tommy hung the phone up, "There, let's get out of here."

Chapter 3

The afternoon heat was building while Officer Stanton Smith sat in his squad car outside the drugstore. It was a boring late summer Saturday afternoon while he was doing his best from nodding off to sleep. As a way to hold off the drowsiness, he would watch flies coming in and out of the open windows. Counting them as they came and went.

Just as his eyes started to close, the radio caused him to jump.

"Car one one five"

"This is one one five," Stanton said trying not to yawn.

"Call the station please."

"Ten – four"

"What the hell do they want now," Stanton said to himself as he opened the squad car door. He walked into the drugstore to see the young, attractive cashier counting the money on the counter. "You shouldn't be doing that, someone could come in and grab the whole till," Stanton said with authority. She placed her hands down on the glass counter, "With you sitting out there all afternoon?" The officer gave an uncomfortable smirk, "Can I use your phone, please?"

Without saying a word, the cashier reached under the counter to retrieve the phone and placed it on the counter. Stanton picked up the receiver then keyed in the number. "It's Smith," Stanton said. A woman's voice came back to him, "We just had a hang-up call. Probably just a prank… anyways, they said they found a body."

Officer Smith turned away from the cashier and asked softly, "A body?" There was a long exhale, "I'm sure it was kids goofing around, but he seemed pretty adamant and gave where to find it. He said along the tracks, far south of the station. Look for a sign that says forty-one." Stanton grabbed his notepad from his shirt pocket and wrote down the description, "I'll go check it out… let you know over the radio what I find."

Stanton placed the receiver down on the phone, "Thank you for use of the phone." The cashier slightly rolled her eyes then went back to counting the money. "Would you like me to stay until you're finished?" Stanton asked. The women looked up, "No, now you made me lose count!"

The officer walked out into the heat to see the town dead just like he left it a few minutes before. He got into the squad car, backed out and drove down the main drag toward the old train station. As he came to the tracks, a yellow Pinto passed him going in the opposite direction. He turned on to the gravel pad then grabbed his walkie before exiting the car.

"This is at least something to do," Stanton said out loud as if someone was there to hear him.

He walked to the tracks to see nothing was coming. As he started walking south on the tracks, a mirage hovered over the rails causing them to blur into the distance. Stanton walked carefully down the center of the set of rails looking for both the sign and anything out of the norm.

He came to the block signals, looked around, but did not find anything but a broken lens on the ground. "Someone must have shot it out," Stanton said out loud then looked up to the signal to see that a new lens was in its place. He continued his slow pace down the tracks until he found the milepost sign. Through the weeds he could see the path that cut into the woods and marshland.

Stanton carefully looked around before entering the weeds; the grasses were thick and an occasional thorn bush bristled out. He knocked the weeds down with his boots to better gain access to the trail. Once there, he looked around seeing only the trail and more weeds. "I don't see a thing," he thought to himself. A warm breeze blew through the trees causing the sun to dance around the underbrush. With the breeze came a strong, earthy smell; a smell that caused Stanton to stop and take notice.

The wind was coming from the southwest, so that was the direction he started to move in. With the assistance of his boots, he crushed down the weeds and grasses. He was only in six steps when he found what looked to be a freshly dug hole in the ground. He moved the dirt around, but only found dirt with a particular odor.

Stanton pulled the portable radio from his belt and pushed the button, "Dispatch… this is one one five."

"Go one one five."

"This appears to be unfounded. Someone has been digging in the woods, but I do not see anything other than dirt."

"Ten- four"

Stanton placed his walkie back onto his belt then turned to walk back to the trail. He noted clumps of dirt spread throughout the weeds, as if flung with little care. As he stepped away, one clump of earth caught his eye. He bent down to pick it up. The dirt felt very cool in the hot, humid air. It too had a particular odor to it. He crumbed it in his hand allowing the dirt to break apart and filter through his fingers. As the clump became smaller, something hard appeared.

Stanton opened his hand and with his thumb moved the remaining soil around to find a gold ring. It was small in diameter; like something a teenage girl would wear. On it was a tiny amethyst stone. He cleaned the dirt off to see if there was an inscription, but there was none. He found that the gold itself was just plating, because in one spot the gold was worn away.

He stepped back to the hole and knelt down. He moved the dirt allowing his fingers to sink into the soft soil. At first his pass he did not feel anything, but as he moved his hand back, he felt something. He put his fingers around the object and gently pulled it out of the earth. As the object arced out of the soil, he knew exactly what it was, a rib bone. It was short in length and small in diameter. "Son of a bitch," Stanton said out loud.

He grabbed the radio from his belt and as he was pushing the button he said, "One one five… send me the ten – seventy-nine to my location."

"Say again one one five?"

"I need the coroner to my location, now. Send a detective also."

"The Coroner? Ten – four"

Stanton gently placed the bone back right where he pulled it out. He walked around in the grasses and weeds; knocking them down to look for clues. Amongst the weeds were more clumps of dirt, some were almost ten feet from the grave. Nothing appeared to be significant, but he knew that was not his decision to make.

He walked back to the railroad tracks to see the distant glow of a headlight. As the train came closer to the distant crossing, it blew its horn. The sound, even at the far distance caused Stanton to jump. He stood in the weeds as the locomotive quickly came toward him. As it and the rest of the train passed, the wind generated cooled the middle-aged police officer. As the caboose passed, Stanton removed his radio once again to call the dispatcher.

"One one five."

"Go one one five."

"Can you ask the phone company to run a trace on the phone call your received?"

"Ten – four. The requested units are in route to your location."

"Ten – four dispatch"

Stanton just placed the radio back onto his belt when another unit called him

"D - seven to one one five"

"Go ahead D - seven," Stanton said as he quickly jerked the radio from his belt.

"I am at your squad car, where are you located?"

"Take the tracks south. I will stand between them so you can see me."

"Hope there are no more trains, officer."

Stanton looked down the tracks to see the caboose now fading into the mirage and nothing coming on the other set of tracks. He did as he said he would and walked onto the roadbed and stood between the tracks waiting for the detective to arrive. Shortly he could see the figure of a man walking toward him as cars passed on the crossing.

As the man came closer, he could see the light blue shirt the man wore, covered with sweat stains. "Officer Smith?" the man said slightly winded. "Yes, Sir. Stanton Smith," he said while trying not to stare at the large white rings growing on the light blue shirt. "God damn is it hot out today," the detective said, "I am Detective George Norris by the way." The sweaty man reached forward to shake the officers hand, but stopped short when he noticed the dirt on his hands.

"Have you been digging around the scene?" the detective asked with a raised tone. "Yes sir. The caller stated there was a body, but nothing was found but an open hole in the ground. I picked up a chunk of dirt and found a ring in it," Stanton said as he retrieved it from his pocket to give to the detective. The detective took the ring and studied it carefully. "Looks to be from a young woman or teenager. Very cheap… probably costume jewelry. Is this all you found?"

Stanton slightly shook his head, "No. After I found this I examined the hole more carefully. I ran my fingers through the soft earth and pulled out what looks to be a rib bone. I placed it back down where I found it."

"Okay, show me the hole, as you call it," George said while wiping sweat off of his forehead with the back of his left hand. He followed Stanton into the weeds and then onto the trail. "There… just through those weeds is the hole. Looks to be freshly dug up, but other than the one rib, there is no other sign of anything," Stanton said.

The detective walked into the weeds to find the hole as Stanton described. He bent down to pick up the rib. "I have no idea if this is human or not. Shit, it could be anything… You wanted the coroner just because of this?" George asked with an angered tone. "I only ran my fingers through the loose soil, I do not know if there is not more buried deeper," Stanton said pleading his case. George walked around looking at the soil.

"There are only one set of shoe prints and I am guessing those are yours," George said, "lift up one of your feet so I can see the tread." Stanton did what was asked of him and placed his left boot so the detective can look at it. "Yep, looks like a match," George said, "Okay, so let's say a body is or was here, how did it get dug up? There are no animal prints. The clumps of dirt look as if they are from a spade. If it was just dug up, where are the person's foot prints? The dirt looks to have been shaped or flattened out except for where you ran your fingers. Maybe they used the back of the spade to level the dirt."

Stanton looked at the hole then the surroundings, "The weeds were trampled down when I came, but I did trample them more. Perhaps some shoe prints can be found under the weeds?" George looked down and then moved some of the weeds with his shoe, "I don't know. Perhaps the trail offers something." He walked back out of the weeds then looked at the dirt path, "I can see something, but this dirt is rock hard. The chance of someone sinking in enough to make a print is slim."

A call came from the tracks that cause both men to look up. "Is anyone there? Someone call for the coroner?" the voice said. George piped up, "Yes, follow my voice through the weeds onto the dirt path." A thin, wiry man walked through the weeds carrying a black bag like that of a doctor. "Hi Eric, how's June doing?" George asked with an upbeat tone. "Oh, she's good. Staying with her sister in La Crosse this week, giving me some peace and quiet… Hello officer. Don't seem to know you," the coroner said. "Officer Stanton Smith this is Coroner Eric Locke," George said, "Eric we haven't much other than a ring and a rib bone. Haven't dug around to see if there is more buried."

"Where is the bone?" Eric asked. "Here near the grave," George said while stepping into the weeds. He bent over, picked the bone up then gave it to the coroner, "Is it human?" Eric studied the bone, "It does appear to be, but I'll have to do further analysis to confirm. If human and depending on the location in the rib cage, I would say this is from a teenager, maybe slightly younger." George pulled the ring out of his pants pocket, "This was the ring found. I would think this is from a teenage girl."

Eric took the ring and studied it, "Looking at the loop size, yes, a teenager. I have shovels in the back of the van. Officer, could you retrieve them for me?" Stanton nodded in agreement then took off through the weeds. "He's kind of green, isn't he?" Eric asked. "I would say so, at least when it comes to a death investigation. Don't have too many of them around these parts, thankfully," George said, "I guess someone called this in, said they found a body. Other than a bone and a ring that were not out in plain sight, there was no body. So where did it go?" Eric looked around, "Looking at the coloration of the soil, something was here. Something that is now gone. Perhaps your caller took the remains?"

"If that is the case, why call?" George asked. "Might be one of those guys who like to toy with the police," Eric said with a chuckle. "No, my gut tells me someone placed this body here so as not to be found. Somehow it was found and the person who placed it here took it to rebury or at least hide," George said then smacked a mosquito that was biting his neck.

Stanton was within a few yards of the crossing when he was called on the radio. "This is one one five."

"The phone company came back with that trace. Said it was a pay phone at the old train station."

"The train station? Okay, ten-four"

Stanton went to a white van that was parked next to his squad car. He opened the back door to find two shovels laying on the floor next to a stretcher. He picked them up then closed the van door. As he turned around he looked toward the old train station in the near distance. Across the tracks was the Economy Grain and Feed where a man was loading his truck with a tow motor. After looking for oncoming traffic, Stanton jogged across the road and railroad tracks. He walked up to the truck the man had just finishing loading.

"Hello Officer, what can I do for you?" the man asked. "Did you happen to see anyone using that payphone over at the old train station?" Stanton asked. The man looked over to the station, "That one over there? No, I do not remember seeing anyone." Stanton placed the points of the shovels down onto the ground, "It would have been about an hour or so ago."

The man shook his head, "No, sorry Officer. I do not remember seeing anyone over there." Stanton picked the shovels up, "Thank you anyways. Anything else seem out of the norm today?" The man shrugged his shoulders but did not say anything.

Stanton started to walk away when the man shouted, "Officer… there was these two guys…" Stanton turned around quickly, "Two men?" The man took a handkerchief out of his pocket and wiped his forehead and neck down, "Yeah, over where you are parked there. I had another truck in then… maybe two hours ago, I believe. It was a puke yellow car, a Ford maybe. Well two guys got out, a real fat one and a real skinny one. They took off down the tracks."

"When did they return?" Stanton asked. "Don't know. After I loaded him I went into the office to cool off. The car was still here then," the man said as he pointed toward the squad car. Stanton pulled out his notepad from his pocket and started to write down what the man told him. "Do you remember what they were wearing?" Stanton asked. "No, sorry, I can't. One had a hat on but I do not remember which one. Just a baseball hat I guess," that man said. "Okay, if you think of anything else, please call the station and ask for Officer Smith," Stanton said as he placed the notepad back into his pocket. The man shook his head in agreement while again remaining quiet. As Stanton started to walk away he looked at the shovels in his right hand, "Hey, did they have anything with them? Like a shovel?" The man squinted as he thought, "Yes… yes they did. They had one of those old foxhole shovels. I remember now. I saw the skinny one with it and thought to myself, I haven't seen one of those since I was in France during the war."

Stanton shook his head, "Thank you for the help. You going to be here for a bit? I may have someone who would like to speak with you." The man looked at his watch, "Yes, about another forty-five minutes or so." Stanton waved then took off at a fast pace back to the detective and coroner.

In no time he was down the tracks and telling the detective what he had learned. "A fat man and a skinny man... no clothing description other than one had on a baseball hat and they had a foxhole shovel. Well, it's a start... I guess," George said, "Officer, you are a might younger than us old men would you like to move some of that dirt around for us?" Stanton was not enthused but was willing to do what was asked of him.

Stanton stepped down into the hole carefully then looked back to the coroner, "Just start digging?" The corner pointed to one corner on Stanton's right, "Start there and carefully, gently, start to pull the soil back. If there are more bones, I do not want to disturb them until I can get some photographs." He did as he was told and carefully started to pull the soil back. As he did, the earthy smell took a much more unpleasant odor.

"I know that smell anywhere," George said. "Yes, but I think it was from the decomposition of what used to be here. I do not see any signs of the body, no more bones," Eric said. Stanton continued to pull back the soil gently, creating a small hill that was now covering his boots. "That smell... Oh man, is it horrible," Stanton thought to himself. "Stop," Eric said sharply," Right near the tip of the spade... see that?" Stanton looked down, "What?"

"I see it, a tooth," George said while removing a small paper envelope from Eric's bag, "Take this and use it to carefully put the tooth inside without touching it with your fingers." Stanton took the envelop and bent over to find the tooth. Right were the men pointed it out, the tooth laid on its side. He opened the flap of the envelop and used it to scoop the tooth inside. He passed it to Eric who quickly allowed it to slide out to be seen, "This tooth was loose before the victim was murdered... God, she still had a baby tooth."

Stanton was now feeling that he wished he was not there. He took the shovel and continued to move the soil. As he did, nothing was seen but the black fertile earth and the occasional off-color spot. "That staining was caused by the decomposition," Eric pronounced. "How long you think she was dead?" George asked. "I don't know. The smell leads me to think she was here for not too long of period. We've had some good rains that past few weeks. The moisture would bring the bugs out... they would make short work of a small body," Eric stated with his best educated guess.

George looked to Stanton who was now a very flushed white, "Why don't you climb out of there and go get some fresh air." Stanton shook his head, "No, no... I'm fine." Eric pointed to the officer, "You may be fine but if you vomit in my crime scene, I'll have you catching dogs until the cows come home." Stanton pushed the shovel off to the side and stepped out of the hole. As he walked toward the tracks, Eric jumped down and started to sift through the soil with his bare hands.

Stanton made it to the tracks and seeing nothing was coming, sat down on the closet rail. The sun was beating on his head causing it to turn a dark red in little time. He didn't want to look like a wimp, but the creosote smell of the wooden ties was far better than the smell of human rot. The sound of insects buzzing silenced the sound of the men talking and occasionally laughing as they worked the crime scene. Stanton looked to his watch to see that about fifteen minutes had passed. He stood up to walk back to the hole when the two men emerged out of the weeds.

"There was nothing else to find," George said, "You can clear if you like. I would like your report on my desk by Monday morning." Stanton shook his head in agreement then asked, "Now what?" Eric gave him a blank look, "What do you mean?" Stanton pointed to his bag, "What about the girl, how do we find what happened to her and more importantly who buried her?"

"Well we don't have much to go on. I will look at the missing reports and if any fit the age range I think she, if it was a she, was in. I will then ask for dental records, but one tooth is very hard to match since it was in good condition. If it was cracked or broken, it would be easier to match… that is if it was on the x-ray or in the dental files,"

Eric said with conviction, "Sorry Officer, but we may never know who she was."

"There must be something that can be done!" Stanton exclaimed with disbelief. "Officer, this is not a movie, this is real life. We do not solve murders in sixty minutes. We can only do what we can with what we have... which isn't much," George said bluntly. "What about the two guys who were seen coming down the tracks?" Stanton asked. "What about them? They could have been doing anything. I will talk with the gentleman at the feed store, but I think that is a dead end," George said as he started walking down the tracks toward his car. Stanton stood his ground in disbelief as he watched the older men slowly disappear down the rails.

Chapter 4

With a shower of gravel and clouds of dust, Sir Francis flew into his driveway. He slammed on the brakes managing to skid to a stop inches from the rear bumper of Randy's sports car. "God damn you!! You almost hit my fucking car!" Randy yelled as he stepped out of the Pinto then slammed the door as hard as he could. "You!" Francis yelled, "You and your stupid scams. I hope the police are not on their way here right now to arrest us!"

"The cops are not on their way here. They don't know anything about that body. Shit, we didn't even do anything wrong!" Randy yelled as he checked his car carefully. "We unearth a body!" Francis yelled as he gestured wildly with his hands. "So, we found a body. Is that illegal?" Randy asked innocently. Francis held his fists in the air as he let out a blood boiling scream. "You are the dumbest person placed on this planet! Do you know that?!" Francis yelled like a bratty child, "No, I take that back. I am the dumbest for putting up with you and your stupid get rich quick schemes! Even when you were in diapers you were stealing coins from my piggy bank."

Randy clinched his teeth, "Well stupid here is the one who made a simple con into a business that has kept that gut filled for over twenty years." The yelling emulating from the parking lot caused Sasha to come out to investigate. "Well the cut was never fair! You're driving an MG while I drive a

47

phlegm yellow Pinto!" Francis yelled back. "Hey, what's going on?" Sasha asked. "Oh look! Your newest vagina has arrived. Please tell me, how much did my brother promise to pay you for your services?" Francis asked of the stunned woman.

Sasha stood with her mouth wide open not knowing how to defend herself. "Wow, look at that mouth. Now I know why my loser brother felt compelled to give you a job," Francis said with venom. "Leave Sarah out of this," Randy stated. "It's Sasha!" Francis yelled, "You don't even know her name!" Sasha threw her arms in the air, "I don't need a job this bad. You two are nuts!" Randy tried to stop her as she was walking down the driveway toward the street, "Leave me alone... you weren't even that good in bed. I only screwed you because you said you had a job for me." Randy stood slack jawed as he watched the firm, well sculptured derriere of the woman walking to the road. "Let her go," Francis yelled, "there is one like her on every block after ten o'clock."

"Well thanks a lot, asshole," Randy said to Francis, "I was actually feeling something for her." Francis smiled, "That feeling can easily be cured with penicillin. Now I am going inside and pray no one turned us into the cops." Randy grabbed the shovel out of the car, "No one called the cops! Whoever was yelling, wasn't yelling at us... I wonder who he was yelling at?"

Francis shook his head, "Don't know... he said you shouldn't be on the tracks... wait..." Randy looked off to the side as he computed the answer in his brain, "Someone was on the tracks... right near us?" Francis's eyes grew large, "No he said, what are you kids doing on the tracks." At once the brothers stated in chorus, "Those kids!" Francis pulled the baseball hat off of his head then threw it at his brother, "You and your stupid scams. Those kids probably saw the body and have already ratted us out to the cops!"

Randy shook his head, "You keep thinking we did something wrong. All we did was do a little exploring... so we came across a shallow grave. There is no crime in that." Francis walked right up to within a hairs distance from his brother, "There is when you're trespassing on private property and you do not disclose that you have found a body. You better pray those kids are at home right now eating potato chips or beating off to some music video."

Randy stepped back from his fuming brother then smiled, "You are not seeing the big picture here." Francis' eyes had become pinpoints as the anger boiled in him, "The big picture? What the hell is the big picture?" Randy stepped back toward his brother and said in a charming tone, "That kid might actually be physic." Francis walked past Randy, picked his ratty old hat up off of the ground and once again threw it at his brother, "Who the fuck cares?!"

Randy picked the baseball hat off of the ground and knocked it against his leg to release the dust and dirt. He then gave the hat to his brother. "Just imagine if he really has physic powers... Think of how we could exploit that." Francis shook his head, "There you go again; another scam, another con. He's a fucking kid who probably saw swamp gas that he thought was a ghost. There are no ghosts! There are no spooks or spirits of whatever you want to call them! God, you would think you would know that by now." Randy shook his head in disagreement, "He had to have seen something. Right near where he saw the ghost, we found her grave. Shit, her hair was even braided like he said the ghost had."

Francis shook his hat toward his brother while staying mute with raging anger then turned and walked inside the house with more anger than one man could bare. Randy stood there and yelled to the now closing door, "We could be rich! Who knows what that kid could tell us... maybe even vault combinations!" Randy watched as the door slammed shut following with the sound of the deadbolt latching. He looked out toward the road to just see Sasha in sight, "Oh Shit... Sarah!"

"Why are you just picking at your food?" Elizabeth asked Sam. "He's being his normal nerdy self," Danielle said with a chuckle. Sam looked at his sister then back down to his plate of mashed potatoes, corn and an undisturbed pork chop. "Sam, listen to your mother and eat your dinner," Michael said bluntly. Sam looked up to his father, "I'm not really feeling well. Can I go lay down?" Sam closed his eyes as he grabbed his stomach with his right hand.

Michael looked to Elizabeth then back to Sam, "Your stomach hurts?" Sam looked down to the plate then back to his father, "My stomach... I think I'm going to be sick..." Sam jumped up from his chair and ran for the half bathroom under the stairs. In the distance the remaining members of the family could hear Sam vomiting. "I knew it, the flu is going around," Elizabeth said as she stood up from her chair. "I better not get sick because of that little pest," Danielle said bluntly, "I have a date tonight." Michael looked at his daughter then shook his head in disbelief, "Your compassion speaks volumes of your character."

Elizabeth went to the bathroom door waiting for it to open. "Honey, are you okay?" Elizabeth asked as she lightly knocked on the door. There was a moment of silence then Sam answered, "I'm fine... I just want to go to bed." Elizabeth twisted the doorknob then gently pushed the door open, "Go on up, I'll check in on you in a little bit." Sam did as he was told and went upstairs directly to his bedroom.

Sam closed his door then sat on the bed. From there he looked out his window to see the sky turning a dark amber color as storm clouds approached. He laid back on the bed without taking his clothes off. It wasn't long before he slowly closed his eyes. All Sam could see was the remains of the body. He could even smell it with such clarity, he could taste it. Every time that smell came back to him, his stomach felt as if it was trying to crawl out through his throat. He did his best to clear his mind; to think of anything other than that rotting body in the woods.

Sam started to drift to sleep as he slowly cleared his mind. With the veil between awareness and sleep lifted, he dreamt of his crush, Cindy. A dream started that seemed so realistic, so vivid; he knew it must be true. Cindy was sitting at the foot of his bed as he woke. The breeze from the window caused her long hair to flow to her back and twist around as if it was braiding itself. Sam sat up and reached for her hand. As Cindy came closer, she started to fade. Sam tried his best to grab her hand, but it was as if the length of the bed was starting to expand. The harder he tried, the further away she was.

"Cindy, reach for me," Sam pleaded. She tried by reaching out to him, but it was just no good. A large rumbling noise was starting to take the room over. Cindy was speaking, but Sam could not hear because the rumbling was now deafening. Suddenly Cindy began to glow with an intensity that caused Sam to shield his eyes with his right hand. Cindy's form was now completely faded in the brilliant light.

So bright was the light that Sam could even see the bones in his hand. He closed his eyes, but it was no good. His ears felt as if they were bleeding from the rumbling that was so strong he also felt it in his chest.

As if a switch was flipped, in an instant the sound stopped and the blinding light disappeared. Sam opened his eyes to see he was no longer in his room. He was now in the woods however it was not like the woods as he knew it. There were no bugs, there were no musty smells. The trees were not wildly grown like normally seen in the woods; it was as if they had been grown to create geometric shapes. Even the leaves seemed perfect, far too perfect.

As unsure as he was, Sam decided to explore his new surroundings. As he walked, his feet were silent. You did not hear the rustling of fallen leaves or the cracking of branches; there was just silence. The silence in itself was overwhelming and frightening. As Sam rounded a tree he saw a young woman. However, it was not Cindy, but the spirit he had seen the night before. She floated near a field of vivid wildflowers. Sam was so scared, but yet, he was now feeling at peace in this place. As he came closer, she turned to him, yet unlike the night before the spirit now had a face; a very beautiful face. "You've come to see me," the spirit said.

"You're the one from last night… in the woods," Sam said. "Yes," the spirit said with a sweet voice. "You were the one found today, weren't you?" Sam asked. "No," the spirit replied with a now somber tone. "Who are you?" Sam asked. The spirit turned to the flowers and looked out across the thousands of acres of beautiful, brilliant colors, "I'm forty," she said. Sam walked to the floating woman and asked, "Forty? Your name is forty?"

The spirit turned to him, her face was now that of a skeleton that howled, "No!" Sam stepped back, "Who are you?" The spirit shot toward him then grabbed his arms with her boney fingers, "Cindy!" Sam was in pure horror, as he tried to get away, the boney fingers dug into his skin. "You're not Cindy! Let go of me!" Sam pleaded. "Find me… I'm forty!" The skeleton yelled as insects started to crawl out of its mouth.

Sam used all of his strength to break free of the spirit. With a large cracking noise, the arms of the spirit ripped free of its body yet still were heavily clamped onto Sam's arms. As Sam yelled and screamed, the rumbling returned. As if a cannon was fired next to him, a deafening roar came at his side causing him to jump out of his bed to his feet. The room was now dark until a brilliant flash of lightning caused the room to glow briefly followed by a cannon like rumble.

Sam's heart was racing, he was lightheaded and his limbs were shaking. Rain was beating against the window and the wind was causing his house to creak and moan. Sam looked out the window to the

54

dark yard just in time for another flash of lightning. Much to his fright, the lightning illuminated many young women and girls standing in the yard. Sam ran to the window placing the palms of his hands on the glass. He waited for another flash; seconds went by… then the wanted flash came, yet now they were all gone.

Sam ran to his desk and pulled a note pad out of a drawer. He opened it up and with a pencil wrote, "Cindy 40" He placed the pencil down then went back his bed. He sat down while listening to rain beat on the house. His head hurt from the dream and the confusion it was causing. From the hallway he heard, "Sam… Sam!" When he turned to answer, there was another brilliant flash followed by the view of his nightstand as if on its side.

"Sam, how are you feeling?" He rolled over to see his parents standing at the foot of his bed. "I was asleep," Sam said. "Yes, you were really rolling around. Were you having a nightmare?" Elizabeth asked. "I really do not remember," Sam said. Elizabeth walked up and placed her left hand on his head, "You don't really feel warm. Maybe you got too much sun today?" Sam yawned, "I guess so. I'm tired but I don't feel like sleeping." Michael walked to the window, "Looks like a storm is coming. Bet it will keep you up anyway."

"Well we're heading to bed, "Michael said, "If you need anything, come get us." Sam yawned again, "Okay. See you in the morning. Please leave the light on for now." Once his parents left the room, Sam got out of bed to take his clothes off. He threw his shirt into the corner of the room where his book bag laid against an old toy chest. Next, he took his jeans off and went to throw them over the back of his chair. As he did so, he noticed his notepad on the desk. As seen in his dream, the notepad read, "Cindy 40" A shiver went down his spine as he said to himself, "It was just a dream... it was just a... dream." He placed the notepad back into the drawer then walked to window. He looked out to the dark yard as flashes of lightning could be seen on the horizon.

He cracked the window to get some fresh air then sat down on the floor and laid his head against the window trim. He looked down the block to the small ranch home were Cindy Stewart lived. His school boy crush was becoming full unrequited love. The distant rumble of thunder caused him to look out toward the horizon where the flashes were becoming brighter and more frequent. He could feel himself becoming drowsy. His head started to slump when a bright flash of lightning caused his eyes to open. He looked out to the yard to see the young women standing there once again. Each one held a sign, like that of the milepost along the railroad tracks, each one had a different number. He could see their faces; he could see their pain. His heart was again racing when another bright flash came so vivid he was blinded.

Sam opened his eyes to see the white ceiling of the living room. He turned his head to see his father watching a college football game on the television. "Hey, sleeping beauty... mom wants you to set the table," Danielle yelled from the dining room. He looked back toward the ceiling trying to understand what had just happened. "Sam, you heard your sister. Go get moving on that table," Michael said. Sam pulled himself up from the couch, "I have to use the bathroom first... I'll be right there!"

Sam went up the stairs to his bedroom. He opened the desk drawer to find the notepad blank. "Forty... what the hell is forty. Man, what a fucked-up dream," Sam said to himself. He went back to the hallway so he could go to the bathroom. As he passed through his doorway he heard in a whispering voice, "Forty."

Chapter 5

"What is forty?" Tommy asked. "Don't know, she said she was forty. She was really bitchy about it too," Sam said while flinging rocks out onto the road. The pair were walking down a neighborhood street on a sultry Sunday afternoon. "Was her name Cindy or do you think she was Cindy?" Tommy asked as he threw a rock at a beat-up stop sign. Sam shrugged his shoulders, "I really don't know. That was the most screwed up dream I have ever had." Tommy chuckled, "At least it didn't have any clowns in it." Sam picked up another rock to throw at the stop sign, "Nope."

"She wasn't the Cindy you like to dream about, was she?" Tommy asked with a chuckle. Sam remained quiet as he sat down on the curb. "You know; you are too into that girl. She only likes the jock types," Tommy said with conviction. "I don't know if she really likes anyone. She always hangs with the girls. Every time I try to talk with her," Sam said but was interrupted promptly by Tommy. "Mary Beth jumps in to stop you?" Tommy said in an angered tone. Sam shook his head, "Yeah, every damn time."

"Mary Beth Collins is a real bitch. I think she is butch anyways. You know, that might be why she cock blocks you all the time, she wants Cindy to herself," Tommy said then started to laugh. Sam looked off down the street and remained quiet. "I heard my parents talking last night, the cops did find the body," Tommy said.

"How do they know? Did they actually say the cops found a body?" Sam asked surprised. "Well they didn't say anything about a body, but the cops were asking questions. I guess my mom was talking with my aunt. She heard it from a friend who works down at the gas station. He heard it from a farmer out on Summerville road who heard from some guy at the feed store. I guess a cop came over asking questions to the guy," Tommy said winded. "How did you keep that all that straight?" Sam joked, "What questions did he ask?"

"He asked if he saw anyone using the pay phone at the old train station," Tommy said in a low tone. Sam's eyes grew large, "Shit, they know about us!" Tommy shook his head, "No. Luckily the guy didn't see us at all, but he did see something." Sam placed his head down, "What?" Tommy looked over, "He saw a skinny man and a fat man going down the tracks."

"Fat man and a skinny man?" Sam asked, "That bogus physic!" Tommy shook his head, "Yep. But he didn't know who they were so the cops really don't know anything. My mom had the radio on this morning, but there was no news about a body being found." Sam could see two boys coming up the sidewalk, "Looks like your brothers are coming. Why didn't they come out with you early?"

"Johnnie overslept as usually and Donnie had extra chores," Tommy said then laughed. "What's so funny?" Sam asked. "Donnie got caught beating off in the old outhouse last night," Tommy said through busts of laughter. "Oh fuck, who caught him?" Sam asked wide eyed. "Our dad… told him he was doing it wrong!" Tommy said then fell backward into the grass laughing.

"Doing it wrong? There is a wrong way? What is the right way?" Sam asked surprised, "Did he tell your mom?" Tommy sat up, his face red from laughing while tears streamed down his face, "Yep. Right in front of everyone." Sam shook his head, "Man that is screwed up! You would think your dad would be okay with that." Tommy laughed, "I am sure he is, but he likes to bust our balls as much as he can."

Johnnie and Donnie walked up to the pair then sat on the curb with them. "I'd shake your hand, but I don't want to run home to wash it," Sam said to Donnie with a straight face. "Fuck off!" Donnie said with a blushed face. "Chill out man, we all do it," Sam said. "Yeah well our mom's don't know it… until now," Donnie said embarrassed.

"Hey, Sam had a dream about a bunch of women ghosts," Tommy said with a humorous tone. "Oh, did you have sex with them in the dream?" Johnnie asked with a big smile. "No… It wasn't that kind of dream," Sam sad. "Well at least you didn't have to change the sheets then," Donnie said while trying not to laugh.

"Get this; it was the same ghost he saw the other night. Said we didn't find her body but another. Said she was forty," Tommy said. Donnie looked to Sam, "Forty? What the hell does that mean?" Sam shrugged his shoulders, "Who knows, it was just a dream anyways."

"I don't know, you really saw a ghost the other night because her body was right where you saw her," Johnnie said, "Maybe she is forty years old?" Sam looked over, "No, she didn't look forty years old. I guess she was Danielle's age or a little older." Tommy piped up, "You weren't thinking of Sam's sister when you were beating the bishop, weren't you Donnie?" Sam threw his head in his hands. "No, I was thinking of Miss Kemp." As if it was rehearsed, all four boys stated out loud, "Yeah…"

"She is far too sexy to be a teacher," Tommy said, "I have stroked it out to her way too much." Sam laughed, "I bet every guy in class has beat off to her at least once." Tommy laugh, "Yeah, I bet she makes Mary Beth wet." Sam looked over then rolled his eyes.

"I just was thinking, remember there was the sign that said forty-one near where the ghost was… there are signs all along the tracks with numbers like that," Johnnie said. "So, what's your point?" Tommy asked. "Maybe she is near the forty sign," Johnnie said. The boys all looked at Johnnie, "Well, it's a thought at least."

Tommy shook his head, "You know, you might be on to something. Why don't we go over there and take a look!" Sam looked to the sky that was growing darker by the minute, "Looks like another storm is coming. We don't even know where the forty sign is, if there even is one."

Johnnie looked over, "There is one. Should be one mile south, those signs mark the miles." Sam looked to him, "One mile? We would have to go another mile farther south, shit, not with rain coming." Donnie shook his head, "Yeah we need to be home soon anyways. Sunday is bath day. I want to be the first one in the tub." Sam looked at Tommy, "Bath day? You guys really are hillbillies." Tommy smirked back, "I prefer white trash. It gives us a touch of class." All the boys laughed as a police squad car drove up the street.

"Man, the cops, I wonder who called them?" Donnie asked. "Maybe they heard you were beating off?" Tommy said with a chuckle. "Chill out guys, he's just patrolling." Sam said. "There is no such thing when your father is Cletus Jones," Tommy said with a gritty tone.

The squad car pulled up to the curb with a howl of the brakes. The door opened and a very large police officer stepped out wearing dark sunglasses. "Afternoon boys… we all taking a break under the shade of this nice chestnut tree?" the officer asked. The triplets kept their heads down while Sam looked up to the imposing man, "Yes sir." The officer leaned back against the grill of the squad car, "Well, you seem like a might proper young man... how come you hanging out with the sons of Cletus Jones?" Sam shrugged his shoulders, "Because they are my friends."

The officer took his sunglasses off, folded them and placed them into his shirt pocket. "How about you boys? You are might far away from the homestead, ain't ya?" the officer asked with an inquisitive tone. Tommy looked up, "We haven't done anything wrong officer. We're just sitting here talking." Sam looked over to Tommy to see him becoming bright red. "You know, your old man was just about your age when I first arrested him. Yep... caught him breaking into the general store. You know what he said?" the officer asked. All the boys remained quiet. "He said he wasn't doing anything wrong... just like you said right now. Well, your father must teach you boys well," the officer said.

Tommy was starting to get up from the curb, but was stopped swiftly by Sam. "You have the fighting spirit just like your old man," the officer said. A roll of thunder came from the south. "Sounds like a storm is coming... I hope you boys don't get wet on your way home. Now, us officers keep a close eye on this town. You all remember that, okay?" the officer said as he walked back to his squad car.

Sam could see that Tommy was shaking with anger. The squad car pulled away from the curb with only inches to spare as it passed the boys. "I fucking hate my father." Tommy said. Donnie looked over, "Fuck you asshole! There is nothing wrong with our father." Tommy looked back to his brother, "How many times do the cops stop us? How many times do you see women hold their purses tight as we come close? How many times do the teachers look to us when something happens in class? That's all because of who our father is!" Tommy said with pure anger.

"All of you, just chill out. He just stopped to get a rise out of you. Don't let him succeed," Sam said remaining calm. "I can't stand it. I hate this town. I hate how we are looked at like pure shit even though none of us have ever done anything wrong," Tommy said as he held back tears. Sam raised his eyebrow to his friend. "Okay, something that we have ever been caught for," Tommy said with a straight face.

Drops of rain slowly started to fall on the boys. "Come over to my house," Sam said, "You guys can't make it back home without drowning." Donnie looked to the sky then back to Tommy. "No, we will go over to our aunt's house. She only lives a few blocks away," Tommy said, "Why don't you come with?" Sam nodded his head in agreement, "Okay."

As the boys started to walk down the block a man sat in his car watching them. As they ran from tree to tree while the rain started to fall, he sat with his hand out of his car window with a lit cigarette between his fingers. When they turned down the next block, he started his car, pulled away from the curb and slowly came to the stop sign. He looked down the road to see them walking up to a small bungalow. The boys waited on the steps, until the door opened and all four went inside.

The man turned down the street and looked to see the address; one fourteen. He made a mental note of it, took a drag off of the cigarette then proceed to drive away as the rain started to beat down on the town.

"Aunt Summer, this is Sam," Tommy said as they walked into the living room. A Stones record was on the turntable spinning, waiting for the tone arm to drop. "So, what brings you boys over?" Summer asked. "The rain," Donnie said. As Summer walked, Sam took close notice. Tommy hit Sam gently on his back then whispered, "Hey, that's my aunt. Quit looking." Sam looked to his friend then smiled.

"Well, you guys can go do what you want, I have a project to get done," Summer said as she lowered the tone arm onto the record. A few pops and cracks came from the speakers, then 'Start Me Up' started to play. She turned the volume up while the boys could feel the bass thumping in their

chests. "Hey, let's go down to the basement,"
Tommy said to the gang. Sam was the last to leave
the room as he watched Summer sit down at the
dining room table surrounded by books and papers.

The boys went through the kitchen then
down a flight of stairs to the cool, musty basement.
"Your aunt is hot!" Sam proclaimed just loud
enough to be heard over the music. "She is my
mom's youngest sister. She's in college… goes for
that book learning," Tommy said then laughed as
Donnie and Johnnie took turns jumping on an old
bean bag chair. "Hey, why have I never met her
before?" Sam asked. Johnnie piped up, "Don't
ask…" Sam looked to Tommy who just shook his
head. "She doesn't like our dad," Donnie said, "so
we only see her when we come over here. This was
our grandparent's house before they moved to
California."

"There is tons of stuff down here that they
haven't moved to California yet," Tommy said,
"Grandpa has lots of neat stuff to look at." Sam
watched as the boys opened old cardboard boxes
and pulled out pictures, books and other paper
goods. He then looked up to the floor boards that
felt as if they were about to splinter from the loud
music. Sam thought of Summer then of the boys'
mother, Martha. He never thought she was that
attractive, but if you took away the ratty clothes,
washed away the occasional bruise on her and
maybe ever seen her smile; you would see the close
resemblance to her younger sister. Sam now realized

just how tough their lives are living under Cletus Jones' roof.

"Hey Sam, come look at this," Tommy said. Sam sat on an old area rug next to Tommy who had a giant scrapbook in his lap. "Grandpa kept anything about this town that he thought was interesting or historic," Tommy said then pointed out a picture of the train station. "I never saw that building when it wasn't bordered up and falling apart," Sam said. Tommy turned the page to find yellowed newspaper clippings. "Man, look at some of those haircuts from the sixties!" Donnie laughed. "They put in the paper when they opened the automatic carwash?" Sam asked, "That's news?" Tommy turned the page to more clippings. Seeing nothing of interest, he turned the page again when Sam stopped him by shouting, "Stop, go back."

Tommy did what was asked of him and turned the page back. "Look, there," Sam said pointing to a picture of a young woman beside the headline, 'LOCAL WOMAN MISSING' Sam started to read the article aloud, "Miss Beverly Larsen was last seen leaving her job at the local bowling alley Saturday night. Her car was found on Porter road east of the CNW railroad tracks. The key was still in the ignition. No other personal effects or clews were found."

"What's so big about that?" Donnie asked. Sam sat, his eyes looking toward the blank cinderblock wall. "Yesterday in that dream… I saw a bunch of women standing on the lawn holding signs. I swear to God she was one of them…," Sam said softly. "That is fucking creepy," Johnnie said. "What did the sign say?" Tommy asked. "Twelve… I think," Sam said. Tommy looked at the article, "This is from nineteen-seventy. We weren't even a year old yet."

"The article say anything else? Did they ever find her?" Sam asked. Tommy skimmed through the text, "No this looks like it came out only a few days after she disappeared." Sam grabbed the scrapbook from Tommy and quickly looked through the old articles. "Nothing," Sam said, "Nothing more about her."

The music went low then the sound of Summer walking around was heard. "Hey, I wonder if Aunt Summer remembers this?" Johnnie asked. "We can go ask," Tommy said then stood up off of the floor, "Come on, let's go ask her."

The troop of boys went up the stairs to find the young woman on her knees in front of a library of records. "Aunt Summer," Tommy said, "do you remember this?" He handed the scrapbook to the women who now had an unpleasant look on her face, "Why are you digging through this old crap?" Tommy pointed to the article of the missing woman, "Do you remember this happening?" Summer read the article then saw the date, "I was only six when this happened. I've never even heard of this woman. Why are you interested?"

"We are doing a report on Riley for school," Johnnie said, "We wondered if you would remember that, but I guess you are too young." Summer shook her head, "Yes, way too young. I hope you put all this stuff back where it belongs. Dad would be mad if he knew you were thumbing through it." She closed the scrapbook then handed it back to Tommy, "Go put this away where you found it."

"Do you think the newspaper would have old articles to look at?" Sam asked. "They would, if they hadn't gone out of business in the mid-seventies. Down at the college they have tons of old newspapers on microfilm. They may have those," Summer said as she was thumbing through the records. "Could you take us tomorrow?" Tommy asked. "Um, you have school tomorrow and I am sure your mothers would not let you skip," Summer said bluntly.

Tommy thought for a second, "You could call us out." Summer turned toward him and stated brusquely, "No." Tommy, ever so persistent said, "Come on, you are the cool aunt. You always let us play records and stay up watching scary movies when we were little." Summer could feel herself being pressured, "Okay, but, all of you can't be called out. The school would know for sure something was amiss. Tommy, come by tomorrow morning and you can go to the college with me." As Johnnie and Donnie made sounds of disapproval

Tommy asked, "How about Sam? He is my partner on the report."

"Well if Sam wants to go, his mother can call him out. Come by with Tommy in the morning," Summer said as she stood up from the floor. Sam took notice as he could see down her shirt as she did so. "Guys," Summer said, "I know you are not doing a report but it's probably best I don't know what you are up to." Tommy chuckled uncomfortably, "Why do you say that?" Summer pulled the record off of the turntable and said, "When you have a report for school, they expect you to do the research after school not outside school when you are supposed to be in class. But I remember how boring that school was…"

"Does that sound good to you?" Tommy asked Sam. "I'm sure my mom will be fine with it," Sam said. "Oh, I'm sure she will be…," Summer said with a touch of humor, "Looks like the rain stopped." Tommy looked to his aunt, "I guess you're telling us it's time to go."

Summer smiled, "You always were the smart one. However, clean up whatever mess you guys made before you leave." Tommy shook his head, "Come on guys." As the brothers left, Sam stood behind to admire the young woman. "Follow them…," Summer said pointing toward the kitchen. "Yeah… okay," Sam said while blushing.

As Sam reached the bottom of the stairs, the brothers were about to come right back up.

"You don't need to ask her for her number, we already know it," Donnie said with a geeky laugh. "I ripped the article out," Tommy said, "If anyone asks tomorrow, I was puking my guts out. You guys understand?" Johnnie and Donnie shook their heads in agreement. "That's good for them, but what about me?" Sam asked. "I'll call and say I am your father. They won't question that." Sam shook his head then said with a chuckle, "I hope your voice doesn't crack when you are talking."

The boys went up the stairs then opened the back door. "We're leaving, Aunt Summer!" Tommy yelled. "Be here at seven tomorrow morning. I have an early class," Summer replied from the dining room. The boys walked out into the damp, humid air. "We can cut through the back yard to the alley," Johnnie said. As he and Donnie took the lead, Sam and Tommy stayed a few paces back.

"Your aunt is so cool. She's so beautiful also!" Sam said. "You have no chance little boy, she's twenty," Tommy said. As they came to the side street, a green Dodge passed the boys, leaving in its wake a smell of stale cigarettes. "We better head home," Donnie said. "Yeah I better also," Sam said, "I'll meet you here tomorrow morning." Tommy shook his head in agreement. As Sam started to walk away from the boys he turned, "Hey, you're sure your aunt wouldn't like me?" Tommy shook his head and said bluntly, "She's like our mom; she only dates assholes."

Chapter 6

Detective George Norris walked down the dark, dank hallway through the basement of the county building. His destination was the county morgue which resided in a corner past the electrical room and the records vault. George walked through a pair of squeaky steel doors to find Coroner Eric Locke sitting at his desk smoking a pipe.

"So did you find anything out?" George asked as he sat down on a padded stool. "The rib is from a female who I estimate was between eleven and fourteen. Judging by the tooth found, I would say closer to eleven," Eric said then took a puff on his pipe. George looked at the ring sitting inside a clear plastic bag on the desk. "Could the ring size help determine age?" George asked. "Possibly, but the weight of the girl would be more of determination of finger diameter than age," Eric said.

"I was really close to your estimate; I put a teletype out for a missing girl between the ages of ten and fifteen. I haven't had any replies. The only known missing girl in that age range was from three years ago over in Beaver Creek. She was never found," George said sounding depressed. "Well that couldn't have been her. The soil discoloration and smell leads me to believe that body was not there for long. I wonder why no one has reported her missing?" Eric asked with disbelief.

"She could be a run away, from a youth home, maybe even from a nut house," George said. "Sure, but in any one of those cases you would think the authorities would be notified," Eric said, "Do you have any other leads?"

"I talked with William Teep at the feed store. He was the one the officer talked with the other day. He really couldn't see much from where he was and his vision is for shit. The two guys he saw could have been anyone and could have been doing anything. Unless something drops into my lap, there's nothing more I can do with this," George said.

"Well that body has to be somewhere and unless the killer or whomever it was that took it has a strong disposition, that smell would bring a man to his knees. It's quite possible she has been reburied in that area. It should really be searched," Eric said then took another puff on his pipe. "I know, but my boss would not let it go any further. See, Sheriff Walker is up for reelection and they do not want stories coming out in the press," George said then shook his head in disbelief.

"Stories? What kind of stories?" Eric asked. "Bad press. A child being murdered under his watch. God forbid it shows we do our job and find not just who she was but who murdered her," George said, "Last night I was thinking of another theory." Eric sat up in his chair with a large creak of the wooden frame, "What's that?" George looked at the ring again, "She was murdered by a parent. That would account for why there are no missing person's report." Eric slowly nodded in agreement, "Yes that would. You should check the local schools. See if someone has not reported to school yet this year."

George stood up, "Well I will try but if I get caught, it could be my job. Of course, what good is being a detective if I cannot do my job just because of an election?" Eric smirked, "Wouldn't be the first time an elected official bent the rules just to make sure their butt is covered at the polls."

"Are you two coming or what?" Summer yelled from the front door. "Just a minute!" Tommy yelled back from the kitchen. Sam stood next to him, his fingers crossed. Tommy quickly dialed the number and waited while the line rang. Sam could hear the reply of the answering machine followed by Tommy in his best deep voice say, "Hello this is Mister White, my son Samuel will not be in today. He has a touch of the stomach flu. Thank you." With that Tommy gentle placed the yellow receiver down onto the hook of the wall phone.

"Samuel?" Sam asked, "I am only called that when I am in deep shit." Tommy replied, "If we don't get moving, both of us will be in deep shit!" The boys ran through the house to see

74

Summer waiting at the door. Sam took careful notice of her tight blue jeans and her white blouse. As they walked to the jeep Tommy whispered, "Quit looking at her already! You are creeping me out."

The boys climbed into the rear seat of Summer's Wagoneer. As she backed out of the driveway, she stopped to let a green Dodge pass the down the street. "Keep an eye out for speed traps, we are running late," Summer said as she floored it down the street. "When we get there, I'll drop you off at the library. Go inside and ask for Susan, she has short black hair and is about Tommy's height. She will make sure no one bothers you," Summer said as she took a sharp curve causing the boys to slide around on the back bench.

"Now listen; do not jack around, do not talk loudly, do not be idiots. Understand?" Summer commanded as she looked at the boys through the rear-view mirror. "We will be good," Tommy said with fake sincerity. "I'll give you bus fare when we get there. I have lab, so I won't be coming home until four or five tonight. When you are done with your research, take the bus back to my house," Summer said while braking sharply for a stop sign, "You remember where the key is?" Tommy shook his head, "Under the flower pot next to the peeing statue in the backyard."

Sam looked over and asked, "Peeing statue?" Summer looked back, "Yes, peeing statue.

My dad won it at a golf outing." The boys held tight to the door handles as Summer pressed down on the accelerator as she came to a yellow traffic signal. "Ha! It's still yellow," Summer said with pride, "We are here. The library is just over there. I have a few minutes until class starts."

She stopped in front of a red brick building overstated by large white stone steps leading to a pair of wooden doors. "Here's a few dollars for the bus," Summer said while handing the money to Tommy, "Remember, be good while you're here. I don't want to have to beat your ass later."

The boys jumped out of the jeep and before Sam could fully close the door, Summer drove off. "Okay I have a plan," Sam proclaimed. "Yeah, what's that?" Tommy asked. "I'll be bad so she has to beat my ass tonight!" Sam said with a snicker. "In your dreams my friend, in your dreams…," Tommy said with a stressed tone.

The boys swiftly walked up the front steps then enter the building through the pair of wooden doors. The building smelled strongly of old books, with a slightly musty smell. To the right of the boys was a small counter where a young woman with jet back hair was standing writing in a notebook. "I've heard attractive women hang out with not so good-looking women," Sam whispered, "but that broad is downright scary!" Tommy shook his head in agreement, "Let me do the talking."

"Hello, are you Susan?" Tommy asked. "Yes. Oh, you must be Summer's nephew," Susan said with a pleasant tone, "She said you need to look at newspaper articles for a school project. Follow me upstairs, that is where they keep the films." The woman came out from behind the counter wearing a short miniskirt. As she walked up the stairs to the second floor, the hormone driven boys kept a few steps back admiring her creamy white legs.

"Over here are the microfilm machines. Do you know how to use them?" Susan asked. "Yes, I do," Sam said. "Good, well everything is computerized. Just go to that computer over there and type in what you are looking for. It will tell you what film to look at for that article. It only goes by names, so it is limited. The films are in these cabinets next to the computer," Susan said as she flipped the computer on. The screen flashed green as the computer booted. Within a few seconds a prompt came up asking for search criteria.

"That's all you should need. If anyone asks why you are here, just tell them to come see me, okay?" Susan said in her sweet, pleasant voice. "Yes, thank you very much," Tommy said pleasantly. As the woman walked away, Sam started typing the name in 'BEVERLY LARSEN'.

"Could you believe that woman? I could see her panties!" Tommy said with astonishment. "Yep. Her face might not be too good, but those legs make up for it," Sam said, "It says we need roll fifty-five." Tommy walked over to the cabinets to find the drawers numbered. He swiftly opened the drawer that said '50-69'. Tommy looked inside the organized drawer to find the roll, "Here it is, work your magic with the machine."

Sam opened the cap to pull the film out. He placed it in the film holder then turned the crank handle. "Okay we should be set," Sam said then flipped on the light. The screen showed the first page of a newspaper that was upside down and the text reversed. "Yep, you know what you're doing…," Tommy said then laughed. "I just need to flip the film around, chill out," Sam said embarrassed.

Sam quickly fixed the machine then started to look for the article, "I think it said June third." Sam quickly spun through the film, "June second. Just a few more pages, okay, June third." They scanned the text as Sam slowly turned the handle. "There," Tommy said while pointing to the screen. "That's the same article your grandpa had," Sam said, "Hold on, I think the computer had a few more dates listed."

"Look at the fifth," Sam said out loud. Tommy looked up then held his index finger to his lips. Sam shook his head in acknowledgment. Tommy turned the knob looking for June fifth as Sam came to sit back down. "I don't see anything," Tommy whispered. He continued to turn the knob until Sam said, "Stop, right there."

'RILEY WOMAN NOT FOUND, FAMILY DISTRAUT' Sam scanned the article, "Looks like the headline said. They haven't found her and nothing new was found to indicate what happened to her." Tommy looked at the other articles that showed nothing of importance to them. He slowly turned the handle just enough to see; 'RILEY MAN FOUND GUILTY OF BATTERY' Tommy put his head down, "I can't believe it."

Sam looked over, "What's up?" Tommy pointed to the article then stood up to walk to the computer. Sam read the article out loud softly as possible. "Cletus Jones has been found guilty of battery for an incident that happened last April at his parent's farm. Jones, twenty-one, battered his mother and father in a drunken rage when asked if he could help with the spring planting. His father, Charles, spent three days in the county hospital with a broken rib and eye socket. Cletus will be held at the county lockup for a period of six months to fulfill the sentence."

Sam shook his head then looked to Tommy who was staring out the window. "I told you he was an asshole," Tommy said softly, "There was one more article, but we need another roll of film." Sam remained quiet as he rewound the film then placed it back in its canister. He gave it to Tommy who was waiting with the next roll. "It's June second," Tommy said. Sam loaded the film as Tommy closed the cabinet drawer.

Sam wound the film rapidly looking for June, "Okay, the second." The boys scanned the pages one by one. At the end of that day's paper, near the bottom, was the article they were looking for; 'ONE YEAR PASSES FOR MISSING RILEY WOMAN' Sam scanned the tiny article. "All it said is that she is still missing. Nothing new; no clues," Sam said. "I will bet you anything she is at the twelfth mile marker," Tommy said. "That is…" Sam said as he did the math quickly in his head, "Twenty-nine miles from here."

Tommy turned the light inside the machine off then said, "Well, there is still mile forty to look at. Why don't we head back to town and go out to search?" Sam shook his head, "No, we will get caught for truancy." Tommy gave him a disappointing look, "Truancy, big deal. Come on, let's put this film away and get moving. The bus should take us close to the tracks; we'll walk down to the mile mark."

Except for the boys and the driver, the bus was empty. They did not say much as they bounced down the road toward Riley. Sam could tell Tommy was still sore about the old article involving his father. As the bus rounded the curve onto Main Street, Tommy took the cord into his hand. After a quick stop for an elderly woman in the crosswalk, the bus continued through the town. As it neared the tracks, Tommy tugged on the cord to notify the driver they would like off.

As the bus slowed to a stop, the boys waited near the door. When it opened they jumped off onto the sidewalk. "Oh shit!" Tommy said, "That lard ass cop from yesterday is just down near the TV repair shop… quick, jump behind this car." Sam did as he was told and scrunched down behind a beat-up station wagon with Tommy.

"Did he see us?" Sam asked. "No, I don't think so," Tommy said, "Let's go behind the buildings then we can run to the tracks." Sam did as Tommy said as he was both scared and energized. The thought of getting away with something was getting to be an adrenaline rush to him. They went behind a small diner then the feed store. They came out at the tracks right across from the old train station.

"The coast is clear," Tommy said, "Let's make a run for it." As Tommy went off sprinting across the road, Sam stuck close. The made it across the road, past the wig-wag signals and onto the gravel roadbed in less than two seconds. "Damn, you should go out for track," Sam said windily to Tommy. "It helps when running from the cops," Tommy said with a chuckle, "Let's get moving down the tracks."

The boys walked down the rails while keeping an ear out for trains and the police. They passed the forty-one marker without even looking off toward the shallow grave. As the sun beat down on them, they made the mile in no time. "Oh my God, we are so fucking stupid!" Tommy said out loud. "What?" Sam asked with haste. "We don't have a shovel!" Tommy said as he hit himself in his forehead. "Well, we can at least look around for anything odd," Sam said.

The area around the forty-mile marker was just like that of the forty-one marker; tall grasses, weeds and the dense forest just down the embankment. The boys split up walking up and down the embankment looking for anything odd. "Found an old shot gun shell," Sam said as he held it up for Tommy to see. "Yeah, found a few here too. I think guys are taking shots at the insulators on those old telephone poles," Tommy said.

"Man, this all looks the same to me," Sam said. As Tommy walked down the embankment to Sam, he heard someone whistling. "Who is it?" Sam whispered. Tommy held his hand out then carefully climbed the hill to see a scruffy man walking the rails toward them. "It's Trailer Tim," Tommy whispered down to Sam. "Who?" Sam rebutted.

"Trailer Tim, he lives out in an older truck trailer near the river. My parents told me he is bat shit crazy, but I think he is just off a bit. I talk to him whenever I see him," Tommy said, "Come on, let's go say hello." Sam gave a queer look then followed his friend up the hill.

"Tim!" Tommy yelled to the old man, "It's me, Tommy Jones." The old man walked over; his white hair was blowing wildly in the breeze; his skin was dark from years of not being washed. The clothes he had on were about twenty years out of date and the pants had more holes than fabric. "Tommy, Tommy, Tommy… yeah… I remember, 'member, you," Tim said with a mumbled stutter. "This here is Sam," Tommy said while pointing out his friend. "SSSS Sam, nice, nice, nice, to meet you," Tim said.

Carried on Tim's left arm was a model steam engine. The paint was faded allowing spots of the raw metal to show through. "That's Tim's engine. It's just like the one he rode through here when he was younger, isn't it Tim?" Tommy asked. "Yessss, yess, just like it. Rode the rails, rails, rails, for many years. What are, are, are, you boys doing out here?" Tim asked.

"Um, looking for a ghost," Tommy said with a half-smile. "Ghost, ghost, many, many of them in these wood, wood, woods," Tim said with wide eyes, "Come out at niii, niii, night." Sam felt very uneasy by the unkempt man, but found the courage to ask, "Have you seen anyone burying bodies out here?" Tommy looked to Sam with horror.

"Bodies? Nnnn, nnn, no, no, no bodies," Tim said, "But be careful, careful, caaaarfull of Red." Tommy raised his eyebrow, "Whose red?"

83

Tim pointed down to the rails, "Track, track, track foreman. He beat me last fall, fall... beat me last fall, he did." Sam looked to Tommy, "The man in the truck." Tommy shook his head in agreement, "Tim, does he have a yellow truck?" Tim shook his head rapidly, "Yes, yes, yes... yellow truck. Beat me with a wrench, wrench... beat me he did."

"Why did he beat you?" Sam asked. "Came from town, town, town, one night. He was out here by himself, 'self, working on the tracks, track, tracks... He said I scared, scared him. So he hit me with a wrench, wrench... hit me he did." In the distance a horn could be heard. "We better get off the tracks, a train is coming," Sam said.

Tommy and Sam went down the embankment, but Tim just crossed onto the other mainline. "He's going to get killed!" Sam yelled. "Leave him; he does this all the time," Tommy said, "I think he likes the feeling of being so close to the moving train." As the engines approached, the engineer laid on the horn to worn the old man. Sam and Tommy watched as the four giant engines passed followed by with at least one hundred mixed freight cars. The sound was deafening as the wheels screeched along the rails.

Sam was watching in a sense of awe until a voice broke over the sound, "Forty!" Sam looked to Tommy then yelled, "Quit fucking around!" Tommy looked back, "What?!" Sam looked down to see the caboose coming. As he looked past Tommy he heard again, "Forty!" Once the caboose passed and with it all the noise, Sam said, "Quit messing with me!"

Tommy looked to Sam, "Messing? How?" Sam's face turned bright red, "You kept saying forty!" Tommy shook his head in disagreement, "No man, I did not say anything. I just watched the train go by." Sam looked as his friend with disbelief but was interrupted by Tim, "That, that, that was fun!! I, I, I miss riding the rails." Sam looked up to the old man, "I bet it was fun back then, wasn't it?" Tim shook his head, "Yes, yes, yes... but I, I have to go... boys. Oh, oh, oh, they said to tell you forty."

"What the fuck man?" Tommy blurted out, "Who told you to say that?!" Tim shook his head in an angled fashion, "The, the, the voooices, vvv, voices." Sam climbed the hill then asked, "What voices?" Tim smiled showing his brownish, yellow teeth, "The women. All, all, all the women talk to me. They, they, they love me... the women do." Tommy looked up to Sam and while shaking his head in short bursts stated, "This is not fucking happening... What the fuck is going on?"

Tim started walking toward town as the boys watched him. Without turning around, Tim said, "Forty... She, she, ssshe'ssss forty." Tommy ran up the hill and then around the man so as to face him, "Where is she buried?" Tim turned back toward the mile post sign, "Forty." The old man started walking again but was stopped by Tommy once more, "Tim, at your trailer, do you have a shovel?" Tim shook his head, "Yes… a shovel I, I , I have." Sam walked up to Tommy, "What are you thinking?" Tommy gave a blank face, "Can I borrow your shovel?" Tim shook his head then proceeded to continue down the track.

"Are you crazy?" Sam asked. "Listen, something really fucked up is going on out here and I want to find out what it is. Let's dig around that sign a bit, see if we find something," Tommy said, "Come on, his trailer is about a quarter mile down the tracks." As Tommy starting walking Sam stayed still. Tommy looked back, "Are you coming or what?" Sam stayed mute while walking slowly toward his friend.

The boys walked down the tracks toward the Deer River. As they came to an iron truss bridge, Tommy pointed down the river, "There, see the trailer?" Sam looked down the river to see a white trailer sticking out of the woods. "That's where he lives?" Sam asked.

Tommy started walking down the embankment toward the river's edge. As Sam followed, he felt as if someone was watching him. He turned around quickly, but no one was there. "What's with you, come on!" Tommy yelled. Sam turned back around and jogged to catch up with his friend. Once past a few bushes, the full trailer came into view. The white sides still shone brightly in the sun yet the logo of a local dairy was well faded and just barely visible on its side. A makeshift staircase constructed of logs and branches lead up to its rusting doors.

"Oh, this place smells," Sam said bluntly. "Well look at Tim. The man looks like he never had a bath in years. Can't expect his house to be clean, can you?" Tommy said with a chuckle, "Let's look under the trailer to see if a shovel is there." Sam decided to look under near the flattened tires only to see weeds and trash. "Looks like the trash man hasn't been here in years," Sam said.

Tommy dug under the trailer with his bare hands bringing out old tin cans, pop bottles and anything else that the mind could imagine. "You better be careful," Sam said, "You don't want to have to get a tetanus shot!" Tommy looked up then went back to digging. "I don't see a shovel, perhaps its inside." Sam said. "Go on in, I'll be right there," Tommy said while fully under the trailer turning over old street signs and the occasional car bumper.

Sam walked up the creaking stairs to find one of the doors slightly open. It took as much courage as he could muster to try to open the door. The door was heavy but he pulled as hard as he could and with a loud grunt he opened it just enough to walk through the gap. "Holy Shit!" Sam exclaimed. Tommy came running around trying not to fall over the junk he had just unearthed, "What is it? What's in there?"

Chapter 7

Summer walked up the steps to her house then stopped to get the mail from the mailbox. She went to turn the knob to find it locked, "Susan said they left. I thought for sure Tommy would leave it unlocked." She pulled out her key, unlocked the door then went inside to the find the house quiet. "Tommy? Sam? Where are you two?" Summer asked as she threw the mail on the couch, "Lab got called off so I got to come home early. You guys want to go get a burger or something for lunch?"

She walked into the kitchen to find it silent and vacant. "Tommy?" Summer asked again. She looked down the basement steps to find it dark. "Damnit, I told him to come right back here," Summer said out loud, "Ugh, I have got to get these jeans off; so damn hot."

Summer went down the hallway then into her bedroom where she opened her dresser to pull out a pair of gray shorts. As she unbuttoned her jeans, she could hear the floor squeak in the living room. "Tommy? Are you out there dicking around?" Summer asked. Once again there was nothing but silence. She walked out into the living room to find it as she had left it, vacant.

Summer unzipped her jeans as she walked back into the bedroom. She slipped the jeans off and as she went to grab the shorts from her bed, she felt as if someone was watching her. She spun around quickly to see no one there. "Too many long nights," Summer thought to herself. She slipped on her shorts, tied the string to make the waist tighter, and then returned to the kitchen. She opened the refrigerator and after inspecting its contents said, "Well nothing is missing so those two never came back. If they get themselves into trouble I'm screwed."

Summer pulled out a pitcher of tea then took a glass from the cabinet next to the refrigerator. After filling the glass, she walked into the living room then sat on the couch next to the mail she dumped when she first came home. She placed the glass on the end table and as she went to pick up the mail, she heard the floor creak in the hallway. "What the hell?" Summer said out loud, "Tommy, if you are fucking around, it's not funny!" She sat silent listening for any little sound, but she only heard silence.

She quickly turned her attention back to the mail, "Electric bill… gas bill… phone bill. Ugh, I'm so glad dad still pays all of these." Behind a flyer for the pizza shop down on Main Street, there was a sealed blank envelope. Summer looked at it then said, "There is no address, no stamp, what the hell?" She ran her finger under the flap to open it. Inside was a white piece of paper. Summer pulled the paper out to see two digits written in blue ink. "What the hell is this?" Summer said out loud. She placed the paper down on the couch when she heard the floor creak again.

Summer jumped off of the couch and went to the kitchen, as she yelled "Who the hell is in here?!" No one was in the kitchen. She turned on the light at the bottom of the basement steps then slowly walked down into the cool, musty air. As she got to the point where she could easy look around the basement, she did not see anyone or anything but the dimly lit basement.

She was about to return upstairs when she remembered the walled in root cellar beneath the stairs. Summer quietly stepped down the steps and with her bare feet, she stepped onto the cold, damp basement floor. The only sound was the occasional drip from the faucet in the utility tub and her taking a soft breath. She slowly walked to the root cellar door, took a deep breath then pulled the door open as fast as she could. Much to her relief, no one was in there.

Summer closed the door then loudly heard the sound of someone walking swiftly through the first floor. As she passed her father's workbench, she grabbed an old hunting knife that hung on the pegboard. Next to the workbench, a black rotary phone hung. She picked the receiver up to find no dial tone. "Fuck," she whispered. Quickly she hit the hook three times and listened again, but the line was dead silent. She placed the receiver back on the hook then slowly walked to the stairs. She looked up to the door wide open into the bright kitchen. With the knife firmly in her hand, Summer found all of the courage she had and ran up the stairs determined to stab the first person she saw. She looked around the kitchen, "Who is here? Come out!" As she listened, she could hear her heart beating rapidly.

Suddenly the front door opened. She ran as fast as she could to the living room to find the door wide open. She carefully walked out the door to see no one in the yard. The only sound was that of a bird chirping in a maple tree on the side of the house. Summer stood just inside the door frame shaking while she clung to the knife.

Suddenly in the distance there was the sound of tires squealing. She peeked back out and looked down the block in the direction the sound came from, but she did not see a car. Summer went back into the house, closed the door then locked it. Her heart was still racing and her hand ached from holding the knife so tight. She looked to the couch to see the white envelope lying where she threw it, but the letter was gone. She looked on the carpet, on the end table even under the cushions; the letter was nowhere to be found.

"Sam, what's in there?" Tommy yelled as he climbed the stairs. "Come in here, you are not going to believe this," Sam said with a sense of awe. Tommy walked into the dark trailer. He closed his eyes so they could better adjust to the low light.

91

"Look," Sam said as he pointed into the trailer. Tommy opened his eyes to see not the inside of a shipping trailer, but what looked to be a well furnished, clean and organized home. The furniture was old and fairly worn, but in good condition.

"I do not believe this," Tommy said with complete awe, "I would have never believed this unless I saw it with my own eyes." Sam found a flashlight lying on a card table, "I wonder if this works." With a large click, the flashlight illuminated the trailer. "Look at the pictures," Tommy said pointing to a small table. Sam looked closely, "I think that is Tim... look how young he was."

Tommy picked one up and asked with amazement, "Who is the woman and the little girl?" Sam shrugged his shoulders, "Maybe he was married?" Tommy put the picture down and picked another large one up, "Holy shit, he wasn't lying, look!" He handed the picture to Sam, "Wow, look at that locomotive he is standing next to. He was an engineer?" Tommy laughed, "All this time I thought he meant he was a hobo or something."

"Let's find the shovel then get out of here. I feel like we broke into a house or something," Sam said. Tommy shook his head, "Yeah, it's kind of creepy, isn't it?" Sam placed the photo back down carefully as Tommy walked further into the trailer. Past the tidy parlor section was an immaculate sleeping area. "Boy that bed looks to have been slept in for many years," Tommy said. "Yes, I think he needs new sheets or at least wash them once a decade," Sam said, "I don't see a shovel in here either." Tommy pointed beyond the bed, "Maybe he has tools and stuff behind those rugs."

"Maybe we should just go," Sam said. "Come on, what do you think is behind the rugs, the bearded lady or something?" Tommy said with a chuckle, "If you're chicken, I'll do it." Sam gave him a blank face, "I'll do it." He walked past the sleeping area to the makeshift curtains made from old area rugs. He swallowed a bit of saliva in his mouth as he opened the curtain. As he past the curtain he used the flashlight to illuminate the dark area. The boys stood silent as they saw the walls and ceiling plastered with photographs of women and girls.

"What the hell is this?" Sam said out loud, "These are women from around Riley." Tommy looked closer at the black and white photographs, "That's Emily from the drugstore. There's the doctors wife... Look! Miss Kemp!" Sam shook his head, "It's like he hides in bushes or something and takes their pictures. This is screwed up!" Tommy started to laugh, "Come look at this."

Sam walked over to the picture Tommy was pointing to showing a young couple making love in the backseat of a car. Sam looked around to see women he didn't know and many he did. Many more were of classmates; some were playing in their yard, others were swimming at the city pool. "Tommy," Sam said softly, "Come look at this."

Tommy walked over to the photograph Sam was pointing to. Tommy focused his eyes on a group of four girls playing in a yard; the oldest one was very close to him. "Mom," Tommy said with anger in his voice. "I guess the little girl is your Aunt Summer," Sam said. "Yes, the other two are my Aunts Kim and Samantha. This photograph must be way older than us."

Sam looked over to a small table covered with bottles and glass trays. "He must develop the film himself," Sam said pointing to the bottles. "He would have to. If he went to the Fotomat, the whole town would know about this," Tommy said. "How does he pay for all of this?" Sam asked. "Scrap. That's what my dad told me. Tim collects junk metal and turns it in for money," Tommy said.

The flashlight started to flicker then died. "Crap!" Tommy said. Suddenly Sam felt a cold breath on his neck, "What the hell was that!" Tommy looked into the darkness, "What?" Sam stayed quiet, his breath shallow and his heart starting to race. "Sam? Are you there?" Tommy asked. "I just felt someone blow on my neck," Sam said softly. Tommy tried to feel his way to the wall so he could find a way out. As he moved his feet shuffled on the wood floor. "Tommy is that you?" Sam asked with his legs frozen to the floor. "Yeah, I'm trying to find a way out," Tommy said.

Sam tried to move his feet, but it felt like someone glued them to the floor. Without warning he heard a woman's voice in his ear, "Find me." Sam screamed, "Oh my God!" He made his legs move with great force and ran toward what he thought was the correct direction. In doing so, he hit Tommy in the back with his right hand causing him to spin around like a top. Sam hit the back of the rugs with his face. He tried desperately to find where they parted. Finally, he found the end of one rug and with the strength he didn't know he had, ripped the threads that held the two rugs together.

Bright sunlight poured in blinding both of the boys. Sam ran toward the light going through the trailer then down the stairs. Tommy came out behind him, "What the fuck happened?" Sam was trying to catch his breath, "You heard! You had to have heard her!" Tommy looked to Sam, "Heard who? All I heard was you screaming then you hit me in the ass with your hand... fag!" Sam shook his head while he struggled for breath, "You had to have heard her... come on, you had to have."

Sam started to cough as he tried to catch his breath. "Man, calm down... breathe," Tommy said with a touch of worry. Sam tried his best finally calming his breathing while his heart still raced. "What did you hear?" Tommy asked. Sam looked at him, "It was a woman... the same voice I heard in my dream and when the train went by. She said, find me." Tommy shook his head, "I swear man, I didn't hear it." Sam placed his hands on the sides of his head, "I think I'm going nuts."

Tommy went up the stairs then closed the trailer doors. He came back down to see Sam starting to cry. "Just chill, you're not nuts. Just relax," Tommy said. "Let's get the hell out of here. I don't want to do any digging. Let's just go back to your Aunt's and wait for school to get out," Sam pleaded. Tommy shook his head, "Yeah, this place creeps me out. Sam... you don't think Trailer Tim killed those women in your dream, do you?" Sam looked at the trailer than the surroundings, "I don't know. He is odd and he loves taking pictures of women. Let's get hell out of here."

The boys followed the river to the bridge then went up to the tracks. As they walked toward town, they remained quiet. They past the fortieth milepost without even taking another look at the surroundings. As they came closer to town they could see someone working near the block signals. "You don't think that is the guy from the other day, do you?" Sam asked Tommy. "I don't know, but this is the only way to go unless we take the trail out and then the highway back into town," Tommy said. "Hell no, if we have to, we'll make a run for it. Besides, I want to stay away from that trail," Sam said.

They passed the forty-first milepost with only a glance to the trail from Sam. As they neared the block signals, Sam said, "That's not the same guy, thank God." As they approached, the man climbed a steel ladder attached to one of the signals.

They walked beneath him hoping he wouldn't notice.

Just when they thought they were in the clear, the man said, "Shouldn't you two be in school?" The boys turned to the man slowly to see him replacing the light bulb. "Are you a cop?" Tommy asked with a brash attitude. The man laughed, "Do I look like a cop?" Sam shook his head, "No." The man climbed down the ladder, "So you have nothing to worry about then."

"We skipped today. Had some stuff to do," Sam said. "Well, be careful around these tracks, even if there isn't a train, you can still get hurt," the man said with authority. "There is another guy who works on the tracks that yells at everyone, Red," Tommy said. The man looked at the bulb as he cleaned it with a rag, "Red? I don't know a Red... Oh, I bet you mean Wally Smith. He has a red crew cut." Sam shook his head, "Yeah, I heard he's a real bad ass. Trailer Tim said he hit him with a wrench."

"Well, be between us three, stay away from Wally. When he came back from the war, not all of his screws were still there," the man said. "Do you know Trailer Tim?" Tommy asked. "I know the legend of Tim. I've talked with him as he walked by, but he was from before my time," the man said. "Is it true he was an engineer?" Sam asked. "Yes. He was based out of Greenly," the man said as he climbed the ladder. "Do you know what happened to him?" Tommy asked.

The man placed the bulb in its holder, closed the cast iron door then placed a pad lock on it, "Well from what I was told he was one of the last holdouts from the steam era; just hated the idea of diesel locomotives. He was on a run one night when his house caught fire. I guess his wife and little girl perished. So they gave him some time off but when he came back to work, his engine was gone. He asked what happened to it and they told him the scrapper's torch got it; he was to be trained on a shiny new F7 starting that day. Well that was the last death Tim could take. He walked out of the yard and was never heard from again. He showed back up about twenty-five years ago living in an old trailer near the river."

"Man, everyone in town just thinks he's crazy," Tommy said, "What a messed-up story!" The man came down the ladder then sat on one of its rungs, "Yeah, it's a sad story, if it's all true." Sam shook his head, "Yeah." The man stood up then picked up his tool bag from the ground, "Well boys, I need to get down to thirty-nine."

Sam looked at the man, "Hey, those signs with numbers, what do they mean?" The man threw the bag over his shoulder, "Those are the miles from Greenly. Right now we are a little over forty-one miles from Greenly. It helps the engineers know where they are if they are not used to this subdivision." Tommy looked down the tracks, "So the closer you get to Greenly, the lower the numbers go?" The man shook his head, "Yep. Anyways, I'll see you boys around."

The man walked to his yellow truck and slowly got in. He rolled the window down then said to the boys, "Wally, or Red, as you call him. Stay away from him... way away. He doesn't even like me to be out here working. He acts like this is his personal kingdom."

The man backed up the roadbed to the crossing then left. "Even after seeing all of those creepy pictures, I feel bad for Tim," Tommy said. Sam shook his head, "Maybe that's why he takes those pictures. Maybe they remind him of his family. Maybe that is his family now." Tommy started walking, "Come on. Let's stick to the rear of the stores so no one sees us. Hopefully Aunt Summer has some food, I'm starved."

The boys were careful as they went through the business district of Riley. At each road they crossed they looked vigilantly not for passing cars, but police cars. They were coming up the street when they noticed multiple police cars with their lights flashing.

"Shit, they are right in our way," Sam said. Tommy looked carefully, "Man, they are right near my Aunt's house. Do you think someone ratted us out to the cops?" Sam shrugged his shoulders, "The only ones who knew were your brothers and your Aunt. I doubt any of them would do that." Tommy started walking again, "Let's get as close as we can then we can dart behind one of the houses if we need to."

As the boys made their way closer, there was a small group of people talking on the parkway. As the boys passed carefully Tommy heard one of the women say – "I can't believe we had a break-in on this block. That's never happened before."

Tommy whispered to Sam, "Did you hear that?" Sam looked over, "I wonder whose house got hit?" As the boys passed the group of people they could make out that the squad cars were right in front of Summer's house. "Oh Shit!" Tommy said out loud, "They are at my Aunts!" Before Sam knew it, Tommy took off running toward the house. Sam swiftly took off after him, "Hold up!"

Tommy ran as fast as he could down the block. As he ran up the yard, Summer walked out of the house. "What happened?" Tommy asked winded. "Someone broke in... Where have you been?" Summer asked in a loud whisper. "I'll tell you in a bit. Did they get anything?" Tommy asked. Summer shook her head, "I don't think so."

As Sam walked up, Officer Stanton Smith walked out. "Ma'am, you are sure nothing was taken?" Stanton asked. "No... no nothing," Summer said with a touch of fear in her voice. "Well there were no signs of a break-in. Have you loaned a key to any one, perhaps an old boyfriend?" Stanton asked with a raised brow. "No," Summer said bluntly.

"The key in the back." Tommy said. Summer looked over, "Oh, we have a key hidden. It's in the backyard." Stanton held his hand out, "Why don't you show me where it is." As Summer lead the way, Stanton, Tommy and Sam followed. As they walked up the driveway, Stanton said, "Oh, this is why you phone didn't work. The person cut the cable." Stanton showed the cable hanging on the side of the house with the other end dangling from a small metal box.

Summer rounded the house where a two-foot-tall statue of a peeing angel sat in a mulched bed directly behind the house. "Here, under this flower pot," Summer said as she bent over to pick the pot up, "It's gone. The key is gone!" Stanton looked around the mulch, "I do not see it anywhere. Which door was it for?" Summer placed the pot down, "Both the front and back door, they are keyed the same."

"I will ask the dispatcher to call a lock smith for you. You will need these locks rekeyed this afternoon," Stanton said, "Please look over everything in the house again and if you find anything missing, no matter what, please contact us." Summer shook her head softly, "I will, trust me."

"Well, there isn't much more for us to do. I will ask that a patrol car comes past here at least once an hour, more if they can," Stanton said.

"Thank you... boys go on in the house now. I will be right in," Summer said.

Tommy and Sam did as they were asked and walked up the back step. "Man, can you believe this?" Tommy said. "I know, I thought your father was the only one who broke in to homes in this town," Sam said with a chuckle. "I should knock you one for that comment, but unfortunately it's the truth," Tommy said as he exhaled.

The boys went into the kitchen were Tommy proceeded to see what Summer had in the refrigerator. "Lettuce, carrots... green beans? What the hell?" Tommy said in disbelief. "Check the freezer, that's where we keep the hot dogs," Sam said with a reassuring tone. Tommy opened the door, "This thing is empty except for ice and a bottle of vodka. She needs someone to buy her some food."

Summer walked in the back door, closed it gently then asked, "Where the hell have you two been?!" Tommy looked to Sam then said, "We did our research then left... not that long ago." Summer was turning a light shade of red, "I don't need lies right now. Where have you been?"

"We did do our research, but it's not for school," Tommy said. Summer sat at the small breakfast table, "I'm listening." Tommy looked to Sam, "Tell her about the ghost." Before Sam could say a word Summer interrupted, "Ghost? I can't believe this, a ghost? Are you kidding me? How old are you two?!" Sam looked completely embarrassed in front of the attractive woman. "It's true but there is much more to it," Tommy said, "He had a dream and that article we showed you yesterday, about the woman missing, well that was the woman in his dream."

Summer looked at Sam, "So you had a dream last night about…" Sam stopped her, "I had the dream Saturday night." Summer looked at the boys with a curious look, "You're telling me you dreamed about a woman and just happened to find an article about her the next day… I think I need a drink…"

"There were many women in his dream," Tommy said. "Oh, you had an orgy in your dream," Summer said with a blank face, "Little perv." Tommy shook his head, "No, just listen to me, they were all dead." Summer stood up, pulled a glass out from the cabinet then asked, "Dead? They are all dead? Your friend dreams about dead people. That's nice…" Sam felt so embarrassed, "Yes. They were all murdered." Summer pulled a bottle of whisky out from the top of the refrigerator then poured a bit into the glass.

"So you dreamed about murdered women and just happen to find the article about one of them in my basement… great," Summer said then took a sip of the whiskey, "So what else was in your pleasant little dream?" Tommy looked over to Sam then said, "They were all numbered. We think the woman in the article was the twelfth because she had a number twelve on her. The ghost Sam saw was number forty-one." Summer's face turned white like that of a ghost.

"What's wrong?" Tommy asked. Summer threw the glass into the sink causing it to shatter. She ran past the boys going directly to the living room. The boys took off behind her to find her ripping the cushions off of the couch. "What are you doing?" Tommy asked. Summer next pulled the end table away from the wall, "It has to be here!" Sam backed up against the living room wall while the young woman turned the room upside down. "What? What are you looking for?" Tommy asked stressed. Summer was on her knees looking under the stripped couch, "It's not here! Fuck!"

Tommy walked over to her side, "Aunt Summer. What are you looking for?" She looked up to her nephew and said winded, "In the mail was a blank envelope… inside was a piece of paper. When I heard someone in the house I was looking at it… fuck he must have taken it." Tommy asked wide eyed, "Took what?!" Summer sat back on her feet and exclaimed, "The letter!" Sam walked to Tommy's side and asked, "What did the letter say?" Summer was starting to look flush again, "Forty-two."

Chapter 8

"We are hoping to speak with our father, he just passed away," a young woman said in a somber tone. Suddenly the table started to rise and shake as wall sconces brightened then dimmed. "Ah, I see a man; he is in the room with us right now!" Sir Francis said with wide eyes and a bellowing tone. The young women gasped with the news as one of them looked around the dark room, "Dad! Is that you? Please, tell me where he is!"

"Please, remain calm he is telling me. He is walking around the room very slowly looking at his beautiful daughters," Francis said, "Laura, your husband, he is hard of hearing, yes? You need to shout for him to hear…" One of the women looked up with wide eyes, "Yes! Oh dad, it is you! Oh, thank God. Is he well?" Francis placed his right hand on his forehead, "Your father… he says he is sorry. He says he was weak when you wanted him to be strong. He tried to fight it, but his strength was not enough to overcome. He is sorry he is not there for all of you."

The woman started to sob, "I know you did your best dad." The table quickly settled back down to the floor as Francis said in a soft tone, "Your father… he is with another man; a very young man." One of the women looked to Francis, "David? David, is that you." Francis quickly looked to the corner of the room, "Yes… he says his name is David. He is here with great love for his sisters. He

105

wants you to know he and your father are well on the other side."

One woman stood up, "Where is he?" Francis looked to a dark corner of the room, "To your left, in the corner. The young man… he stands with your father." The woman walked over then sung her arms wildly into the air, "You son of a bitch! You died because you are selfish! Now you show up with the man you made sick!" One of the other women jumped up and grabbed her angered sister. "Please ladies… they are fading away… Please control your sister! Oh… oh no, I am afraid they are gone," Francis said.

"Can you bring them back?" One woman asked with haste. "I am sorry… the God's they say not today… perhaps… tomorrow. When your hearts are open again… tomorrow I am sure," Francis said with a hint. "We will be back tomorrow. Hopefully our father will come back to us," one of the women said through bouts of sobs.

Francis stood up as his turban was starting to slide to his right. He walked over to the angered sister then placed his hands on her shoulders, "You are in much pain… much anger. I feel you need your own session to help you reconnect with your brother. His pain has infected you… you need to be cleansed of this pain. I can help with that." The woman looked toward her sisters, "I am so sorry… I am so angry that David killed himself."

The sisters came over and as Francis removed his hands from her, they hugged the now sobbing sister. "The Gods, they are rejoicing that your hearts are healing from this pain. Please, come see me in the morning. I know we can reconnect with your father and brother. Please let the healing continue," Francis said with an uplifting tone.

As the women left the room, Francis walked behind them, "Ladies if you decided to come back tomorrow... I will give a ten percent discount." As the women walked out into the bright sun, they remained quiet. Francis retuned to the room to find Randy counting the cash, "Four women at fifty bucks a piece! Nice!"

"How did you know the one woman by name?" Francis asked puzzled. "I may have happened to bed her one night after her deaf husband needed to work extra shifts at the mill," Randy said with a chuckle. "And the brother?" Francis asked with a humored tone. "This was right after he hung himself from the overpass. She was messed up... and really good in the sack," Randy said then laughed as he recounted the money.

"You are one sick man," Francis said as he ripped the money from Randy's hands, "I'll put this in the cigar box so I know where it is." Randy shook his head, "Hey, if I haven't had screwed her, I would have not known things that really sold them on your abilities." Francis looked at his brother dead on but remained silent. "Come on, you sold it good. I bet we don't just get them back tomorrow, but I bet we can soak them for two or three more sessions!" Francis remained quiet as if in another world.

"I found out some more about those kids and you ain't going to believe it," Randy said proudly. "Kids?" Francis asked puzzled, "What kids?" Randy shook his head, "What kids? The ones that lead us to the rotting body!" Francis sat down on his chair then removed his turban, "I know what kids, idiot. Why are you wasting time on this?"

"Because that one kid really has a gift... a gift that could make us very, very rich." Randy said as he leaned on the table with both arms. "Luck, that is what the kid has and you had bad luck when you forced me along to find buried Indians," Francis said. "Well I still don't know who that kid is, but I did find out who the three zombies were with him," Randy said, "and guess who their father is..."

Francis pulled out a deck of cards and placed them on the table, "Who, like I really care..." Randy sat down then grabbed the cards from his brother, "Cletus Jones. The guy we fence stuff for." Francis looked up, "Jones? He has kids... that's right, he has triplets. So, why should I care about this?" Randy started to get mad, "He might tell us who that kid is. We need that kid!" Francis grabbed the cards back, "We are conmen. We run a con we do not baby sit children. Quit fucking worrying about some zit faced kid!"

Randy stood back up, his face red, "That kid saw a ghost that lead us to her body! Who knows what that kid could tap into!" Francis leaned back in the chair causing it to groan, "Randy, forget about the kid. It's that simple, forget about the fucking kid." Randy pulled at his hair, "Ugh! We have a golden opportunity right here, don't let it pass by!"

Francis shuffled the cards in his hands as his brother fumed. "What are you going to do? Kidnap the kid and keep him in the basement?" Randy sat back down, "I haven't thought that far ahead yet… Maybe we can trick him to thinking that he needs to help us." Francis shuffled the cards out for solitaire, "Help us? Help us do what?" Randy thought silently for a few seconds then said, "We tell him we…. shit! I'll think of something…"

"What were you doing over there anyway?" Martha asked Tommy. "Sam and I were working on a report for school," Tommy said with a naive tone. "Don't lie boy. Summer, what was he doing there?" Martha asked with a stressed tone. Summer was sitting with her sister and nephew at a dirty table covered with papers and unopened bills. "They had a report for school so I took them to the college to do research. I gave them money for the bus when they were done because I was supposed to have lab but it was called off," Summer said while watching flies buzz around the room.

"Cletus, you find it yet?" Martha yelled down the hallway. "Hold on!" was the response. "I don't know if this is the real solution," Summer said but was closed down quickly by Martha. "You want to be killed in your sleep? Raped? You don't know who that was in the house," Martha said with anger, "God damn, you are a young woman without a man there to protect you!" Summer was very offended by the last statement, "I don't need a man to protect me!"

"No but you do need this," Cletus said while holding a Colt revolver in the palm of his hand. "I don't even know how to use a gun," Summer said with conviction, "I could kill someone with that thing!" Cletus smiled with chew stained teeth, "That's the point, to kill someone. Come on outside, I show ya how to use it." Tommy jumped up from the chair then yelled, "Come on guys! Dad's gonna show us how to shoot a gun!"

Cletus walked out the door while twirling the gun around on his right index finger. The triplets were the next out the door followed by Red, their basset hound. "Well I guess they need me too," Summer said with a somber tone, "are you coming?" Martha stood up, "No, I'm going to get dinner started. Summer, I really hope you take what happened to you seriously. The eighties are a dangerous time."

Summer looked at her older sister whose face showed her age plus some, "I do take it seriously but having a man doesn't solve everything. Why don't you come out here and watch me shoot?" Martha turned around then opened the pantry door, "No you'll be fine. If Cletus doesn't have his dinner ready by five he's a real bear." Summer stood up from the chair, walked to her older sister then hugged her. "What is that for? Haven't hugged me since you were a little girl," Martha said with surprise. "It's because I haven't hugged you since I was a little girl," Summer said.

Summer let go of her older sister then walked out into the hot afternoon sun. "Come on Aunt Summer!" Johnnie yelled from the side of a weather-beaten barn. Summer walked along a dirt path cut through the overgrown lawn. She came to the side of the barn where the ground slowly fell into a valley about a half mile away. "We can shoot out here all we want and not hit anyone… unless we want," Cletus said with a laugh.

Summer gave a smirk but wanted to have nothing to do with Cletus. "Come over here and I show you how to hold it," Cletus said. Summer was reluctant to do so but slowly walked to the grungy man. "Come here and stand right in front of me," Cletus said while waving at the young woman with the gun in his left hand, "Stay right there." Cletus stood close behind Summer then held the gun in front of her with his left hand. "Take the gun in your left hand and wrap your fingers around the grip," Cletus said as his hot, stale breath hit her hair.

Summer did what was asked of her, but was feeling sick from the smell of his breath. "Now put your right fingers on top of the others except for the finger next to your thumb, hold it out for now," Cletus said. Summer did as she was told but felt quite ill when Cletus place his fingers on top of hers. "This gun has a kick, I'll hold your hands until you get used to it," Cletus said while whispering into Summer's right ear, "Look right over the top of the barrel and aim toward that old oak tree down there. Put your finger on the trigger and when ready, pull it back."

Summer lined up on the trunk of the old tree about seventy-five feet away. Her stomach was tight from the having Cletus so close to her, but then she remembered her sisters face. She remembered how Cletus abuses her and with that a small fire grew inside of her. She looked down the barrel, but she did not see the tree, she saw Cletus's face. She quickly pulled back on the trigger and with the roar of a cannon, the gun fired. She could feel the gun trying to go upward but Cletus's hands held it firm.

Quickly another roar happened to her side, but this time of the boys cheering. "Look! She hit the tree dead on!" Tommy yelled. "Awesome!" Johnnie yelled. "Calm down guys, let's give her another try," Cletus said sharply, "Okay Hon, aim

112

again then pull the trigger." With that the flame grew bigger. Summer pulled the trigger and hit the tree within an inch from her first shot "Man, she is good!" Tommy yelled, "Almost as good as you, dad."

Cletus removed his hands but stayed close to her body, "Okay you know what the kick is like now, take another shot without me holding your hands." Summer looked down the barrel again, pulled the trigger and did her best to keep the gun from flying upward as it went off. "See, has quite a kick!" Cletus exclaimed then laughed, "You boys see where that shot landed?" Tommy piped up, "Yep she hit the tree dead on again!"

"Well seems like we have a natural here. Take another shot when you're ready," Cletus said as his hot breath hit that back of Summer's head again. Summer lined up but just as she started to put pressure on the trigger, Cletus ran his hands down her sides causing her to jump as she pulled the trigger. The bullet went down past the oak tree where a line of trees seemed to meet the horizon. As the bullet sailed through the leaves, a flock of birds flew out.

"Keep your greasy hands off me," Summer yelled with venom. Cletus laughed then said, "I was just making sure you could react under pressure. Looks like you need to practice some more… Someone breaks into that house again, they ain't gonna stand still so you can line up on them."

113

Tommy looked at his father with resentment; he knew his father touched his aunt just only for his own personal satisfaction.

"Go back over near the boys," Summer said as her ears rang from the gunfire. Cletus did as he was told but not before ogling her rear end while saying with a lusty tone, "Damn the Graham girls all have those same curves." Summer relaxed herself and with a swift motion, raised the gun and pulled the trigger twice. The boys watched as the bark at the dead center of the tree exploded. "Dead on!" Tommy yelled.

"I think you need to reload the gun," Summer said bluntly. "Damn boys, I guess your aunt here is a gun slinger!" Cletus said as he took the Colt from Summer. As he was reloaded the cylinder Martha yelled from the house, "Dinner!" The boys took off running toward the house as Summer followed. "Don't you want to shoot a little more, darling?" Summer stopped then slowly turned to her brother in law, "I think I can handle the gun just fine and so help me God, you call me darling one more time, I'll use you for target practice." Cletus started to laugh, "Damn all you girls have the same attitude also... just need to be broke like a horse."

Summer felt that flame turning into a holocaust in her soul, "Broke? Is that what you do to Martha when you beat her? You're just breaking her?" Cletus lost his grimy smile, "What you saying?" Summer smirked, "I'm saying you treat my sister like an animal. The one who needs the gun for protection is her." Summer turned then started to walk the path back to the house. She made it about ten feet when gunfire broke the relative silence. Summer whipped around to see Cletus holding the gun up into the air.

"You ever talk to me like that again, that will be the last thing your sister will ever hear," Cletus said with a cold attitude. Summer walked back and said bluntly, "You ever hurt her or any of those boys again... I'll make sure they never find your body." As Cletus stood there stunned by the woman's audacity, Summer quickly swiped the gun from his hand. "Oh, by the way, thank you for letting me borrow this," Summer said with a smile. She turned around once more to go to the farm house. When she walked in the door she saw the boys sitting at the table looking at her with pure silence.

"How was school today?" Michael asked Sam. "School? Um, it was good," Sam said then took a sip of his milk. "How about you, Danielle?" Michael asked as he took a spoonful of mashed potatoes from a bone white bowl. "School is school... we have the fall dance coming up next weekend. Can I go?" Danielle asked bluntly. "It's up to your mother," Michael said while the thought of his daughter dating was eating at his stomach lining.

Elizabeth looked toward her husband then to Danielle, "Of course you can go. Who is taking you?" Danielle shrugged her shoulders, "Haven't been asked yet, but I know someone will." Sam piped up, "Yeah there has to be someone desperate enough!" Danielle looked to her little brother as she rolled her eyes, "You will never have to worry about going to school dances, nerds are not allowed."

"Before you two get going, stop," Michael said firmly. Danielle looked to her little brother who responded with his tongue darting out. Michael stopped with his fork in midair while he stared his son down. Sam quickly pulled his tongue back into his mouth then turned his attention to his dinner. "How was your day?" Elizabeth asked her husband. "Busy as usual. That building is still blistering hot; I cannot wait for fall. Oh, do you remember Stanton Smith from school?" Elizabeth looked up from her plate while cutting her chicken, "The name sounds familiar, but I can't place him."

"He was on the varsity baseball team with me; well he's a patrolman for the city now. I just happened to see him at the gas station when I stopped on the way home. He was telling me a young woman a few blocks over... had someone break into her house when she was gone. I guess she came home and didn't even know the guy was there until he made some noise. He cut her phone line and everything," Michael said then took a sip of his beer.

Sam listened with his undivided attention hoping his father did not know that he was at the house. "That's horrible! What is this town coming to?" Elizabeth asked. "Well make sure to keep the doors locked when I am not home," Michael said, "I guess the woman had a key hidden outside the intruder found. Glad we don't do that."

Sam took a bite of his chicken then asked his father, "They have no idea who broke in?" Michael looked to his son, "Don't talk with your mouth full, son. And no, none of the neighbors saw a thing. Don't worry; it's probably just an old boyfriend of the woman." Danielle looked up to her father to see him staring right back at her.

"That just scary... imagine a man creeping around a house in broad daylight," Elizabeth said, "You two be careful when you are going to school tomorrow morning. That man may be a maniac or something." Michael took another sip of his beer then looked to his son, "Next year you will be in high school Sam. Perhaps you should try out for wrestling or football." Sam darted his head up from his plate then asked, "Why?"

Michael looked at his son, "Because, you need to be toughened up a bit. The world is a dangerous place. Don't you want to be able to defend yourself? You never know when Russia might pull something..." Sam shrugged his shoulders, "They tell us in school that fighting is never the solution." Michael shook his head then looked to his wife, "See what those softies are teaching our son... Sam, never go around looking for a fight, but if one comes looking for you... you need to be able to defend yourself; especially if you are in the right."

"Michael, he's just a boy," Elizabeth said. "He's a wimp," Danielle said then laughed. Sam could feel himself growing smaller in the room. "He's not a wimp but he does need to be able to deal with the older boys in high school," Michael said bluntly, "I loved wresting... builds character, muscle and the ability to defend yourself."

"Oh, those guys in wrestling always smell so bad!" Danielle said, "Well... Sam already smells so he would fit right in." Elizabeth gave her daughter a stern look then said, "Quit." Sam looked up to his family, "I'm fine. I don't need help learning how to fight and the last thing I want is to be in sports!" Michael placed his fork down on his plate with enough force to cause his wife to jump, "Listen to me, you will be in sports. No son of mine will be going through school without participating in sports." Sam pushed his chair back then stood up, "I guess you will need a new son then because I will not be playing any sport."

Chapter 9

"We are almost out of time today," Miss Kemp said with her back to the blackboard, "I would like all of chapter two read tonight as there will be an open book quiz tomorrow. Pay special attention to the footnotes; they contain important information also. Tommy and Sam, please stay after so you two can schedule your make up test." Tommy looked back to Sam who was sitting behind him and whispered, "Do you think she will spank us?" Sam giggled loud enough for Miss Kemp to look in his direction.

The bell rang announcing the end of the school day for the students who left with the rush of prisoners freed from life sentences. "Why did they have to have a test yesterday?" Sam asked Tommy as they walked toward the teacher's desk. "I know, just our luck," Tommy said with a disappointing tone. "Boys we had a test covering all of chapter one yesterday. So it pretty much covered the beginning of the revolutionary war. Unfortunately, I have an appointment this afternoon, would both of you be able to stay after tomorrow to take the test?" Miss Kemp asked as she was removing her purse from the putty beige desk.

The boys looked to one another then Sam said, "That should be no problem Miss Kemp." The young, attractive teacher opened her purse, looked inside then closed it quickly when she saw Tommy peeping in. "Good tomorrow it is…," Miss Kemp said but was interrupted when a man walked in the classroom. "Rachel are you… boys… good to see you. I hope I was not interrupting anything," the man said. "We are finished here, they were scheduling their make-up test for tomorrow afternoon," Miss Kemp said, "see you tomorrow boys. The test should only take about twenty minutes should you need to make arrangements to get home."

Tommy and Sam took their books then walked out of the room into the vacant hallway. "Did you see that shit? She's boning the fucking gym teacher," Tommy whispered. "How do you know they are boning?" Sam asked as they passed through the doors to the parking lot. "He's so high class; he makes her buy the rubbers. I saw them in her purse along with a pack of camels," Tommy said then pointed toward the front of the school, "Look, there they go. He must not be able to wait to jump her bones." Sam looked over to see their teacher getting into a convertible with the gym teacher, Mister Neer.

"I thought he had a wife," Sam said. "He does and a couple of kids too," Tommy said, "It's always those jock types that get the hot chicks." Sam shook his head, "Don't even bring that shit up, my old man wants me to join either wrestling or football next year. Fuck that shit…" Tommy smirked, "Old man wasn't a jock so you need to be?" Sam shook his head, "Worse, he was a jock and now I have to be just like him. He says I need to be toughened up." Tommy laughed, "Toughened up? What he wants you to be a Marine or something?" Sam rolled his eyes but remained quiet.

Johnnie and Donnie came from across the parking lot on their bikes to also see the attractive teacher leaving with the gym teacher. "Did you guys see that?" Donnie yelled to Sam and Tommy as he rode up to them. "Yeah, she's boning him," Tommy said disappointed. Johnnie stopped his bike quickly making a skid mark on the worn asphalt.

"Damn, that's as long as the skids in your shorts," Tommy said with a laugh. Johnnie placed his left foot on the ground then lifted one cheek off of the bicycle seat only to let out a loud blast, 'Pfffffhhhhhtttttttt' Sam swiftly turned his head away from the discharge, "Damnit, I'm down wind of that!" Tommy started to laugh, "Now I know why he has skids… Damn, you had the pizza for lunch!" Tommy then held his nose with his right hand while waving his left hand in the air.

"What you guys going to do this afternoon?" Donnie asked. Sam shrugged his shoulders, "Don't know, I have a bunch of homework because of yesterday. Like I want to do that." Donnie opened his back pack to pull out a pack of cigarettes, "Anyone want one?" Tommy shook his head, "Yeah, I'll take one." Sam looked back to the school, "Let's get moving guys, I don't want to be seen by the principal. He's always looking out to nail us for something."

The group of boys moved to the side street where the bike rack is. "I have to get my bike," Tommy said, "Where's your lighter?" Donnie passed a purple tinted clear plastic lighter to his brother then said to Sam, "Tommy tell you Aunt Summer has a gun now?" Sam shook his head, "No. Where did she get it from?" Tommy took a drag off of his cigarette then said, "Our dad. He showed her how to shoot last night… you should have seen it! She hit that old oak tree in the pasture five of six times."

Sam got a small grin on his face but remained quiet. "What's up with you?" Johnnie asked. Sam got straight faced then blushed a bit. "What's up?" Tommy asked. Sam found the encouragement then asked, "Do you think your aunt would ever like a guy like me?" Johnnie and Donnie giggled, but Tommy thought about the question poised to him, "Truthfully I don't know. Now if you were her age, maybe. But you're just a kid to her… even though your equipment is ready for her."

Johnnie looked down the street, "Shit, get rid of your cigs quick, a cop is coming!" Tommy and Donnie quickly threw their cigarettes into the bushes just beyond the bike rack. The boys pretended to be perfect citizens as the squad car passed by slowly. "Thank God he kept going," Tommy said. "Hey I forgot to tell you that my dad talked with that cop that was at your aunt's house," Sam said. "Shit, did he tell your old man we were there?" Tommy asked. "Naw, didn't even mention two boys were there. Which is good because I would not be able to walk right now if my dad knew I skipped school," Sam said.

"Let's go back out to the tracks," Tommy said as he was trying to recover his cigarette from the bushes. "For what?" Donnie asked. Tommy pulled himself out of the evergreen bush with his cigarette still lit, "Sam and I were trying to look for another body." Donnie shook his head, "No more of that dead body and ghost shit... let's go over to the theater and sneak in." Sam piped up, "I don't know Tommy, maybe we should just leave it alone."

Tommy took a long drag then blew the smoke out of his nostrils, "You know something is out there. Something that wants you to find it... remember it has talked to you." Sam shook his head slightly in agreement, "I know... but we didn't see nothing and we don't have shovels to dig. Let's just forget about it." Tommy shook his head, "Forget it? No man... and the shovel... I hid one on the trail this morning."

Sam gave Tommy a blank face, "What about the guy who works for the railroad?" Donnie interrupted the negotiations between the two friends, "They are off in another world, let's go see a movie, Johnnie." Tommy looked over to his brothers, "If you guys want to go... go. We don't need your help anyway." Sam looked to the two brothers leaving sore, "You pissed them off."

123

"Well?" Tommy asked with a raised brow. "Okay, but you didn't answer my question about Red," Sam said. "No problem, we can see up and down the tracks for a few miles each way. We'll see him coming, that bright yellow trucks sticks out good," Tommy said with complete assurance, "Come on, let's go to your house so you can grab your bike."

The boys walked swiftly to Sam's house then carefully pulled his bike out of the garage hoping Sam's mother would not see him. As they went down the side of the house, Sam's mother saw the boys passing. "Where are you two off to?" Elizabeth asked through the open kitchen window. Sam looked up startled by his mother, "We are going off riding for a bit." Elizabeth bit her lip a bit then said, "Your father is working late tonight. Remember he wants you here when he's not..." Sam looked down then back up to his mother, "Okay... Sorry Tommy, maybe tomorrow... I hope."

"Tommy, why don't you stay here for a bit, no reason for you to leave," Elizabeth said with a helpful tone. Sam looked to his friend, "Want to hang out for a bit?" Tommy thought for a second, "I... I better be getting home. Thank you anyway Misses White." Tommy walked his bike toward the sidewalk where he mounted it then rode away. Sam feeling defeated, returned his bicycle to the garage by pushing it in the door allowing it to fly into his father's workbench where it turned over on its side.

Sam came up the back steps, walked in the door then passed his mother silently. "Hey, don't look so down," Elizabeth said, "Dinner should be ready in an hour or so." Sam continued walking into the dining room then to the stairs. As he started to climb them his sister came in the front door. "Could you tell your criminal friend to quit looking at me?" Danielle said with an angered tone. "Fuck off!" Sam said then ran up the stairs to his room finally slamming the door behind him.

"What the hell is your problem?" Danielle said out loud. Elizabeth came out of the kitchen to see her daughter looking up the stairs, "What was that?" Danielle smiled, "Your son… all I did was tell him to tell Tommy to quit looking at me. You should see it mom! All he does is stare at my breasts." Elizabeth shook her head, "Well I just told him he couldn't go out with Tommy but I did offer for Tommy to stay." Danielle quickly objected, "Mom! Don't let that little freak in here! He looks at me like a sex maniac or something. He's just like his father. Everyone in town says that you know."

Elizabeth gave her daughter a disappointing look, "He's not a sex maniac and he's not like his father. He's a normal boy whose hormones are out of control. If you don't want him staring at your boobs, try wearing a bra. You can almost see your nipples through that shirt. From now on, your wardrobe will be monitored before you leave for school." Danielle's face turned red, "He's the sex maniac but I have to dress better! I can't believe this!" Before her mother could respond, Danielle ran up the stairs in a huff. Elizabeth waited for her door to slam shut then said, "I never should have had kids."

Tommy furiously rode his bike as fast as he could through the business district of the town. He almost hit a man leaving the bank while weaving to miss a woman pushing a baby carriage. He left the sidewalk and went across the street right in front of a delivery truck causing the driver to yell obscenities toward him while in front of a group of children and their mother.

As he neared the tracks he didn't even look to see if a train was coming as he hit the crossing then rode between the rails of one set of tracks. His body was quickly feeling numb as the bike bounced between the ties and ballast. He came to the trail where he dismounted the bike leaving it laying between the rails. He jumped through the weeds and went down the trail to recover a rusty spade from the bushes. Before he left the trail, he went to the open grave next to the trail. He stared at the hole then quickly left to go back to his bike.

He jumped on his bike for the bumpy mile long ride to the next milepost. As he rode he thought of nothing but what he may find buried in the weeds. His friend's nightmare had become his obsession. He could see the milepost quickly approaching as the warm afternoon breeze started to pick up. When he came to milepost forty, Tommy jumped off his bike then lifted it over the rail only to throw it down in the weeds. He looked carefully for anything that seemed odd, but the summer's growth of weeds obscured the ground completely. Even where the boys looked before could not be seen due to the rapid growth of the plants.

In the far distance Tommy could hear the horn of a train. He paid it no attention as he walked on the ground using his shoes to feel for anything amiss. Minutes had passed as he walked back and forth over a length of thirty feet either side of the post. Soon the rumble of the train was becoming noticeable in the near distance. Tommy was about ten feet from the rails when the engineer blasted his horn to worn the boy.

Tommy turned at the loud noise just in time to see the engineer wave to him as he passed going over fifty miles per hour. The sound of the engines was deafening as they rumbled by pulling a long train of coal cars. Tommy stepped back away from the rails as the swiftly moving cars became unnerving. As he stepped back he noticed he had also stepped down about four inches. Tommy felt around with his feet to discover he was standing in a depression in the embankment.

As Tommy's feet moved around to find the edges, he could feel a sobering excitement come over him. He retuned to his bike to see he had left the shovel on the roadbed right next to the speeding train. It took all the courage he had to walk up within a foot or two of the train to then pull the shovel back with his heel. The breeze the cars created made him feel as if he would be sucked in at any second.

Once he got the shovel in his hand, Tommy ran back to the depression. With little care and little regard for what he was doing, Tommy dug into the earth. With each shovelful he would look into the hole before taking another chunk. Tommy lost all sense of time and his surroundings as he dug.

The heaping piles of dirt were now surrounding him. He was down more than a foot but nothing yet was found but a few beer bottles and a broken glass insulator. As he took another shovel full a voice caused him to break his concentration. "Wwww, what ya doing?" Tim asked from the rails. Tommy looked over, "Looking for a body!" Tim walked down to the mounds of dirt, "Body? A body..." Tommy started to dig again then said, "Yes. A woman... she's buried here."

"Yes... yes... I know. She talks to me..." Tim said softly, "Many wo, wo, women speak to me here... here." Tommy kept his concentration on the earth he was removing. "Ssss, stop boy," Tim said. Tommy looked to the old man, "Why?" Tim sat on one of the piles of earth then started to weep, "She's… she's… she's my friend."

Tommy was starting to get angered when he blurted out, "Like those pictures? Are they your friends too?" Tim looked down to the soil, "I, I, I, I'm old boy… My time may be near… near. They… they… are like friends to me… like my daughter…" Tommy's anger was now turning toward sadness for the old man. "Tim, it ain't right if there is a woman buried here… She's someone's daughter," Tommy said as he started to dig once more. Tim slowly shook his head in agreement, "Yes."

"I… I… I'll go… please tell her I, I, I'm sorry," Tim said softly. Tommy did not acknowledge the old man as he walked back up to the rails. As Tommy took another shovelful Tim yelled from the rail, "There… where you are… she says she's there." Tommy looked back to the old man pointing right at him. "She's there… Cindy is there," Tim said then started to walk back toward the river bridge.

Tommy looked back to the soil and with all his strength threw the spade into the ground. He dug up another shovel full of dirt but nothing was seen. "Crazy old man," Tommy said under his breath as he pushed the spade in again. Tommy worked hard as the late afternoon sun shined down on him.

It was in the sun that something glimmered and caught Tommy's eye. He bent down into the dirt to find what reflected the sunlight. Tommy moved his head around to see if he could catch the light again, but he couldn't. With his bare finger he dug into the soil where he thought the light came from. He pulled a large chuck of soil back to find what reflected this light. He stared down for a second then with the tips of his finger, brushed the soil away from a jaw bone. "A gold filling," Tommy said, "That must have been it."

Tommy used his finger to push more of the soil away to review the full skull of a human. His heart started to race as he realized that Sam was correct; Sam did hear voices telling him that a body was here. Tommy stood up then shook the soil from his pants, "I got to go tell Sam!" Tommy went to turn when he felt a sharp pain to the back of his head. He could see that he was falling forward but he could not put his arms out to break the fall. His head crashed into the grave and as his eyes slowly closed all he saw was that skull.

Chapter 10

Sam went right back to his bedroom after dinner. It wasn't because he was being punished for the swearing at his sister or slamming the door. It was because he just needed to be alone. He felt as if his life was falling apart at the seams. He never knew fourteen would be such a rough age.

Being one who loves schoolwork so much, his homework sat on his desk untouched while he sat on his bed listening to the radio. As the sun slowly went down, so did his eyes. It wasn't long before he was lying on his side snoring with his clothes on. After a short nap, Sam awoke to his room dark and the radio mute. He tried to find his alarm clock to see the time, but it wasn't on the nightstand like it should be.

He slowly pulled himself up in bed then turned so as to stand up. When he stepped onto the floor it felt cold and wet. He tried to focus his eyes in the dark, but it was of no use as the room was just too dark. Sam placed his foot back down onto the wet floor to find it was no longer his bedroom, but the middle of a river.

"What the?" Sam tried to say, but the words just wouldn't form in his mouth. He could feel the water slowly rising up his legs, inch by inch. There was little sound and the harder he tried to speak, the harder the words were to form. In the distance a pinpoint of light could be seen. It seemed to get larger by the second; it appeared to be headed right for Sam!

He tried his best to move in the deepening water but it was so hard to do so. The river bottom was mud that seemed to pull at his feet with a great suction. The light was getting brighter yet he still could not see his surroundings. Sam's heart raced as he tried to move in the water that was now close to his navel.

He knew it was no use in trying to move out of the way of the bright light. He turned his back to the light as he felt himself being hit by a great amount of energy. The feeling was of great pain, fear and sadness. He tried to breathe but each breath was shorter and more painful. He could now feel the water rising toward his chest as his head started to ache. What little vision Sam had was now gone even with the bright light surrounding him.

The water continued to rise now close to his chin. Sam's head was ringing like a bell continuously struck over and over. Then as soon as it started, it stopped. Sam could no longer feel pain or sadness or even fear. The water was now gone and his feet no longer felt like they were stuck in mud. He slowly opened his eyes to see he was back in his dark bedroom. The music was playing on the radio and his alarm clock was back on the nightstand. It read one o'clock.

He reached for the radio to turn it down when the music was drowned out by the voice of a woman. "Sam," the voice said softly, "Sam he found me…" Sam looked to the radio dial dimly lit then said, "Who are you?"

Sam listened as the music started to rise in volume. "Who are you?!" Sam asked. The music continued to play when a voice came from the foot of his bed, "I'm Cindy and he has found me." Sam turned quickly to see a beautiful young woman standing at the foot of his bed. She was the woman he had seen before but now she seemed so real, so lifelike that she had to be in the room with him. "Who found you?" Sam asked. The woman smiled, "Your friend but now you must find him." Sam looked at the woman with fear and asked, "What do you mean find him?"

The room started to fade in Sam's vision. "You already know where he is… your dream tells you where he is…. He found me…," the woman said as everything went black. Sam could feel his heart racing again, "Come back!! Who do I need to find?!" Sam could see nothing; it was as if he was blind. He was struggling to breathe. It was as if the room was losing oxygen. Sam felt as if he was about to faint and quickly there was nothing. Sam's senses were gone. Sam felt as if he was gone.

Without warning, Sam opened his eyes to the bright flashes of lightning and the rolling of thunder. Suddenly during another crash of thunder, a loud banging came at his door. "Sam! Open this door, now!" Michael said as he beat on the door with his fists. Sam rolled out of bed then walked to the door. He unlocked the door only to have it fly open at him. Michael was standing at the door with a drenched Cletus Jones.

"Is Tommy here?!" Cletus yelled, "Where is he?" Sam shook his head, "I don't know… he's not here." Cletus pushed the boy aside as he came in the room looking for Tommy. "Where is he?" Cletus asked as his clothes dripped onto the wood floor. Sam shook his head, "I don't know! I haven't seen him since we came home from school."

"Is there anyone else's house he might be at?" Michael asked his son. "No, no one that I know of," Sam said. Elizabeth's voice could be heard from the first floor, "Michael, the police are here!" Cletus looked to Michael, "My boys missing and you call the cops on me?" Michael could see that Cletus was a force he didn't want to tangle with, "No, I called them to help look for Tommy." Cletus pushed past Sam's father, "I don't need no damn help…"

Cletus came down the stairs to see Stanton Smith wearing a rain coat looking up at him. "What's going on here?" Stanton asked. "Tommy is missing," Elizabeth said. Stanton asked Cletus, "Your son, Tommy?" Cletus shook his head, "He never came home. I came here because their boy is almost kin to my boys." Michael came down the stairs with Sam closely behind. "Do you know where he is?" Stanton asked Sam.

Sam felt as if the whole world was staring at him. "Sam?" Elizabeth asked, "Do you know where Tommy is?" Sam looked down, "I think... but I don't know for sure." Stanton motioned to the boy, "Come down here, we need to talk about this." Sam did as he was told and came down to the landing just as brilliant flash of lightning caused the dark living room to glow. Sam looked into the now dark room, "The river... I think the river."

"What?!" Cletus asked. "I think he might be in the river," Sam said. Stanton looked to the boy, "Why do you think he is in the river?" Sam got real quiet just as another bright flash of lightning came, "I had a dream... I have been having dreams." Cletus was turning bright red, "What did you do to Tommy?!" Stanton turned to the fuming father, "Calm down. Let me handle this. Son, what do you mean you have been having dreams?"

Sam looked the police officer directly in the face, "Dead women... I have seen their ghosts. We found one body near the trail." Michael looked to his son, "What are you talking about?!" Stanton looked to the boy, "Did you make that phone call?" Sam shook his head, "Yes from the train station." Cletus interrupted, "What body? What phone call? Where the hell is my boy?!"

Sam tried to hold back tears, "I had a dream tonight that I was in a river or lake and the water was rising up my body... then she told me that he found her..." Michael now too was fuming, "What are you talking about?" Sam started to cry, "The woman at mile forty! Tommy must have found her body! The river isn't far from there." Michael looked to Stanton, "Was a body found?" Stanton looked to the men, "We found human remains off of the railroad tracks near a trail through the woods." Elizabeth gasped, "A body? I didn't hear anything about this?"

Stanton exhaled, "We only found a bone and a tooth... some jewelry." Sam shook his head, "No! There was a whole body there... a girl." Stanton looked to the boy, "You are telling me there was a whole body?" Sam shook his head, "Yes but she was... she was... it smelled so bad!" Cletus grabbed the officers arm, "Forget about some body, where is my boy?!"

"Where is this mile forty?" Stanton asked Sam. "Down the tracks from where the first girl was found. The woman said she was buried near mile forty. Tommy and I were going there when mom told me I had to stay home... but Tommy never said he was going there alone!" Sam said while sobbing. "Can you take me there?" Stanton asked. Sam shook his head, "Yes."

"Go get a raincoat if you have one. I think I might have one for you Mister Jones," Stanton said as he headed toward the door. "I'm coming too," Michael said as he headed to the coat closet, "I have a coat in here somewhere." Stanton opened the door in time to see a stroke of lightning streaked across the sky, "I will radio the fire department for help."

Cletus headed out the door with Stanton. Michael found an old green rain jacket and while putting it on said to Elizabeth in a soft tone, "We may need to get Sam some help." Elizabeth seemed to lose a bit of color, "Help? Like psychological?" Michael shook his head in agreement as Sam came down the stairs with a bright yellow rain coat. "Let's get moving," Michael said.

They ran out the door into the pouring rain. They went to the squad car then got in the backseat with Cletus. "First time without cuffs," Cletus said with a somber tone. Just as Michael got the door closed, Stanton pulled away from the curb as the tires spun to get traction. "Go to the old train station," Sam said, "We will have to get on the tracks and walk down then."

Stanton blew though the town as lightning flashed and rain poured down. As they drove toward the station they could see the wig-wag signals were lit and oscillating back and forth. "Shit, there must be a train!" Stanton said. As he came toward the feed store he pulled to the curb. Next to the building a switch locomotive was setting out two grain cars.

"Maybe he could take us," Stanton said, "Wait here in the car." Stanton ran to the locomotive that was now at a stop. He held tightly to the slick steel handrails as he climbed the stairs.

He opened the door startling the engineer who was looking back toward the cars. "I need you to take me down the tracks; there may be a boy in danger down there," Stanton said with haste. "A boy? Where?" the engineer asked. "Mile forty... I believe," Stanton said, "I have the fire department on the way with men. There are two men and a boy with me that will come with."

The engineer grabbed a white microphone that was hanging to his side, "Zach cut those cars loose then get in here. We need to head down to forty to find a boy who may be injured." Stanton opened the door and waved toward the squad car shouting, "Come on!"

Cletus, Sam and Michael poured out of the car into the driving rain. As they climbed the stairs Sam slipped but was caught by Cletus before he fell to the ground.

"Dispatch, this is eight zero seven, I need both mainlines closed. There may be a boy injured near mile forty. I am taking a police officer down there right now," The engineer said calmly into the microphone. A tall man in a bright yellow rain suit walked into the cab through the rear door, "The cars are loose." The engineer turned to the group of strangers, "Hold tight." Sam watched with amazement and joy as the engineer moved the run lever to one. He heard the diesel engine start to idle up as the gauges in front of the engineer moved.

With a quick jerk the locomotive itself started to move.

"Zach, get all the flashlights you have in the cabinet. They will need them in this rain," the engineer said as the locomotive picked up speed. "Forty is a little over a mile away, should be there very fast. How do you know the boy is there?" the engineer asked. "I'll explain that later. How far beyond that is the river?" Stanton asked. "Not far at all, maybe a quarter mile," the engineer said.

Sam watched down the rails that were illuminated by the headlight of the locomotive and the occasional flash of lightning. "Hold on, I need to slow now, we are just about there," the engineer said, "Zach get ready to help. I'll set the hand brake." The wheels slowed down then the locomotive stopped just short of the forty sign. Stanton grabbed one of the flashlights from the brakemen then went down the stairs. He jumped down onto the roadbed while running the light around, "Tommy!"

Cletus was next followed by Michael and Sam. "Tommy! Where are you?!" Cletus yelled. A brilliant flash of lightning caused the landscape to glow as if lit by the sun. "There! There is something there!" Zach yelled from the walkway of the locomotive. Stanton looked in the direction with his flashlight to see what appeared to be an open grave, "Dear God…"

The men slide down the embankment toward the water filled hole. Michael jumped in and felt around in the muck, "He's not here." The men were scanning the woods with their flashlights as another flash came from above. "I don't see anything," Michael yelled. Sam looked down the tracks then yelled, "The river!" Stanton yelled to the men, "Come on, let's take the train down to the river." As Cletus went to climb the embankment, another flash illuminated the landscape. "His bike!" Cletus yelled, "His bike is over here." Cletus looked around the bike but there was no sign of Tommy in the pouring rain. "Come on, let's check out the river," Michael yelled

They climbed back onto the walkway as the brakemen yelled in the door, "We need to go to the bridge." The engineer quickly released the brakes then put the locomotive into motion. It wasn't long before he was applying the brakes again. "Ask him to turn this thing off!" Stanton yelled to the brakeman who acknowledged with the shake of his head.

The locomotive stopped just short of the bridge. As they jumped down onto the roadbed the engine slowly rumbled down. Once the engine had stopped, all they could hear was the water rushing under the bridge. "The river must be three feet higher than it was before the storm started," Michael said. "Well? Where the hell is he?!" Cletus yelled to Sam. While Michael could relate to how Cletus was feeling, his fatherly instincts kicked in,

"Hey, don't yell at my son... Sam, do you know where Tommy may be?"

Sam shook his head, "All I know is that there was water that was slowly going up my body. My feet felt as if they were stuck in mud or something." Stanton looked to the group of men, "Split up and take to either side of the bridge, we need to scan the water." Sam and Michael ran to the edge of the bridge where a rusty chain took the place of a guardrail. Michael used a flashlight but it barely made a dent in the darkness of the roaring river. A bright flash of lightning illuminated the sky but nothing could be seen.

Michael turned back toward Stanton and Cletus then yelled, "Do you see him?!" Stanton yelled back, "No!" Sam looked down to see the top of the river just about to lick the beams. "I don't know what you dreamed, but is there anything else you can remember?" Michael asked Sam. He looked to his father as the rain poured into his eyes, "No." Michael grabbed Sam's arms, "Think God damnit! Did you see anything else?"

Sam was trying his best not to cry, "My head hurt real bad and there was a light. A light started out small then got larger until I was surrounded by it... the water was so tall; it was near my chin..." Before Michael could ask a question, the brakeman asked, "The light was it like the highlight on the locomotive?" Sam looked up to the bright headlight of the locomotive then shook his head, "Yes, maybe, I think." Zach looked to Michael, "I think I might know where he is. A few miles down there is a deep stream that parallels the tracks for a maybe a quarter mile, maybe less. Its runs into this river a half mile from here."

Michael yelled to Stanton, "Come on, we need to go down the tracks. The brakeman knows another spot." The men went back into the locomotive while the engineer started the engine. "We need to go to that stream, near thirty-eight," Zach said. Sam was shaking from the cold and dampness as the locomotive lurched forward. He looked out the window as they passed over the bridge. Shortly they were coming to an area not familiar to Sam. "Right there, we need to stop there," Zach said. The engineer quickly applied the brakes causing the engine to slide slightly on the slick rails.

When the engine stopped, Cletus was ready to jump out the door. "Stop!" the brakemen yelled, "Get off the engine near the other rails. This side of the roadbed is held back with a retaining wall. You jump off on that side, you might land right in the stream." Cletus shook his head then headed out the door followed by Stanton and Michael. "Son, you better stay in here, its dangerous out there near that stream," the engineer said, "Take a seat over there and dry off some." Sam did as was asked of him but felt left out.

The men used their flashlights but like at the river, the water appeared as nothing but roaring blackness. A bright bolt of lightning struck a tree not far into the woods. "We may have to head into the engine, this is getting dangerous with the lightning," Stanton yelled over the rumble of the locomotive. "You go inside," Cletus yelled, "I'll find my boy myself." A bright flash of lightning illuminated the sky just long enough for Stanton to see something near a tree that was surrounded by the stream.

Stanton grabbed Michael's arm then nodded toward the tree. Michael shined his light toward the tree to see what looked to be a white shirt against the trunk. "What color of shirt was Tommy wearing today?" Stanton asked Cletus. He shook his head, "I, I don't remember, light I guess… yellow, white… I don't remember." Cletus looked to see Michael holding his beam of light toward a tree in the stream. He looked to see the white against the truck. "Oh God!" Cletus yelled then went to jump into the water.

Michael and Stanton grabbed the man. "No, you'll get swept away!" Stanton yelled as Cletus struggled to get free. "Hey! Do you have any rope in there?" Michael yelled to the brakeman. He shook his head, "No… but we do have some in the caboose! It's back at the feed store." Stanton did his best to hold Cletus and said, "Tell them to go back. The fire department must be there by now. They can come back in that caboose."

Michael ran to the brakeman, "Come on, let's get that caboose!" Stanton held Cletus tight as he cried out, "Tommy! Tommy! Can you hear me?!" The locomotive idled up then slowly accelerated toward town. As they came closer to town, they could see flashing lights of fire trucks near the crossing. Within a short distance of the crossing, the engineer pulled on the lever to blow the horn. "Zach go down there and get ready to couple up the caboose. Sir, you go tell the firefighters to jump in," the engineer said as the locomotive slowly came close to the caboose. Sam watched out the window and down the hood as the caboose came closer and closer as the locomotive slowed finally slamming just into the coupler of the caboose.

Michael ran down to the fire chief waiting in the pouring rain, "Get rope and what else you need. There is a boy in the water about three miles down. We'll take you in the caboose." The chief yelled back to the men who were getting out of the trucks, "Get everything you need for a water rescue then get in the caboose!"

Michael climbed back into the cab to see Sam shaking from the cold. He got down on his knees then hugged his son, "I'm sorry I yelled at you on the bridge. I know you are trying to help." Sam was about to say something to his father when the brakeman crackled over the radio, "We're ready!" The engineer placed the engine into the second position as the wheels spun wildly on the rails. As he pushed a button on the console, sand poured on the rails allowing the locomotive to gain traction and swiftly lurch forward.

Within a few minutes the engineer was applying the brakes as they came to the stream. As they neared, Sam could see Cletus and the police officer waiting. "Sam stay in here," Michael said as he left the cab.

Sam watched as the men poured down the side of the locomotive while Stanton shown his flashlight out to something in the water. One of the fire fighters walked out with a coil of rope over his arm. He tied one end to the handrail of the locomotive while attached the other end to one of the men. Once secured, the firefighters slowly lowered himself into the water. The men held the rope tight as he fought the current to get to the tree.

"Son, you might want to look out the window over there," the engineer said with a somber tone. "Tommy?" Sam said softly. The firefighter got to the tree then pulled at the white object. Out of the water a head appeared. "Tommy!" Cletus yelled as Stanton and Michael grabbed him once again. The firefighter struggled to free Tommy from the tree and its tangled branches. "Pull me back!" the firefighter yelled over the sound of the rushing water.

As he was pulled back toward the tracks, he did his best to stay afloat. "He's stuck in the limbs I believe. I cannot free him," the man said while looking up from the torrent. "Is he alive?" the chief asked already knowing the answer. "No," the firefighter replied. "You two, get tied onto the rope, maybe all three of you can free him," the chief said. Cletus no longer fought but was now slowly slumping down. They gently allowed him to sit on the rail. "My boy…," Cletus said. Sam watched from the locomotive while the man known no higher than being a criminal, sat on the rail crying over his son.

The firefighters made their way to the tree in hopes of freeing Tommy. Sam watched the men work but felt nothing, no sadness, no anger, nothing. The men worked until one man said, "Okay, pull us back!"

As the men fought their way back, two of them pulled Tommy through the water. When they came to the retaining wall they tried to lift Tommy's body up. "Holy shit, he can't be this heavy," one of the men said out loud, "You guys grab a hold as we push him up." As two men on the roadbed pulled on Tommy's lifeless body, the three below pushed him up.

"What the hell?!" one man exclaimed, "Officer, get over here!" As they laid Tommy down on the ties, you could see that his legs were bound together with many wraps of a large steel chain. "What the hell is going on?!" Stanton exclaimed with disbelief.

Chapter 11

The sun was beating down on two men and a woman who were digging through mud and muck. Coroner Locke stood above them from the railroad roadbed observing their delicate work. "Eric," Detective Norris said walking toward the elderly coroner, "Have you found anything yet?" Eric looked to his friend then said, "Take a look for yourself." George looked down to see the full skeleton of an adult human lying in the mud.

"Male or female?" George asked. "Female for sure, the bone structure is correct and we found her clothes lying perfectly folded near her feet," Eric said while shading his eyes from the sun with some papers. "Her clothes? Where are they?" George asked. "I placed them in an evidence bag for you. Blue jeans and a top printed with the logo of some rock band. I would say characteristic of someone in their late teens or early twenties," Eric said.

"The boy they pulled out of the stream down the tracks, have you looked at him yet?" George asked. "Just a preliminary look; I have the autopsy scheduled for just after lunch. I can tell you whoever killed him first knocked him over the head with something rounded and very heavy. That would have incapacitated the boy so he could then wrap the chains around his legs," Eric said then looked up as a train passed the men slowly on the far track. "Thank god they are shuttling us back and forth with that switch engine and caboose. This is one hell of a walk for this old man," George said with a small laugh.

"George, is it true some kid dreamed about where this woman would be?" Eric asked. "Yes, according to the officer. I am going to talk with the boy at ten; his parents are bringing him to my office. You know I have seen some weird shit in this job, but a kid who dreamt about where a body is located, that's really out there," George said, "I guess he and the kid who died were heading out here to find the body, but the dreamer couldn't come. For him that was lucky, we would have two boys' dead plus this woman."

"Oh, you should know we had a news helicopter flying over us a little while ago," Eric said, "I had them throw a tarp over the body until they left." George shook his head, "Fucking ghouls. I am going to take off for the office. Call me when you are ready to start the autopsy of that boy. I'll make sure not to be there…" Eric chuckled, "You never change, do you? After all these years a little blood and you're face down on the floor." George shook his head then laughed, "Thank God when my kids were born, fathers stayed in the waiting room. I feel sorry for men today."

Sam could not sleep when he and Michael returned just before the sun rose. He was told to get some sleep, but it was no use. Because of him, his best friend was now dead. He wanted to cry, he wanted to scream; but he couldn't. He just laid there in bed as he stared out the window. A little after seven he heard the sound of school mates walking by. He wondered how they would take the news. He wondered if they would even tell them yet. He wondered if they would learn the full story.

He tried to close his eyes once more time but then there was a soft knock at the door. "Sam?" Elizabeth asked, "Are you up?" Sam rolled over toward the door, "Yes." She opened the door to find the boy staring back at her with a blank look upon his face. The lack of emotion was scaring her more than anything. "You need to get dressed and washed up, we have to be at the police station at ten," Elizabeth said, "I have some oatmeal heating up for you."

Sam looked at his mother then asked, "Are you and dad mad at me?" Elizabeth did her best to hold back tears, "No Honey, no. We are glad you are safe." Sam looked back at his mother with the same blank stare he has had since they pulled Tommy out of the water. "I wonder how Donnie and Johnnie are feeling." Sam said with somber tone. "I am sure they are very sad as are their parents," Elizabeth said, "Well, we better get moving." Sam sat up in bed, "I'm not hungry mom. I don't feel very well." Elizabeth tried to muster a small smile, "Okay. You can eat later once you're feeling better."

Elizabeth left Sam to get ready by going downstairs to find Michael sitting at the breakfast table with the newspaper and a cup of coffee. "He's getting ready… I am so worried about him," Elizabeth said then started to cry. "I am too, but we need to hold it together for him," Michael said as he stood then walked over to embrace his wife, "He has some things he needs to account for. That is what scares me."

Sam came down to the kitchen to see his father holding his mother while she had her head on his father's chest. "Get something to eat," Michael said. "He's not hungry," Elizabeth said while wiping the tears from her eyes. "Let's just go. I want to get this over with," Sam said bluntly.

"Well, I guess we will go then," Michael said with a somber tone. Elizabeth did her best to wipe away the last of the tears as the three walked out the back door. As they walked to the station wagon, Elizabeth noticed someone near the driveway. "Michael, there's someone hanging out near the street," Elizabeth said. Michael looked down the driveway to see a middle-aged man wearing a baseball hat standing on the sidewalk right next to their driveway. "You two get in the car, I'll go see what this is about," Michael said.

He walked down the driveway to the man who seemed adamant about not moving from the spot he held. "Can I help you?" Michael asked. "No, but I can help you if you heed my advice," the man said. "Advice? Who the hell are you?" Michael asked with a raised tone. "I'm sure the police will be interviewing your son shortly. Before they do… tell your son that he knows nothing and he is to tell the police that he truly knows nothing," the man said then started to walk away. "My son will tell the truth," Michael said, "and no one will tell him to do any different." The man looked back to Michael, "If he tells the truth, no one will be able to save him."

The man turned back then continued to walk down the sidewalk. "Hey! Who are you?!" Michael yelled to the man, "I'll tell the police about this!" The man never looked back to the angered father but did raise his right hand in the air so as to acknowledge the statement.

Michael went to walk back to the car only to see Elizabeth standing there witnessing the event, "Didn't I tell you to get in the car!" She stood there trembling, "That man just threatened Sam." Michael gently grabbed her arm, "I will let the police know, but do not say a word to Sam, understand?" Elizabeth shook her head in agreement, "What is going on?" Michael saw Sam sitting in the back of the car looking out the window into the backyard, "I don't know. I don't think Sam knows either."

George sat at his desk looking out the open window to the partly cloudy day. Now that the storms have passed, the air has taken a more autumn feel. He started to close his eyes when a

151

knock came at his door. He spun around in his chair to see a teenage boy and his parents looking back at him. "You must be the White family," George said with an official tone. Michael slightly shook his head, "Yes I am Michael, this is my wife Elizabeth and this is Sam."

"I'm Chief Detective George Norris. It is pleasant to meet everyone, but I truly wish it was under different circumstances," George said as he placed his reading glasses on, "Please everyone take a seat." Sam started to walk into the room but was swiftly stopped by his father. "Why don't you and your mother wait in the hallway for a minute, I would like to talk with Detective Norris for a moment alone." Elizabeth guided Sam out of the room while Michael closed the door behind them.

"Mister White, there is no need to shut…," George said but was swiftly stopped by Michael. "I need to speak with you alone. I do not want Sam to hear this," Michael said with an urgent tone. George leaned back in his chair, "Go ahead." Michael sat down on an old oak chair, "When we left to come here a man was waiting for us in our driveway. When I approached him, he told me to tell Sam that he knows nothing… told me if Sam told the truth no one could help him."

George leaned forward in his chair then grabbed a pen from a golf ball shaped pencil cup, "What did this man look like?" Michael closed his eyes to better remember. "Middle aged, sandy colored hair but he wore a baseball hat… some team I have never heard of… Maybe five-ten, one hundred fifty pounds." George wrote the description down on a pad of yellow paper, "Did he have an accent, um, scars, tattoos?" Michael shook his head, "He sounded normal… well normal for Riley. I didn't see anything else odd about him. He spoke like he was quite sure of himself."

"Okay, does your wife know about this?" George asked. "Yes, she witnessed it too, but she will not tell Sam either," Michael said. "Good, why don't you let them in so we can talk to your son," George said. Michael stood up, opened the door then waived his family in.

"Sam… It is nice to meet you. Let me start out first saying that you have done nothing wrong and that you are in no trouble. I would like to talk with you about the dreams you said you have had," George said doing his best to sound upbeat for the teenage boy. "Let's start with the trail. You said you had a dream about a body being buried by the trail….," George said but was stopped by Sam. "No, it was a ghost," Sam said bluntly. Michael looked to Elizabeth with a blank look. "Um, take me back to the beginning," George said sounding flustered already.

"I was late for home when I was coming from Tommy's house. He told me about the trail through the woods. So I took it and when I got close to the tracks, I saw a ghost," Sam said with sincerity. George sat stunned then asked carefully, "So you saw a ghost and that caused you to dig for a body?" Sam shook his head, "Oh no, I didn't dig her up."

"Her?" George asked, "The ghost was a woman but you did not dig her up?" Sam looked to his father then back to the detective, "I told the boys the next day so Donnie said we should go see Sir Francis… he would be able to talk to the ghost." Michael looked to his son and asked with a raised tone, "That con artist with the billboard in his front yard?" Sam shook his head, "Yep, him."

"Okay so you told, um, Sir Francis… and then who dug the body up?" George asked. "Sir Francis and some other guy… We followed them and saw them dig the body up," Sam said, "Then someone from the railroad came and scared us away." George was trying frantically to decide if he should be writing this all down, "So you ran, who took the body?" Sam shrugged his shoulders, "I don't know… Sir Francis and the other guy ran down the trail. I think…"

George leaned back in his chair and took a deep breath of the fresh air blowing in from the outside. "So where does the dream come in?" George asked. "The woman I saw on the trail, I dreamed of her. She told me that wasn't her we found. She was forty and her name was Cindy," Sam said with a somber tone. "Forty? She was forty years old?" George asked trying to understand the

154

teenager. "No, well at the time I didn't know that… she was buried at mile forty. The girl buried at the trail was at mile forty-one," Sam said while starting to feel very uneasy.

"The woman we found today is named Cindy?" George asked. "What? You found another body?" Michael asked swiftly. "Yes. Tommy Jones must have found her body… that is probably what got him killed," George said. Michael's eyes grew large, "You mean the hole I jumped in last night was a grave?!" George slightly shook his head, "Sam, can you describe the woman you saw in your dream?"

Sam shook his head a bit, "Very beautiful… on the trail her hair was braided tightly, but every other time I saw her, her hair was loose, long." George picked up his telephone and typed in four digits then wait for a response, "This is Norris. Get on your little computer and search the missing person's database. Look for any young women named Cindy who was say fifteen to thirty with long hair. Call me as soon as you have something."

"You believe me?" Sam asked with a guarded tone. "Son, I have been in this profession long enough to expect the unexpected. Now, last night you had a dream about Tommy. How did you know where he would be?" George asked. "It wasn't Tommy in the dream. It was me. I could feel the water rising up my body and I couldn't move my feet, it was like they were stuck in mud. The water kept getting higher then there was a bright light. It started small and kept getting bigger, like it was coming for me! Finally, the light hit me and the water was gone… I was back in my room."

George looked at the boy with a stunned look, "That was the whole dream?" Sam shook his head, "No, when I was back in my room, Cindy came to me. She was so beautiful… more beautiful than I have ever seen her. She said that he found her, but now I need to find him." George looked at Sam, "So you didn't know it was Tommy?" Sam shook his head, "No. I didn't know. She just said him."

George was just about to ask another question when the phone rang. "Norris," George said. He listened to the person on the other side while his face slowly lost its color, "Look to see if you have the handout on file if not call and get a facsimile of her photo. Then get it up to me immediately." George placed the phone back down to see the family looking back at him.

"It seems there was a young woman reported missing last year near Whitney. She went to a rock concert with her friends but was lost in the crowd… she was never seen again. She was nineteen years old, had long strawberry blond hair… and her name was Cindy Keppler," George said with disbelief. "Do you think that was the woman in Sam's dream?" Elizabeth asked. George took a deep breath, "Before I came here this morning I visited the area where they were exhuming the body. The coroner told me clothes were found… the shirt was for some rock band."

Elizabeth looked at her son, "You sure she said her name was Cindy?" Sam shook his head, "Yes… she was so pretty. Almost as pretty as Tommy's Aunt Summer." Michael looked over to his wife then rolled his eyes. "Well Sam is there anything more you dreamt about?" George asked. Sam shook his head, "A lot more."

"I had another dream, out on the lawn, many women and girls were standing with number signs," Sam said. "Number signs?" Elizabeth asked. "Yes, just like the mileposts on the railroad tracks. The other day we were out talking when it started to rain so we ran to Summer's house," Sam said, "Well down in the basement Tommy's grandfather has tons of old stuff so we were looking through it. Well we found an article about a young woman who was missing; she was one of them on the lawn."

George grabbed his pen, "You're sure she was in the dream?" Sam shook his head in agreement. "Do you remember her name from the article?" George asked. "Beverly… I think her last name was Larsen," Sam said. George wrote the name down then picked the phone up, "I have another for you to find; Beverly Larsen… Sam, do you know where she was from and when she disappeared?" Sam thought as hard as he could, "A bowling alley here in town in nineteen… seventy I think." George turned his attention back to the phone, "Did you get that? Okay, pull whatever you have."

"I actually remember that," Michael said, "remember I was on the bowling team then." Elizabeth shook her head, "Yes I remember her too. I'm pretty sure she was a waitress in the bar." George scratched his head, "You two have better memories than mine, that's for sure… Sam, is there anything else you can remember about Beverly?" Sam looked to the floor, "She's twelve." There was a little silence then Elizabeth said, "Sam look at the detective." Sam looked up, "She's twelve… she's at mile twelve." George looked at the boy stone faced, "You are telling me that at mile twelve on the railroad line we will find this woman's body."

Sam tried not to look back at the floor but at the moment was feeling like a freak, "Yes." Just then a knock came at the door. "Come in," George yelled loud enough to cause Sam to jump. A young female police officer opened the door, "This is the information you were asking for, Detective." She handed two folders to the detective then swiftly left the room closing the door behind herself.

George opened the first folder to find a missing person's flyer for Cindy Keppler. He turned it around then handed it to Sam, "Is this the woman from your dream." Sam took the flyer than looked at the photograph. He felt such sadness fall upon him, "Yes." Michael took the flyer from Sam, "I cannot believe this… I just cannot…"

George opened the other folder to find the police report about Beverly Larsen. Inside the faded, coffee stained folder was a driver's license photograph of the woman. He handed it to Sam, "This is the woman you said is buried at mile twelve." Sam looked closely at the small photograph, "I think so. I am pretty sure." George reached into his back pocket to pull his wallet out, "Sam, here's some change. Down the hall is a break room. Why don't you go down there and get a candy bar, maybe some soda too. I would like to speak to your parents alone."

Sam looked to his mother. "Go ahead," Elizabeth said. Sam took the change from the detective then opened the door. "Down to your left and please close the door," George said. Sam did as was asked of him and softly closed the door behind himself.

"You know... I've been around the block many times in this job. Sometimes I have something that surprises me... there may be no surprises after this," George said then took a sip of his now cold coffee. "Detective, I don't know what to say. He is a good boy. He's never been in trouble... does his chores. Yes he talks back sometimes, but that is common at his age," Elizabeth said. "I can see that in him. He is a good boy, but what he knows and what he has told us here... well it's beyond logic," George said, "Has he been hanging around any adults? Any strangers?"

Michael shook his head, "His only friends are the Jones boys. I'm no fan of their father, but he seems to treat the boys better than he does his wife." George leaned back in the chair, "Cletus Jones... how many times has that name came across this desk." Michael looked to his wife then back to the detective, "Do you think Cletus had anything to do with this? Do you think he told Sam all of this?" George raised his eyebrow, "Frankly Mister White, I don't know what to think or believe any more."

When Sam closed the door, he left it open just enough to hear the conversation. He stood in the hallway listening closely through the door; however, he did not hear someone coming up behind him. "How are you doing?" came a voice that caused Sam to spin around. "Sam, right? Sam?" Stanton Smith asked. "Yes Sir," Sam said. "I am guessing your parents are talking to Detective Norris?" Stanton asked. "Yes, he gave me money to go to the break room. I guess I better go there," Sam said.

"I'll take you," Stanton said, "It's this way." The officer led the boy down to a small room at the end of the hall. Inside were two tables with four chairs each and three wood grained vending machines against the back wall. "Would you like something?" Stanton asked. Sam looked at the coins in his hand, "A grape soda." He handed the coins to Stanton who placed them in the coin slot then pushed the button for the grape soda. The can popped out the bottom to Sam's waiting hand.

"Come have a seat, I would like to talk with you a bit," Stanton said as he sat at one of the tables.

"Sam, I know you've been through a lot and I do not want to make it worse for you. Your friend Tommy… he and you were at that woman's house the other day. You should have been in school… why were you there?" Stanton asked. Sam looked the man in the eye, "She took us to the library at the college so we could do some research." Stanton looked at the boy, "Research?" Sam took a sip of the soda then said, "Yes. I saw someone who was in one of my dreams so we did research about her."

"So you weren't there when Miss Graham came home?" Stanton asked. "No," Sam said, "We didn't come home until after you were there." Stanton placed his hands on the table and tapped his fingers a bit. "Last night you knew about the remains we found but you said it was a whole body." Sam shook his head, "Yes forty-one." Stanton raised his eyebrow, "Forty-one?" Sam took another sip of soda then carefully belched under his breath. "Yes, she was at mile forty-one on the railroad. The woman Tommy found was at mile forty. That is why I said we had to go…," Sam paused then said, "Mile forty."

Stanton could tell the boy had something on his mind, "What is it, son?" Sam looked to a calendar hanging behind Stanton, "Beverly was twelve. Cindy was forty. There was a girl at forty-one… All the women with numbers." Stanton looked at the Sam, "What is it?" Sam's eyes grew large, "Summer, she's forty-two!" Stanton grabbed Sam as he flew out of the chair, "Forty-two? What are you talking about?"

"The other day, Summer had a letter that said forty-two. When the man or whoever ran from the house, he took the letter!" Sam yelled, "Don't you see?! Summer is forty-two… she's next!" Sam broke free of the officer's grip then ran down the hallway. He opened the door to the detective's office and flung it open with great force. The door swung wildly into the wall just missing his father head. "All the women! They are all buried near each mile marker and Tommy's Aunt Summer is next!" Sam exclaimed. "What are you talking about?" Michael asked.

"Summer had a letter in the mail it said forty-two on it. When the man left her house he must have taken it with because she could not find it. The women are buried at each mile marker and Summer is going to be forty-two! You have to help her!" Sam yelled. George's eyes grew wide, "Are you telling me at every marker there is someone buried?" Sam shook his head, "I think so." George looked to Stanton standing in the doorway, "Don't let anyone know about this, no one. Sam… if you're right… God help us."

Chapter 12

Detective George Norris walked up to the small bungalow on Ash Lane then knocked on the door. As George waited for a response, he looked around the front of the house and then the neighborhood for anything odd or amiss. He knocked once more than said, "Miss Graham, this is Detective Norris of the Richland County Sheriff's Department."

George waited for a minute then decided the woman was not home. He walked to the driveway of the house then proceeded to the backyard. Nothing appeared to be odd and no vehicle was in the driveway or the garage. He felt the only other place she may be was at the Jones' homestead. As he walked down the driveway he noted that the phone line cut the other day had been repaired.

As George opened the car door he glimpsed to the street to notice a green car going by but did not give it a second thought. Just as he looked to back out of the driveway, he noticed a Wagoneer with its turn signal on. He put the car into drive and drove toward the garage allowing room for the Wagoneer in the driveway.

George stepped out of the car to see a young woman in the Wagoneer looking him over. He removed his badge from his belt then held it up for the woman to see. She rolled the window down and asked, "Can I help you?" George passed his badge to the woman, "Miss Graham? I am detective Norris." Summer passed the badge back to the detective, "This really is not a good time."

George shook his head slightly, "Ma'am I understand that with the passing of your nephew, but we believe you may be in danger at this moment." The innocent look left Summers's face, "What do you mean?" George noticed a neighbor peering out the window of his house causing him to say, "Let's go inside where we can speak."

Summer stepped out of her Wagoneer then found the house key on her keyring. George followed the young woman to the door keeping an eye on his surroundings. She opened the door then walked into the kitchen, "What is this about? Does this have to do with Tommy?" George pulled a chair out from the breakfast table, "Please, sit down." Summer looked at the older man with a blank stare, "I do not need to sit. What is going on?"

George sat down, "Well if you do not want to sit, I will. My knees are killing me. Do you know Sam White?" Summer smirked, "Yeah, Tommy's friend. I think he has a crush on me." George chuckled, "I think he does too. Well he stated that on the day that your house was broken into that you had a letter stolen. A letter that had the number forty-two on it." Summer looked off to the side then back to the detective, "Yes… it was a sheet of paper placed in a blank envelope that was in my mailbox... What is this about?"

"Do you still have the envelope?" George asked. "I might, let me look," Summer said but was stopped by George. "In a minute. Tommy died we believe because he found the grave of a murder victim. That victim was buried at the fortieth mile marker on the railroad. The other day we found human remains at the forty-first mile marker." Summer looked at the detective with skepticism, "What, you think that paper means I will be a buried at the forty-second mile marker... whatever the hell that is..."

"I do not want to take the risk," George stated, "Do you have somewhere you can stay? Possibly with family?" Summer giggled, "Sure... my sister Martha. You know the one married to the town slime ball... Last thing I want to do is fall asleep anywhere near him." George rubbed his chin, "Do you have anywhere else?"

Summer opened the refrigerator and pulled out a bottle of soda, "Would you like one?" George smiled, "Yes... Thank you." Summer pulled a bottle opener out of a cabinet drawer then opened the bottles of soda. She gave one to the detective who swiftly took a sip. "My parents now live in California. I have a sister who works for the state department at the embassy in Paris. My third sister is married with five kids and lives in Texas. Only Martha and I are left here," Summer said with a somber tone then took a sip of soda, "So either I stick it out here alone or go take my chances on being raped by Cletus Jones."

"Perhaps you should take a trip to see your parents," George stated. "Um, no. I have school and Martha needs someone stable in her life right now. The only reason I am here is because I want to see if I have a dress that will fit her for the funeral. God damn!" Summer said while trying to hold back tears, "She doesn't even have a fucking dress that doesn't like it's been in a tornado. You know... why the fuck does she put up with Cletus?!"

George could feel the anger and pain the young woman was in. "I will have a car stationed out front for protection," George said. "Come on... for how long? Do you even know who killed Tommy? Is it the same person who killed whoever he dug up?" Summer said as her anger started to boil. "We think it's the same person, but we have no idea who it is. We do know that someone got into this house and more than likely was giving you a warning." George said sternly.

"Stay here, I'll be right back," Summer said. She walked out the back door then proceeded to the Wagoneer where she had left her purse. She grabbed the leather bag only to return to the waiting detective. She opened the bag and pulled out the revolver she got from Cletus. "This is my protection," Summer said as she laid the gun on the table. "I will only guess you obtained that legally and have the proper paperwork," George said with a grin. "In the long run, I really do not care," Summer said without worry. "Do you have extra shells for it?" George asked. "No… only what's in it," Summer said. "I'll give you a box that I keep in my car," George said.

George took another sip of soda, "I will have an unmarked car spotted on the block whenever you are here. They will also shadow you wherever you go." Summer placed the gun back into her bag when said, "That is not necessary." George took a harsher tone, "You do not understand Miss Graham, this is a twofold operation. First part is to keep you alive the second is to catch this bastard. This very well may be the man who murdered your nephew." Summer looked at the detective right in the eyes, "That is a low blow."

"That is reality. I'll go out to my car to get you a box of shells. Get a piece of paper and write down your class schedule along with any other places you think you may be going for the next week," George said, "By the way, do you have a boyfriend or any close male friends?" Summer smiled, "Are you asking for business or pleasure?" George did not take kindly to the question, "Business." Summer smiled, "A girl has to ask."

"Get working on that list, I'll be right back," George said then stood up with a slight groan. Summer went to the living room to find a pad of paper. She looked on the end table, then on top of the television. Next, she went to her bedroom where she found a pad sitting on her dresser. When she lifted the pad, she found the envelop that the letter was placed in. She returned to the kitchen to see the detective had returned with a small green and black box.

"These are more than enough. If someone does get in, make sure you aim for his chest. I'll let the officer who will be watching you know that you are armed," George said. Summer went to hand the envelope to George, "This is the envelope that the letter was in. I don't know if you would want it or not." George took a napkin off of the table and used to take the envelope from Summer, "It may have finger prints. I'll need you to come down so we can take your prints. Please write down your schedule so I can get going."

Sam was sitting on the back porch with an uneaten sandwich lying on a plate next to him. He was not very hungry yet and his head hurt like he has never felt before. The events of last night were flashing through his head. He so wished he could go back and disobey his mother. Maybe if he was there, Tommy would still be alive.

A large cloud caused a shadow to move through the yard just as Sam could hear voices that seemed to be getting louder. It quickly became apparent that his father was yelling at someone from the side yard. Sam took off to see what the commotion was about. What he found he was not prepared for. His father had Cletus Jones pushed up against the house, both men's faces were red.

"There he is!" Cletus yelled with all of his strength, "Come here, I want to know what you did to my boy!" Michael held Cletus to the siding with all of his strength, "Tell your mother to call the police!" Sam stood still unaware he was not moving. "Get going!" Michael yelled at his son.

Sam ran to the backdoor to greet his mother who was coming out to see what all the noise was. "What is going on?" Elizabeth asked. "Call the police!" Sam cried, "Dad has Mister Jones up against the house. Dad wants you to call the police." Elizabeth went past Sam then looked around the corner of the house to see her husband in a stance she had never seen before.

"Did you call the police?" Michael asked. "No, now what is going on?" Cletus was struggling to free himself, "Your boy, I want to know why he killed my son!" Michael was now pushing so hard that Cletus was having a hard time breathing. "Sam did not kill Tommy!" Michael yelled. "How did he know where my boy would be?" Cletus said through gasps for breath.

"Michael let him free!" Elizabeth said, "He's drunk or something." Cletus was trying desperately to get out of the grip Michael had, "I ain't drunk! I want to know what happened to my boy!"

Sam ran into the house to call the police like his father wanted. He picked the receiver up then dialed zero. "This is the operator; how may I direct your call?" came over the line. "Riley police, quick!" Sam exclaimed. The line dialed then a woman picked up, "Riley police." Sam could hear the men struggling outside, "I need the police, one twenty-six Church Street, Cletus Jones is here fighting with my father." There was a slight pause then the woman asked, "Cletus Jones?" Sam was getting frustrated quickly, "Yes!" He could hear the woman whispering to someone but could not make out what she was saying finally she stated, "They are on their way."

Sam placed the phone back down on the receiver than ran back out the door. His mother was still standing where he had left her as she pleaded with both men to stop. "The police are on their way," Sam stated sharply. "I'll get you boy! You'll pay for my boy's death… you'll pay." With that statement Michael swiftly pulled back his right arm then with all of his force punched Cletus in the jaw. Elizabeth's eyes grew wide, "What did you do?" Sam was so stunned he couldn't even mutter a word. Michael let go of Cletus who quickly slumped down into a bed of purple crocuses.

Michael looked to his hand, "Damn… haven't had to do that for over twenty years. Still hurts like hell." Sam thinking he would ease the tension said, "You can see little birds flying around his head!" His mother looked to his with a raised eyebrow, "Go inside, now!" Michael chucked, "You know, you can see them."

Elizabeth turned her attention back to her husband, "What the hell caused this?" Michael looked toward the street as the sound of sirens could be heard, "Hold on, I think the police are almost here." Elizabeth exhaled loudly, "Great... now the police are here. We will have to sell our home after all of this." She didn't know Sam was looking out the dining room window and clearly heard her statement. He sat down on one of the chairs as tears started to stream down his face.

A police officer jogged up to Michael, "We got a call about a fight." Michael didn't say a word but pointed to Cletus. "Cletus Jones... to think I thought I would make it through the month without having to deal with him...," The officer said, "So what happened?" Michael took a deep breath still trying to calm down, "I went to check the mail when Cletus jumped out of that old beater truck and came after me. I don't know if you know, but his son was killed yesterday."

The office shook his head, "Yes, it's all over town... what does this have to do with you?" Michael looked to his wife then back to the officer, "Our son was Tommy's best friend. He helped find Tommy's body last night... so Cletus thinks he had something to do with it. He wanted to see my son, blames him for Tommy's death. Son of a bitch threatened by son's life!" The officer could see the anger rebuilding in Michael. Cletus started to make a sound as he was waking back up from his facial assault. "Let me put the cuffs on him and place him in the car. I'll be right back to speak with you more," the officer said.

He reached to his belt and pulled out a pair of handcuffs. Without saying a word and with little remorse, he grabbed Cletus by the shoulder then flipped him over onto his chest. He pulled his right hand back then placed one link of the cuffs tightly around his wrist. Next, he grabbed his left arm then tightened the other link around that wrist. "Come on Cletus, your favorite cell next to the shower bay is waiting for you," the officer said with a touch of humor.

As Cletus was drug to the squad car, Elizabeth stared at her husband with a blank look. "What's wrong?" Michael asked. "What's happening? Tommy was murdered… there are bodies buried in the woods and Sam… Sam is dreaming about the whole thing?" Elizabeth said while trying to hold back tears. Michael looked up when he caught a glimpse of Sam in the window then quickly looked to his wife and whispered, "We'll talk about his later. Someone can hear us right now."

Elizabeth shook her head in agreement as the officer returned. "Detective Norris just radioed me. He said he will stop back to talk with you shortly… said I am just to take Cletus to the lockup," the officer said with a suspicious tone, "I am guessing you and detective know one another?" Michael shook his head, "Yes… it's a very long story." The officer gave Michael a queer look then said, "I'll have a tow truck come pick up his hunk of crap at the curb. If you need anything else just call us… call the detective I guess."

Michael shook his head as he and Elizabeth watched the officer walk back toward the street. "I think we better go talk with Sam," Elizabeth whispered to her husband. They went inside the house just as the clock was chiming that it was three o'clock. Elizabeth exhaled, "Danielle should be home in a few minutes. Why don't you go talk with Sam while I try to head her off." Michael smiled, "Thank you… I got the easy job." Elizabeth just shook her head with disbelief.

Michael went to the living room to find Sam, but he was not there. Figuring he was up in his room, Michael went upstairs, but quickly noticed the door to the attic stairs was cracked open. After he looked in Sam's room to find it vacant, he went back to the hallway then carefully opened the door to the attic. He walked up the stairs softly and as the attic came into sight, he saw Sam sitting on an old orange crate looking out the window near the peak of the roof.

"It's hot up here," Michael said trying to defuse the growing situation. Sam kept looking out the window, "I opened the window; the air is cool outside." Michael grabbed another crate and placed it next to Sam, "Hope you don't mind that I sit here… the air is nice and cool compared to this stuffy attic." Sam remained quiet as if in a trance.

"Sam… you are going through a lot right now. None of this is your fault," Michael said. Sam kept looking out the window to see school kids walking by including the love of his life, Cindy Stewart. "Sam, look at me," Michael said with authority. Michael looked out the window to see Cindy walking with her older brother Edward. "That's Cindy Stewart, isn't it?" Michael asked. Sam slightly shook his head in agreement but still would not open his mouth.

"You know your mother was about that age when I first laid eyes on her. Your grandparents moved here from Freeport so your grandpa could take a job at the mill. After that I could not keep my mind off of her… well still can't. Of course, I have you and Danielle on my mind now also," Michael said trying to sound fatherly.

"Tommy dying is my fault," Sam said with a somber tone. "No, no it is not," Michael said with a raised tone. "I never should have told anyone what I saw that night or what I dreamed about. Tommy would be alive right now," Sam said while trying not to cry in front of his father. "Sam, I do not know what you saw that night or what you have dreamt about. I do however know where you said they would find… find bodies… they were there,"

Michael said trying to find a silver lining in the black cloud surrounding the town.

"Tommy went out there because of me. I should have never told him," Sam said with a defiant tone, "Now Mister Jones is in jail because of me." Michael could now feel anger building, "Cletus Jones is in jail because he is an idiot. He blames you because it is easier than looking at himself in the mirror and admitting he is a failure. His whole life has been blaming someone else for his mistakes." Sam looked back out the window just in time to see his sister walking up to the house, "Oh great." Michael looked down, "Your mother will deal with her... Sam, look at me."

Sam looked to his father with red, tear filled eyes. "You lost your best friend. You are also dealing with a subject matter that is something a teenager should not have to deal with. You'll get through this, but I will tell you honestly, it will not be easy," Michael said then lost his train of thought by the squealing of brakes. He looked down to see a car had pulled into his driveway, "Now who?" Once the car door had opened, he could quickly see it was Detective Norris.

"Sam I need to go downstairs for a bit. Why don't you relax... here or in your room. It's your decision," Michael said as he stood up from the dusty crate, "We'll pick this up later." Sam looked to his father then looked back out the window. As the cool breeze hit Sam's face, it caused him to feel drowsy.

Michael came down to the living room to find Detective Norris waiting for him, "I heard Cletus Jones paid you a visit." Michael shook his head, "Yes, he threatened Sam." George looked around the room, "Are we alone to speak freely?" Michael shook his head, "We should be." George pulled a piece of paper out of his breast pocket then opened it, "Before I left to come here, the coroner called with the results of Tommy's death. He was struck over the head with a rounded object of both heavy weight and great force. It was sufficient enough to shatter his skull."

Michael sat down on the arm of the couch, "On my God... who could have done this?" George placed the paper back in his pocket, "Well that is not the worse. As you know the murderer wrapped chains on the boy's legs in an attempt to weight him down. Almost sixty pounds worth of chains to be exact. Tommy was still alive when that water flooded the stream. They found water in his lungs meaning he drown... just like in Sam's dream."

Elizabeth walked into the room with a stunned look on his face, "I'm sorry, I walked into the dining room and heard what you said... I just cannot believe this." George shook his head, "There's more... the coroner sent a photographer to the stream hoping the water would have receded so they could get some photographs and find any other clues. When the woman got there, she found the stream was still flooded. The stream flows under the tracks there through a transite culvert. She noted the other side was not flooded. They sent a man in to discover that old railroad ties and other debris were filled in to block the stream. Even if we didn't have that storm, Tommy still would have drowned. The person who killed that boy didn't want him to die swiftly. This person is a sick... very sick."

Michael looked to his wife then back to the detective, "Do you have any idea who did this?" George shook his head, "No. I also do not know who paid you a visit this morning. I talked with Summer Graham and thankfully she still had the envelope the letter came in. The lab will dust it for prints and hopefully find a match in the system, but that could be days. There are only a few days left in the week, why don't you keep Sam home from school until Monday. I will also have an officer patrol your block every fifteen minutes. The sheriff is trying to keep this out of the media, but they already know about Tommy being found and the body. This gets on television and it may spook the killer into hiding or it may just gratify him into doing something."

Michael stood up, "Are you telling me that Sam... my family could be in danger?" George looked to Elizabeth who was now white as a ghost, "I just don't know." Michael rubbed his face, "I have vacation time, I'll take the rest of the week off too. What about Cletus?" George rolled his eyes,

"He's in his second home. Would you like him charged with assault and trespassing?" Michael stayed quiet thinking then said, "No… he has enough problems right now. Just tell him to stay away from my son."

George shook his head, "No problem. I'm going to let him cool his heels for the night and release him at first light. Well I better get going, I wish there was more that I could do."

Michael walked with the detective to the door when George stopped and said, "Oh, there is one last thing that you should know but I need you to keep to ourselves for now. Once you left my office, I called the coroner with who we believed the young woman was in the shallow grave. Well I know the coroner very well and he usually only believes in science and fact, but maybe he is softening in his advanced age… Long story short he personally sent someone over to Whitney for her dental records. When he let me know how Tommy Jones died, he confirmed the remains found were that of Cindy Keppler."

Chapter 13

Randy walked into the kitchen with his head held low while making a long drawn moan. "Oh, another productive night at the bar. Will I find we have a new receptionist this morning?" Francis asked then gave a hearty laugh causing Randy to grab his ears. "After all of these years, I would have thought you would be immune to alcohol," Francis said then bit into a piece of overly toasted bread. "Don't chew so loud… oh my fucking head…," Randy said, "I think I will go back to bed. I'll be up by dinnertime."

"Bed? No, no brother, you have the paper to read," Francis said while passing the folded newspaper to his nauseated brother. "The paper? What the hell for?" Randy asked with his eyes closed. "Open your eyes and then the newspaper," Francis said determined. Randy cracked his eyes open, but seeing the bright sunlight caused his head to hurt even further. "Let me sleep. I'll read the paper later or tomorrow," Randy said with a nauseated tone.

"Open the God damn paper!" Francis yelled losing his cool rapidly. "Fuck! I'll look at the damn paper," Randy said with venom. He opened his eyes doing his best not to let too much light in. It took everything he had to focus on the bold headline in the paper 'RILEY BOY BRUTALLY MURDERED' Randy closed his eyes, "A boy was murdered, what does that have to do with me?"

Francis grabbed the paper then hit Randy over the head with it, "Look at the picture of the boy, you idiot!"

Randy took the paper back from his brother then did his best to focus on the picture. He looked to his brother, "That's one of those kids!" Francis then pointed down the page, "Take a look at that headline." Randy focused on the smaller font headline 'SKELETAL REMAINS FOUND ALONG RAILROAD TRACKS'

Randy's mind was processing far slower than normal do to the hangover. He slowly looked toward his brother who was smiling. "That kid does have a gift, doesn't he?" Francis said. Randy looked back at the paper, "The paper doesn't say anything about these being linked though. Maybe it's a coincidence?"

Francis got up to get a coffee mug hanging from a hook beneath the cabinets. "I made a call to an old friend on the other side of the law," Francis said, "The boy was murdered while digging up the body of a woman from Whitney. She also said there is a rumor going around that some kid dreamed about this and that is how the body was discovered." Francis picked up the coffee pot with a potholder then poured Randy a steaming cup of black coffee.

"So I was right! Ha! I knew it... oh my head feels like shit," Randy said while in delighted misery. Francis placed the coffee mug in front of Randy,

"Sober up. We need to figure out how we are going to get to that kid." Randy looked to his brother, "Oh so now you believe me! I knew that kid had a gift the whole time." Francis took another bite of his toast, "Drink the coffee and sober up already. I need your conniving self up to par on this one."

Randy took a slow sip of the coffee when a heavily handed beat came at the door. "Who the hell is that?" Randy asked, "Tell them to quit… God I don't feel good." Randy placed his head down into his hands as the beating came once more. "I don't know. I'll go see, keep drinking your coffee!" Francis said as he left the kitchen. He walked through to the front of the house just as another beat came on the door, "I'm coming, damnit!" Francis unlocked the dead bolt then opened the door to find a middle-aged man looking back at him; his sandy colored hair showing just under a tight fitting baseball hat.

"Sorry, we're not open yet. The Gods, they need sleep too," Francis said in his best fake voice. The man opened the screen door then pulled a chrome plated semi-automatic handgun from his pants pocket, "That's right and you will stay closed. Get inside slowly and keep quiet. I need to have a word with you and your brother." Francis walked backward slowly with his hands out from his side, "If it's money, we don't have much. Times are slow… inflation I guess"

The man quietly closed the door behind himself, "I don't want your money. Let's go see your brother in the kitchen." Francis slowly turned around but kept his hands out from his side. As Francis walked into the kitchen, Randy asked, "Who was at the door?" Francis knocked his head back slightly causing Randy to look past him to the man with a gun.

"Take a seat, lard ass," the man said then pushed Francis toward one of the chairs. "Who the hell are you?" Randy asked while looking around the table for a possible weapon. "Who I am is not important what you can do for me is," the man said while leaning back against the countertop, "Tell me what those four boys came to see you about." Randy smiled as if trying to charm a woman, "Boys? What boys?"

The man swiftly cocked the gun, "Wrong answer. Would you like to try again?" Francis looked to Randy then to the man, "One of the kids said they saw a ghost. Can you believe it? A ghost!" Francis chuckled hoping to defuse the situation a bit. "Is that what caused you to dig up the grave?" the man asked with a harsh tone. "Grave? What grave?" Randy asked. Without looking where he was aiming, the man pointed the gun down toward Francis's left foot then fired the gun.

Francis fell out of the chair onto his side and immediately grabbed his bleeding foot. "You shot me you motherfucker!" Francis yelled while in pain. "Randy has the chance of answering the question again," the man said. Randy looked down to his brother in pain then back to the man, "Yes... The kid said the ghost had braided hair. I remembered our old man told us there are Indian burial mounds out there. I thought maybe the kid stumbled upon one."

The man reached over and picked up an apple sitting in a bowl. He took one bite of the apple, chewed then swallowed. The man then looked down to Francis who was still on his side but now in a small pool of blood. "What else did the kids tell you?" the man asked. Randy shook his head, "Nothing." The man cocked the gun then pointed it back to Francis. "Nothing man! They didn't tell us shit!" Randy yelled.

"They must have told you where she was buried. I mean, those woods are vast," the man said. "Sure, they said near the trail off of the tracks!" Randy yelled as he could feel his heart beating in his brain. "So they did tell you more," the man said then fired the gun once more this time shooting Francis in the left kneecap.

"You son of a bitch!" Francis yelled as he grabbed his blood-soaked knee. "Who the fuck are you, man? You can't be no cop!" Randy yelled. Francis was trying his best to get up, but the pain was too much. "I would just relax if I were you. The chances of you being able to get onto your one good leg before I remove the back of your head is very slim," the man said with a cold tone.

"What did you do with the body in the grave?" the man asked. "We ran!" Francis yelled before Randy could answer. "Why did you run?" the man asked. "Those fucking kids followed us," Randy said, "Someone yelled at them for being on the tracks so we got the hell out of there." The man took another bite of the apple, "These are really good. Would one you like one?"

Randy ran his fingers under the newspaper to feel the end of a butter knife. The man took another bite of the apple and when he turned to place it on the counter, Randy grabbed the knife. As fast as Randy could, he pulled the knife out and went to lunge at the man. Sadly for Randy, the man's reflexes were far superior to his. As Randy was in midair, the man shot Randy squarely in the chest causing him to fall backward landing on the table then sliding to the floor.

"Poor Randy… to think I was going to let you two live," the man said as he grabbed another apple. Francis looked over to his younger brother lying lifeless on the kitchen floor with a bullet hole directly over his heart. "What is this all about?" Francis cried. The man walked over to Randy then felt his neck, "Randy is no longer with us." Francis did his best to move around but the pain of his left leg was too much.

The armed man walked around pulling drawers out of the cabinets then dumping the contents on the floor. "What the hell are you doing?" Francis asked. The man went into another room where the sounds of breaking glass could be heard. Francis fought the pain the best he could and managed to pull himself up onto his right leg. As he used the counter and cabinets as support, he hobbled toward the back door.

The sounds of things being destroyed was still raging in other parts of the small house as Francis did his best to get the door unlocked. His hands were covered in blood and as he tried to twist the knob, his hand would just slip. Suddenly he noticed that the noise of destruction had stopped. He turned to see the man standing right next to him. "Francis, what are you doing?" the man asked with a monotone.

Francis hopped back from the man not realizing how close he was to the basement steps. "You are going to kill me anyway… who are you?" Francis asked while in extreme pain. The man smiled then kicked Francis' good leg causing him to place all of his weight on his injured knee. He lost his balance then fell backward down the basement steps. He could feel himself hit the basement floor; he tried to move but the pain was far too great.

The man walked down the basement steps while doing his best to avoid the blood stains on the steps. "What unique things do we have down here?"

the man asked. He looked around to see boxes piled up, some reaching the floor joists. "Francis, I am very appreciated by the hospitality you and your brother showed me this morning," the man stated while looking through some of the boxes.

Francis, trying to remain conscious through the pain, slowly turned his head to see the man pulling papers out of the boxes. "You are robbing me? That is what this is about?" Francis asked, his speech slightly slurred. The man looked back, "No but I want it to look that way when they investigate your deaths and the fire." Francis looked back up to see the floor joists, "Fire? Just tell me, what is this all about?" The man pulled a gold lighter out of his pocket then lit the papers on fire. As the papers burned, the man scattered them about the boxes, "I need to go now Francis, it was very nice meeting you."

"I'll take a cheeseburger, fries and an iced tea," George said to the waitress. "Okay what is this all about?" a middle-aged woman asked George. "It's about the sudden crime wave in this small Wisconsin town," George said then took a sip of the complimentary glass of water, "You are not going to believe me, but I need any help that I can."

The woman looked at George who was starting to sweat and said, "I have never seen you like this. Are you feeling well?" George grinned, "As well as I can under the circumstances and you might start feeling like me in a minute." The waitress came out with two bowls of chicken soup then placed them in front of the man and woman. After she left George said, "Karen you know I am a good detective… you've known me for years and we have worked on many cases together."

Karen took a packet of crackers in her hand, crushed them then opened the packet so the crumbs could fall into her bowl of soup. "What's going on with you, did you fall off the wagon?" Karen asked. George smiled, "No, but you might think I have when I get this all explained to you. I have a fourteen-year-old boy who while walking through the woods saw a ghost…" Karen stopped with her spoon in midair, "Ghost? You said ghost… Correct?"

George exhaled slightly, "Ghost… Based upon the tip he and his friends called in we found human remains. He had a dream… a few dreams I guess. That led him to believe there are multiple women buried at one mile increments along the railroad tracks." Karen looked to George then said, "I don't like where this is going."

"Well his best friend went to dig for one of the women and found her skeletal remains but that," George was stopped by Karen. "Cost him his life?" Karen asked with a humble tone. George shook his head, "Yes. I need your help. There is one woman who the boy has named that is buried at the twelfth mile marker on the tracks. I looked on a map; it is just inside our county. I already call the railroad, but they do not want to give me permission to dig up their property."

Karen looked at the detective with a stone face, "You want me to go to a judge to get a warrant based upon the dream of a fourteen-year-old boy?" George put his head down slightly then gave a small chuckle, "I know… but the kid named her and she went missing from Riley in nineteen seventy. I searched to find her parents still live here." Karen looked to George, "You didn't tell them, did you?" George's eyes got large, "Of course not! But I would like to bring them closure. Is there any way we can get permission?"

"I can try, but I really do not think that is possible. There is one judge who I can easily wrap around my finger but he also doesn't like to go out on a limb. If you don't find a skeleton or some kind of remains…," Karen stopped when she heard a siren. "Must be in your lawyer's blood… hear a siren and stop everything," George said than laughed. Karen looked to him with a raised eyebrow, "You ask me for help then make fun of my profession…" George became humbler, "Karen, think of it this way, you're not helping me, you're helping a family find closure."

The siren grew louder causing both of them to look out the window as a fire engine flew by.

"Wow, the volunteer department hasn't had two calls in one week for months," George said as the waitress was placing the food on the table. "There is a fire out on route two," the waitress said as she pulled the bill out of her pocket, "The manager is on the fire department. I heard his little radio going off." George looked up to the waitress, "Do you remember the address?" The waitress shook her head, "No, just route two, near the bypass... house fire I think they said."

Karen could see something was processing through George's mind, "What is it?" George looked out as a rescue squad went by, "After lunch I was heading out to route two... go see our town psychic." Karen chuckled, "I know you use unorthodox methods, but you are really getting out there." George leaned in, "I was going to question him and his brother about the body they found after the boy told them were she was. When we got there, the body was gone except for a bone and a tooth."

"Francis and Randy Abraham, the best con men to come out of this area in years," George said, "But I don't see them stealing human remains unless they think they can turn it into money." As Karen was cutting her burger in half with a knife she said, "You really think you'll get an answer out of them?" George looked to her then smiled, "Maybe I wouldn't but an attractive mother who is worried about her missing daughter might..."

Karen rolled her eyes a bit, "And who is this attractive yet worried mother?" George looked Karen in the eye and said with a seductive tone, "The beautiful woman I am looking at right now." Karen took a bite of her burger but remained quiet. "Well?" George asked. Karen took another bite of her burger but did not utter a word. "It will be fun," George said, "You always wanted to learn how to do undercover work."

She swallowed the bite that was in her mouth than said, "I was hoping after lunch we would do under the covers work…" George looked around the busy restaurant then looked back to Karen and whispered, "There is that small motel down the road from there, perhaps after the psychic we can go there." Karen raised her eyebrow, "A romantic you are not, but it's been two weeks since we were last together… okay, but you'll need to tell me what to do." George smiled, "No problem. Finish up and let's get going."

Karen and George finished their meals then drove out toward the route two bypass. "Tell him that your daughter went missing about a month ago. You think your ex-husband took her, but he states he did not," George said. "Okay but how do I get to the body?" Karen asked. George looked over to her only to see the sun shining on her bare legs. "You might want to keep your mind on the road and not my skirt," Karen said with a chuckle.

"Um… tell him… tell him your husband frequents the forest to go hunting. We have not released anything about the remains we found in the woods on that trail. As far as I know, they think they got away with stealing that girls body," George said.

He went to turn onto the bypass but a police car was blocking the road. George pulled up to the officer and asked, "What is going on?" The officer quickly recognized the superior officer, "There is a house fire down the road, Sir." George could see the fire trucks down the road but could not decide where exactly they were located, "We have someone to visit down there. I'll drive around your car." The officer waived at the detective and his attract passenger as they drove carefully around the parked squad car.

"God, they get them younger and younger," George said with disbelief. "Yes they do," Karen said in a seductive tone. George looked over to her with a blank face. "I don't think we'll be doing undercover work today," Karen said, "That's the psychic's house."

George stopped his car behind a fire truck where one of the men was cooling off with a light spray of water. George quickly stepped out before the car was fully in park. "Where is the chief?" George asked. "Over there near the pumper," the firefighter said. "Stay here Karen. I'll be right back," George said to the woman sitting in the car.

He walked past a few trucks and over many large hoses until he saw the man with a white helmet on, "Chief? I'm detective George Norris. Have you seen either of the Abraham brothers?" The fire chief looked at George than stated, "You got here quick, I just requested the police a few minutes ago." George gave a queer look, "I was coming out here to question them on a matter, what are you talking about?" The chief looked back at George, "They will not be answering anything. Their bodies were found in the house and both looked to have gunshot wounds. We've struck the fire, just trying to find hotspots now."

George shook his head then said quietly, "What the hell is going on?" The chief looked at the detective," What did you say?" George shook his head, "Oh, nothing. Let me know when it's safe to enter the structure and tell them not to move the bodies."

George walked back to the car to find Karen out stretching her long legs. "Well I think our plans have changed today, hon," George said. Karen could tell George was perplexed, "What is it?" George walked in closely to Karen so the firefighters could not hear him, "Both brothers are dead. The chief thinks they have gunshot wounds… Something is going on here and it's not right."

192

A man walked up to the couple talking near the car, "What is going on? Was there a house fire?" George looked to the man, "Yes there was a fire in the house over there." George took a second look at the middle-aged with sandy colored hair then asked, "Do I know you?" The man smiled, "I don't think so. I am just passing through town on my way to Greenly." George shook his head then gave a small grin, "I guess I must be thinking of someone else."

Chapter 14

Sam laid in bed staring at the ceiling doing his best to fall asleep. While the creamy white texture seemed hypnotic, it just didn't help. The window was open allowing a cool breeze to swirl around the room in hopes that would help him sleep. He rolled onto his side then pulled the covers up close to his head. He closed his eyes and did his best to take all thoughts out of his head. The air seemed to be getting colder and colder; so cold that he was starting to shiver even under the thick blankets.

Knowing the window was wide open, he threw the blankets off of himself so he could go close the window. When he got to the window, he did not see the outside, but it was as if he was looking into another house. The house was one he had seen before but just couldn't place it. As he looked around the room, no one was present but the television was on showing nothing but snow. A light was on in the hallway but quickly went out, followed by the figure of a woman walking in the dark. As she went to the television to switch it off, Sam could tell the woman was Summer. She had on a long white nightshirt and nothing else. Even in the loose nightshirt, Sam could make out the curves of her very feminine body.

"Summer it's me, Sam," he said but she could not hear him. Once the television was off, the room grew very dark; so dark Sam could not see anything. Suddenly Summer turned the light on in her bedroom causing the cracks around the closed door to glow. Sam yelled again, "Summer, can you hear me?" The light went out in the bedroom and once again Sam could not see a thing.

He heard a noise next to him that caused him to look to his right side. He found that he was no longer in his bedroom, but in Summer's driveway. A figure in black was prying the basement window open. Sam went to stop the man, but his hands passed through the black mass with no problem. He looked back into the window to see the house was still dark. Sam yelled as loud as he could, "Summer!" No lights turned on and the black mass kept working on breaking into the basement.

Sam ran around to the front door to find there was no knob. He pushed on the door as hard as he could but it wouldn't budge. He kicked the door and yelled once again, "Summer! Please open the door!" He decided to try the back door. He ran right through the black mass to the back yard to find a door knob on the back door. He tried to turn knob but it was locked. Thankfully Sam remembered the key under the flower pot. He went down the steps and knocked the pot over with his right hand. Below the pot was a mass of meal and earth worms.

Sam took all the courage he had and dug his hand into the worms looking for the key. He could feel the metal teeth of the key along with the slimy feel of the insects. He pulled the key out then ran back to the door. He unlocked the door but when he tried to turn the knob, his hand kept slipping. He used both of his hand to slowly turn the knob. Finally, the door popped open allowing Sam to push it in with ease.

"Summer!" Sam yelled as he ran through the house. He came to the bedroom door to find it wide open. He searched along the door frame for a wall switch. When he finally found it, he flipped the light on to find Summer gone. "Oh no!" Sam exclaimed. The sheets on the bed looked as if it was slept in and dirty clothes were on the floor near the hamper. The smell, that beautiful smell that Summer has, Sam could smell as if she was right next to him. His heart started racing, his breathing was labored; then a noise came from the basement.

He ran down the steps to see the black mass coming in the window. Sam tried to stop it, but it was no use! Sam's hands would just pass right through. The mass crept through the house with Sam closely behind. "She's not here!" Sam yelled to the mass, but it was no good. As the mass came close to her room, the door to the bathroom opened. Without looking, without hearing Sam's warnings; Summer walked out. The mass grabbed her from behind with his right hand over her mouth and his left arm around her waist.

Sam tried so hard to fight for her, but his hands would just pass through both of them! Sam didn't know how long it was; seconds, maybe minutes, but Summer went limp. The mass threw her up over his shoulder as if she was just a sack of animal feed. Sam reached for her to pull her away trying his best but his hands just kept passing through her.

"Stop!" Sam yelled as he stood in front of the mass. As it preceded outside Sam ran out yelling, "Help! He's kidnapping her! Help!" He used all of the power he had as he yelled yet what came out was weak, soft, useless. Then Sam noticed as he tried to run through the yard after her, he was not running on grass but millions of bugs. All types of bugs that would pop and crack under his bare feet. It was no use, the mass was getting away as Sam was starting to slide in the bugs. He lost his footing then fell over into the bugs; millions of them were crawling all over him. He was panicking as they started to crawl into his ears and up his nose. Then in a flash they were gone.

Sam looked around to see that he was once again in his bedroom. The bugs were gone but that smell... that glorious smell of Summer was still on him. He smelled his fingers and it was as if he had run them through her hair. Sam realized he had just had another dream and Summer was in danger. He jumped out of bed and ran across the hallway to his parent's room. "Dad! Dad! Wake up!" Sam yelled scaring both of his parents to death. "Sam, what is it?!" Michael said with a frustrated tone. "I had another dream... It's Summer, someone is there trying to kidnap her!" Sam yelled while pulling at the blanket over his father.

"Sam it was just a dream, go back to bed," Michael said barely awake with his eyes closed. "I don't have normal dreams!" Sam rebutted. Michael slowly opened his eyes and stated coldly, "I know... we all know. I pray this town never finds out. Now get to bed!"

Sam stepped back looking at his father with anger and hate. "You said it wasn't my fault, but it is... it is my fault Tommy died," Sam said trying not to cry. "Honey, no it is not," Elizabeth said. Sam ran from their room slamming the door behind him. "Michael, what is wrong with you? His best friend died, he blames himself for it and you go and reinforce it," Elizabeth angrily said. "I know, I know, but face it... there might be something wrong with him. Do normal people have dreams about death and ghosts?" Michael asked somberly, "I really think we need to get him help." Elizabeth rolled over placing her back to Michael, "You better go talk to him right now." Michael groaned, "Fine..."

Michael got out of bed, put his robe on then opened the bedroom door. He walked across the hall to find Sam's room empty. "Sam, where are you?" Michael asked trying to keep his cool. He went back to the hallway then down to the bathroom to find it dark. "Son of a bitch!" Michael exclaimed, "He's gone! Damn that kid!"

Sam ran from his house wearing only a pair of shorts. Summer's house was a few blocks away and he knew he would be there swiftly. The night was cool and the moon was shining down on him as he ran as fast as he could. He ran down the block Summer lived on to find it quiet with only a few cars parked on the street.

Sam ran up the steps then beat on the door, "Summer! It's Sam!" There was no response. He tried the knob but it was locked. He ran around the side of the house almost forgetting about the basement window when he felt a sharp pain in his left foot. He raised his foot to look at it in the moonlight. A shard of glass was sticking out of the side. Carefully he grabbed the piece of glass and pulled it out with great pain. Blood was dripping on the pavement but that did not stop him. He saw the window was broken so he hobbled to the back door.

He came up the steps to find the door wide open. The house was dark inside. He felt around for the light switch finally finding three in a row. He flipped all of them with one motion causing the light for the basement stairs, the kitchen light and the back-porch light all to illuminate. He slowly walked into the kitchen almost sliding on the floor from the blood leaking out of his foot. Sam's heart was racing with both fear and adrenaline.

From a spot deep inside of himself he yelled, "Summer!" There was silence. He looked in the bathroom to find it vacant. Next, he tried a door to find an empty bedroom. Sam was shaking now; anger was replacing the fear. He looked in her bedroom door to see the bedroom just like it was in his dream. And just like in his dream, Summer was gone. "Summer! It's Sam!" he yelled once more.

Sam heard a noise in the kitchen so he turned around and ran as fast as he could only to see a man pointing a gun directly at him. "Who are you?" the man asked. "I'm Sam, where's Summer?" Sam said in a defiant tone, "What did you do to her?" The man could feel his hands sweating as he held the gun on what looked to be nothing but a bleeding teenage boy. "I'm a police officer… how do you know the woman who lives here?" the man said while carefully pulling his finger back from the trigger.

"I know her nephews. I know her… someone took her," Sam said as tears streamed down his face. "How did you cut your foot?" the man asked. "On glass in the driveway; he broke the basement window," Sam said.

In the distance was the sound of a man yelling, "Sam!" The man came in the backdoor, "Sam! Are you here?" Sam gave a breath of relief, "In here dad." Michael walked in to see a man with a gun pointing at Sam. "Who are you?" the man asked. "That's my dad!" Sam yelled. The officer carefully placed his gun into a holster on his belt, "This is your son?" Michael could see that Sam was bleeding, "Yes he is my son, what did you do to him?!" Sam pulled a chair out from the table then sat down, "I cut it on glass in the driveway. Where's Summer?"

The officer swiftly checked the rooms, "She's not here, damnit!" He ran to the backdoor to see her Wagoneer parked in front of the garage. He returned to the kitchen to pick up the telephone receiver only to find the phone dead. He slammed it down so hard the phone broke free from the wall plate, "Fuck! I'll be right back." Sam looked at his father then started to cry, "He has her... he has her and it's all my fault." Michael noticed the pool of blood growing on the kitchen floor below Sam, "I better see if she has a bandage or something."

Michael started opening cabinets looking for a bandage when he was stopped by the officer, "Don't touch anything. They will dust the house for fingerprints. I have a first aid kit with me so we can bandage up his foot. Also, Detective Norris is on his way..." Michael looked to the officer who was opening the plastic case, "You were watching the house, weren't you?" The officer pulled out a package of gauze bandages while ignoring the question, "Let me see your foot. This will keep it closed until they get you to the emergency room. I think you may need a stitch or two."

Sam was losing his color quickly after hearing the dire news, "Emergency room? It's not that bad!" Michael looked out the kitchen window toward the driveway as a car rushed up, "Officer, I

201

believe this is for you…" Detective Norris walked in half dressed and his hair a mess, "Officer, go outside and wait in your car for me." The officer handed the end of the gauze to Michael then did as he was told.

"Why am I not surprised to see you two here," George said bluntly, "Tell me Sam, you had reason to believe this would happen, didn't you?" Sam looked to the detective, "I dreamt it… tonight. A black mass took her." George looked to Michael then to Sam, "A black mass? Can you elaborate a bit? And what happened to your foot?" Sam started to feel frightened again, "I stepped on glass in the driveway. He broke the window to the basement. All I saw in the dream was that it was a figure of man. He was all black, no face, no clothes, just black."

"Do you know where he took her?" George asked. "No," Sam said with his eyes filling with tears, "I don't know. I'm so sorry… it's all my fault." George could see the pain Sam was in, "No son, this is not your fault at all. It's that green fool who should have been watching this house. It's late and you need to get that foot looked at. Why don't I have the officer drive you two over to the hospital." Sam looked to his father, "Do I have to go?" Michael was not about to take any lip, "Yes. There could be more glass in that wound."

"Mister White, please come with me outside for a minute. Sam, we will be right back," George said. Sam looked to his father. "It's fine Sam, stay here and off of your foot," Michael said. The men walked out into the night air and out of earshot of Sam. "What is going on?" Michael asked with a stressed tone. George looked to the house to make sure Sam stayed in the kitchen. "I will be placing two officers on your house at all times. Anywhere Sam goes, one will go with," George said.

"Do you really think Sam is in that much danger?" Michael asked. George looked at the father with wide eyes, "A young woman was just kidnapped… at least we think she was. If your son was right, someone took her and someone definitely broke that basement window." Michael looked George right in the eye, "There's more to this, isn't there? What are you not telling me?"

George looked once more to make sure Sam was nowhere near to hear them talking, "Yes there is, much more. Today the confidence men the boys went to see were found murdered in their burning home." Michael stood in awe not knowing what to say. "Um, also that envelope Summer Graham found that the missing was letter in… It was dusted for prints… only hers' were found on it," George said, "Something very bad is going on and we have no clue as to who is doing all of this. Now because of that fucking cop who was doing God knows what, the young woman he was supposed to be watching over is kidnapped. I pray I do not find a fresh grave along the railroad tracks in the morning."

Michael shook his head, "I wish Sam never got involved in this." George looked back toward the house when he saw the officer walking back with a black ski mask. "Detective, I found this two houses over lying on the sidewalk. Do you think it has something to do with this?" the officer asked. George took the ski mask from the officer, "Since it is in the fifty's tonight, I would say there is a good chance it has something to do with the woman that you were supposed to be watching, being kidnapped."

Michael gave a small giggle then looked down as he shook his head. "What's up with you? You really think all of this is funny?" George asked with a cross tone. "Sam said it was a black mass that took her," Michael said then laughed again, "A black ski mask... I cannot believe this! My son had another dream that has come true." George looked to the officer, "Take Mister White and his son to the emergency room so this foot can be looked at. Then take them home."

George looked at the mask in his hand, "I need to see Sam before you leave, come on." He walked into the house with the two men following. "Sam," George said with a more even tone, "does this mask look like what the man had on?" Sam took the ski mask and looked it over, "I really do not know. All I saw was a black mass in the shape of a man. I couldn't tell what he had on. He was just black... all black." George was hoping this would help Sam remember the clothing better.

"The officer will take you and your father to the hospital to get your foot looked at. When you get home, I want you to go to bed and if you dream of anything… I don't care what it is, write it all down and have your father call me," George said with an easy tone. Sam shook his head in agreement, "I really am sorry I did not get here quicker… Summer will be fine, right?" George looked down to the floor then back up to the boy, "Yes Sam… I'll make sure she will be fine." Michael who was standing behind Sam closed his eyes and slightly shook his head at the promise he knew the detective could not keep.

Sam got up from the chair then hopped on his good foot. "I'll carry you," Michael said, "I don't want you to mess up that foot too." George walked around the house looking for any clues. He saw Summer's purse lying on the floor next to her bed. He opened it to find the revolver, "Fuck, she didn't even have time to grab it." He looked up then ran to the front door. As he came out the door, the officer's car was about to pull away from the curb. "Stop!" George yelled.

The officer slammed on the brakes causing Sam to bounce forward out of his seat. "Jesus Christ!" Michael yelled, "You are an idiot, aren't you?" George ran up to the window where Sam was sitting then made a circular motion with his hand. Sam rolled down the window. "Sam, where was Summer when she was taken? Was she in her bedroom?" George asked. "No," Sam said, "She was coming out of the bathroom."

George looked down the street to the occasional car parked along the curbs, "Did he take her to a car?" Sam shook his head, "I don't know... I woke up just after he left the house with her. He held his hand over her mouth and then she went limp. He threw her up over his shoulder with no problem." George looked at Sam, "He held his hand over her mouth and she went limp?" Just as Sam shook his head in agreement, George said, "Chloroform... Okay, thank you Sam. Officer get them to the hospital in one piece."

George walked back into the house just as a white van pulled up. "Detective, is this the house?" a woman asked. "Yes," George said, "I want every print in that house found and taken... and I want it done before sunrise. Look for anything you can find; fibers, hair, even fucking boogers, I don't care. Just get me anything that I can use to find the kidnapper."

Chapter 15

George was wearing a freshly pressed gray suit while sitting on a rock hard wooden bench. He softly watched as people were mulling around the marble lined hallway carrying papers and briefcases. Occasionally someone would laugh out loud causing him to jump a bit while trying desperately to keep his heavy eyelids open.

He could feel himself slowly falling asleep when the door next to the bench opened. "George," Karen said wearing a conservative blue dress, "George?" He opened his eyes then looked over to see Karen looking back at him, "Sorry. Having two hours of sleep is not enough for me." Karen smiled, "Come in."

George got up from the bench sore but did his best not to allow Karen to notice. He walked into an office to see a man cleaning his golf clubs. "Your honor," George said with pure politeness. "Karen has told me about your predicament. Thankfully for both of us I know a few people with pull at the railroad; one of which I am golfing with shortly," the judge said. He opened a small bottle of cleaner then placed some of the contents on a white rag leaving George to wait for his answer. "Get your shovel Detective. They will allow you to carefully and discretely search the right of way for the remains. You are to not interfere with any of their operations… and if you find remains… you need not tell the public where they were found," the judge said while rubbing his putter.

George smiled unwilling while saying, "Thank you, your honor. I am really hoping this may provide clues to help us find the missing woman." The judge polished his putter then said without looking, "I do hope you realize what your little friend is alluding to… can cause complications to many elected officials. Last thing we would want is news of a mass murderer or serial killer on the loose this close to the election." George was trying desperately to keep his temper under control, "Oh, of course…" The judge looked up toward Karen, "Miss Brady, I would like you to oversee the operation… just in case this ever comes to court. If there truly is a serial killer in my home town, I want him fried." Karen stayed quiet but gave a tight-lipped smile in acknowledgement.

"Both of you can go now, I have a foursome at ten," the judge said with little remorse. "Thank you again your honor," George said then passed through the door behind Karen. George softly closed the door then said out loud, "Asshole." Karen looked at the detective thin lipped. "What? He is, isn't he?" George pleaded. "He just pulled strings to allow you to look for this woman's remains, but George… how is this going to help you find the woman who was just kidnapped?" Karen asked as they walked down the hallway.

"Truthfully I do not know if it will but hopefully there is something there to help us. We are going on the dream of a teenage boy; sadly, he has been right so far. I'm praying he is wrong this time though," George said as they stepped onto the elevator, "I'll stop by your house so you can get some better clothes on. Maybe those jeans of yours I like so much…" Karen looked to the man ten years her junior then smiled, "Anything for you."

They stepped off of the elevator then George proceeded directly to the information desk. "I want to call Locke," George said. He picked up the receiver of a white phone then pressed zero. "Get me the coroner's office, please," George said then paused, "Eric. Get your men together we have permission. It should be right near the highway K overpass. DA Brady is coming with me… should be there in a half hour… okay, see you then." George placed the receiver down, "Let's go." Karen smirked, "Do you know you almost sound excited?" George smiled back, "To see you in those jeans, yes, yes I am."

As his sedan pulled up to a tiny ranch house, George had more on his mind than Karen. "I'll be back in a flash," Karen said. George reached under the seat to find his gun and its holster. He shifted to the side so he could slide it onto his belt while listening to the local news on the radio. Nothing was said of Summer being kidnapped and he wanted it that way. He felt as long as the people do not have a reason to panic the better for the department.

Just as Karen walked out the door, a green car drove by slowly. The driver paid attention to the woman as she walked toward the detective's car wearing tight blue jeans and a loose green shirt. Karen opened the door to find George nodding off. "I walk out all sexy for you and the only one who noticed was some guy driving by," Karen said with disbelief. George kept his eyes closed then laughed, "I could see you... trust me."

Karen closed the door to the car, "Okay old man, let's get a move on." George looked over to Karen then said, "Why don't you stay at my house tonight?" Karen chuckled, "Is that a new pickup line?" George rolled his eyes, "I have much better ones than that!"

"The local news was on while you were getting dressed," George said as he pulled away from the curb, "Nothing was said about the kidnapping." Karen looked over, "Don't blame yourself for this." George stopped at the stop sign then waited for an elderly man to cross the street with a walker. "I don't blame myself," George said softly, "I do however wish I would have taken this more seriously though. I thought the boy was somehow getting information from the killer himself." Karen looked back to George and stated bluntly, "If he would have come forward in the very beginning, none of this would have happened." As they rounded a curve George said, "Well even if he did, I still wouldn't have believed him. Part of me still doesn't."

George pulled onto the shoulder of County Highway K just short of the bridge over the railroad tracks. "Don't look they are here yet," Karen said. "They'll be here. Why don't we walk down and start looking around?" George asked. Karen opened the door then stepped out into the warm, humid air, "It's going to be a hot one. I thought it was finally cooling down." George slammed the door then walked around to the trunk, "It's going to be warm for a while. I'm not ready for snow."

"Okay, where now?" Karen asked. George pointed across the road, "We can go down there. It's about a quarter mile walk if I'm right." Karen looked to make sure no cars were coming then crossed the road. George opened the trunk to retrieve a black case and a garden spade. "What's in the case?" Karen asked as George walked across the road toward her. "My camera. I know Eric will have a photographer with him, but I think I want to have my own unofficial copies," George said, "Come on down this small animal path."

The couple walked down the path coming to a small ditch that lined the railroad right of way. "No trains at least," Karen said. George looked down the tracks to the south, "See that white sign,

211

that should be mile twelve." Karen looked to George, "That is barely inside the county. If we step across an imaginary line; our butts will be in a sling." George looked at Karen then smiled. "I know...," Karen said then giggled.

"Hello down there!" came a familiar voice from up on the bridge. George looked up, "Eric, get down here, were burning daylight!" Karen stepped up onto the rail and did her best to balance along the head while walking. "What are you? Ten?" George asked then laughed. "I was when my brother came home from the military for the first time and brought you with," Karen said then winked.

George watched as four men walked down the small trail armed with shovels. Behind them was Eric Locke with a new friend. "Awe! Who is this?" Karen asked jumping down from the track then making a beeline to a reddish-brown bloodhound. "This is Floyd. I borrowed him from the state police for the day," Eric said, "He's trained in finding decomposition." Karen petted the dogs head as his floppy ears moved in the breeze.

"Eric, you didn't tell them what we are doing?" George asked. "Naw. I told them I wanted to train some with him. You know, in case I'm allowed to get one," Eric said, "Okay, where do we start?" George pointed down the tracks to the small white sign, "There." Eric looked at him, "That's almost a mile, maybe more. These old knees will be aching tonight." George shook his head, "No its no more than a quarter mile… Stop with the whining already."

The group walked down the tracks while periodically checking behind them for the headlight of an oncoming train. They were just past the bridge when Floyd tugged on his leash so hard Eric was starting to be dragged, "Ha! He found something." They didn't make it far when they all could smell it was not the body they were looking for. "Oh my God, that is bad!" Karen exclaimed. Just on top of the ridge was the bloated body of a deer. "Poor guy must have been hit by a train," Eric said, "Come on Floyd, that's not who we want to find."

They made it to the white sign with black numerals stating twelve. Eric looked around seeing deep weeds, grasses and the occasional bush. "I guess we'll walk Floyd up and down the tracks starting on this side. I have no idea if all this brush will be a problem or not," Eric said, "Here, Ryan, take Floyd and get walking while I talk with the detective." A small framed man took the leash then directed the hound for his first pass.

"I wanted to let you know that the autopsies on the Abraham brothers were not completed yet, but I did look the remains over. The skinny one had a gunshot wound to the heart. The other was shot in the foot and knee. He also had many abrasions and a good bump on the head," Eric said to George, "That one was found at the

213

bottom of the basement steps. Possible he was pushed down."

George watched the men searching the weeds, "I have no idea if their murders are tied to this but deep down I think they are. I am really worried about that kid. If whoever did this knows he somehow dreams about all this, he may think the kid knows who he is." Eric looked back to George, "It's all over the office about the woman being kidnapped. I was surprised you wanted to do this today... with her missing and all."

"I have no choice. I have nothing that leads me to who took her, where she was taken... its eating at me that she could be dead already and... it could be my fault," George said in a somber tone. Eric started to open his mouth to say something when Karen interrupted, "Guys! Come over here!"

Karen was standing about ten feet from the tracks on a slight hill. "Did you find something?" George asked as the two men walked toward her. "I don't know, maybe," Karen said while standing next to a white rose bush, "Look at the area around here. Mostly grasses, weeds, some wild flowers and small scruff bushes. What looks out of place?"

Eric looked around, "Looks all the same to me." George rubbed his chin with his right hand then pointed, "The rose bush. That looks to be out of place, very out of place... Bring that dog over here!" The men led the hound over as George remained pointing toward the bush, "Have him smell around the bush." The hound was allowed to go toward the bush. As he moved, you could hear his nose sucking in the humid air. As be came around to the far side away from the tracks he started to bark.

"Does that mean he found remains?" Karen asked. Eric shrugged his shoulders, "I don't know… I guess so." George quickly lost his humorous tone, "You think? You didn't ask?" Eric looked to George and Karen stunned, "They just said he would let me know when he found something… I had to get out here quickly. Damn, try to help some people…" George shook his head, "Well you could have asked. The way they made it sound, he would talk to you and say, hey, there's a body here!" Karen chuckled then said, "George calm down. Eric's just trying to help."

"Just start digging where the dogs indicated with his bark. We'll keep walking around with him," George said to the men. He took the leash of the dog then handed it to Karen, "You're better with animals than me." Karen chuckled but did not say anything. As the men dug, Karen, Eric and George continued to lead Floyd around. Eric stopped to wipe the sweat from his forehead when he noticed something shining from off of the overpass.

"Hey George, don't look up but listen to me. I think I just saw something reflecting off of the overpass… like binoculars or a camera lens," Eric said. George kept his vision on the dog, "Karen you

215

have better eyes than both of us. Just happen to look up and see if you can see any one up there." Karen nonchalantly looked up to quickly see the reflection of the sun off of something but could not make out who or what it was.

"I saw it, but I cannot tell what it is," Karen said calmly, "Do you think it is a reporter?" George watched as Floyd sniffed through the weeds, "I don't know. Could be anyone. Eric, you think one of your younger guys could cut through that cornfield and come around to the road. Maybe get a look at who it is?" Eric shook his head, "I'll go over and ask one of them to do it."

"Why don't we turn around and walk back the other direction," Karen said. George looked over, "Okay. Hopefully one of those young bucks are fast and quiet enough to catch whoever it is." As the couple went back in the direction of the rose bush, Eric crossed over the tracks toward them. "Ryan is heading though the field to see who it is. I told him not to confront the person but to report back to you," Eric said, "And…" George looked at his friend, "And what?" Eric nodded toward the bush, "Come with me."

They walked over to a now deepening hole in the ground. "They are really deteriorated, but they found what may be clothing. If they are, they looked to be folded like we found in that other grave," Eric said with a slight smile. Karen looked to George, "That kid… he's psychic or something." George

216

remained quiet looking down the rails to see the headlight of a train. "Trains coming. Everyone get away from the tracks until he passes," George said.

As the train quickly approached Eric knelt down in the hole shifting the soil with his hands. "Those things are loud!" Karen yelled to George over the rumbled of the locomotives. George acknowledged by shaking his head in agreement. Suddenly the brakes locked up on the freight train causing sparks to fly off of the wheels. The screech of steel on steel caused their ears to ache. "What is happening?!" Karen yelled into George's ear. As he watched the cars were waving back and forth violently. "Everyone Get back!" George yelled. He reached down and grabbed Eric by his collar pulling him from the hole.

As the cars slowed down, the shaking stopped and only the smell of burned brake pads was left. "Oh my ears! What's going on?" Karen asked. "I don't know, stay here with them. I'll go find out," George said. He took off down the tracks jogging the best he could. As he came near the overpass he saw something he was not expecting. Lying on the roadbed was a human leg, beige pants still covered it and its shoe was still attached.

"Oh my God!" George exclaimed. He looked off to see parts of Ryan spread across a large area near the pier of the overpass. From the front of the train, a man was quickly approaching. "Holy shit!" the man said then made a gagging noise.

217

George carefully walked across the scene to approach the nauseated man.

"What happened?" George asked. "He jumped!" the man said while trying not to see the body parts spread about. "What the hell do you mean he jumped?" George asked bluntly. "We were coming up to the bridge… all the sudden he fell right in front of us. A split second later he would have landed on the engine itself," the man said, "The engineer has radioed the dispatcher for help."

George pulled his thirty-eight revolver from its holster, "Go back to the locomotive and stay there." The man really did not hear what George said, but the sight of the gun was enough for him to reverse course and run back to the locomotives. George looked for another way up to the road that was not open, but there was none. He crept up the side of the pier with the gun firmly in his right hand. As he got close to the guardrail, he hopped over but did not see anyone.

He noticed the trunk of his car was open. While carefully surveying the area, he walked over to see the lock had been popped out, but nothing seemed to be missing. In the distance sirens could be heard. He walked onto the bridge to see blood on the pavement and on the concrete guardrail. On the other side of the bridge two deep skid marks were fresh on the road. George placed his gun back into his holster just as two squad cars arrived.

"We got a call about a jumper, Detective," one officer yelled as he pealed out of his squad car. "It was not jumper... someone threw him," George said, "Radio for an investigative team. I want this bridge looked over for clues. I have a possible crime scene down the tracks. Do not let anyone in or out of this area unless I say so!" The officer shook his head in agreement.

As George headed down the trail, he saw Eric walking up alongside the train cars. "Eric... stay there!" George yelled. Eric looked up to George then asked, "Why?" George came down to the ditch then carefully avoided the pieces of human remains. "We found her!" Eric exclaimed, "We found her! A full skeleton... I thought you would be happy?" George looked at his old friend, "Eric... Ryan is dead."

Eric tried to look pass George but was quickly blocked, "Someone threw him off of the overpass in front of the train." Eric was trying to form words but the sounds did not make anything coherent. "My car was broken into and I've found blood up on the bridge like there was a struggle... that was no reporter looking at us," George said as anger built inside of him. "Why... who was looking at us? Why?" Eric asked.

"Let's go back down to the grave, there is a team coming to look into what just happened," George said as he grabbed Eric's arm. As they made their way back, George was racking his brain as to what they have gotten themselves into. "Eric, why don't you take your men aside and break the news to them," George said. Eric shook his head in agreement as Karen met them.

"What happened?" Karen asked. She knew George well enough to know something was bothering him. "What is it?" Karen asked bluntly. "That kid Eric sent back to the overpass... someone threw him off of the bridge right in front of the train," George said. Karen looked back to the other men who were now sitting on the roadbed near the parked railroad cars. She turned to George and whispered, "You're sure someone threw him off?"

George looked at her, "Someone broke into my trunk... I found blood up on the bridge like a fight or struggle happened... there are skid marks from a fleeing vehicle." Karen hugged George tight, "I'm worried about you... I don't know what is going on, but I am afraid for you." George wrapped his arms around the woman he loves, "Nothing can hurt me. I am worried about the missing woman and that kid... we need to convince his old man to get that family out of town."

Karen pulled back, "I have the cabin up north... they can go there." George gave a half smile, "Are you sure?" Karen laid her head back on George's chest, "Yes." Eric walked up while doing his best to hold it together, "Love birds... we have a job to get done." George looked over to his friend. "We all know about you two. I cannot understand why you hide it," Eric said, "Let's get to the body already. I am ready to go home…"

They walked to the side of the rose bush to see the three foot deep hole that contained skeletal remains. "I'll get the dental records pulled for Beverly Larsen in the morning, but I am sure this is her. That kid is batting five hundred so far," Eric said. George looked down the tracks, "Yes he is. That also means there could be a woman buried at each mile along this route and he has his forty-second victim right now."

"Get photos of everything you can and then get her back to the morgue. I need to talk to the sheriff now. This is beyond us… It's time for the feds to get involved," George said somberly. "What about the boy?" Karen asked, "Do you want the feds to ask him questions. They'll have him locked up in a mental ward as soon as he mentions dreams or ghosts." Eric piped up, "She's right… they'll screw that boy up."

"So what am I going to do then?" George asked. "You're job. The job that you do better than anyone I know," Karen said, "Let's get the kid and his family to my cabin then you will at least not have them to worry about. Eric, have you found anything in the grave that may help point us in a direction?"

Eric looked carefully at the skeleton, "I need to get the bones back to the lab, but other than being buried at a mile marker on the railroad tracks, I really see nothing that will help us." George looked at Karen, "I need that kid to help us. Maybe he needs encouragement in his dreaming to find who is doing this." Karen looked at George, "What do you mean? Hypnosis?" George shook his head, "Maybe there is someone at the college who could point us in the right direction."

Chapter 16

The sound of crickets chirping and flies buzzing about was the only thing Summer heard when she woke up. Her head felt like it was in a vise and her left ankle was burning. When she opened her eyes the dimly lit room was enough to make her head hurt worse. She tried to keep her eyes open but quickly shut them due to the pain.

She placed her right hand over her eyes then opened them widely. Very slowly she unshielded her eyes until they could adjust to the light without causing too much pain to her overburdened head. Once they were fully working, she wanted to close them again after seeing her surroundings.

It looked to be an old factory complete with broken windows and rusting equipment. The concrete floor was damp and covered in spots with thick carpets of moss. Full trees even sprouted up in some areas. An occasional bird flew between the rafters and looked down upon their new visitor. Summer looked down to her ankle to discover the burning was caused by a steel shackle locked on with a brass padlock. A large chain was attached to the shackle then ran about ten feet to a large sprinkler pipe coming out of the floor.

Summer looked down to see she was lying on an old stained mattress that was dotted with cigarette burns. She still had her nightshirt on and was relieved to feel that she also had her panties on. She tried to stand up but once she did, the room started to spin violently causing her to fall back onto the mattress with her eyes closed hoping the spinning would stop.

"Help!" Summer yelled as loud as she could, "Can anyone hear me!" She listened for anyone, but the only ones responding were the bugs. She wanted to cry but her strong will was winning and she knew fighting would be the only way out of this. She tried to stand once more but her head stopped her. She looked at the shackle to see if she would be able to get it off. The crudely formed steel and riveted hinge would make this impossible. She looked around the area for anything she could use to break it or the chain.

Not far away where chunks of steel bar. She crawled toward them but found that the chain would keep them just out of reach. She laid on the moss covered floor and stretched her arms as far as she could, but they were still a foot away. She rolled over onto her side then back onto her hands and knees looking for anything that would help.

Summer was crawling back to the mattress when she heard the sound of a steel door closing in the distance with a strong reverberation throughout the building. "Hello?!" Summer asked, "Whose there?" Summer listened as she could hear the sound of boots coming toward her from a pitch black hallway.

A man walked out from the darkness wearing work clothes and a black mask that covered his whole head. He was carrying a white bag and a styrofoam cup. "Who are you?" Summer asked as she backed up over the mattress going all the way to the cold cinder block wall. He placed the bag and cup on the floor within easy reach of the young woman then started to walk away. "Who the fuck are you?! What do you want with me?" Summer yelled.

The man turned around and said in a calm voice, "I hope you like donuts and coffee. Please eat so you can keep your strength up." He turned back around and as he walked toward the darkness stated, "You can scream all you like. No one can hear you here."

Summer was now shaking with fear and anger. As the man disappeared into the darkness, the sound of the door opening then slamming shut was heard. Summer was afraid to eat what he brought but her stomach was hurting from hunger and whatever he used to knock her out. She reached forward to find hot coffee in the cup. She smelled it for anything odd, but all she smelled was the coffee. With a little sip, she felt it was fine enough to drink. Next, she opened the bag to find two chocolate glazed donuts. Summer bit into one and immediately knew they came from the donut shop in Riley. "I can't be far from home!" Summer said out loud.

"Oh God! I feel like a prisoner!" Danielle said out loud as she sat on the couch watching a boring game show. Elizabeth looked up from a book she was reading, "You could do your homework you know." Danielle looked over then exhaled, "Why do I have to be stuck here just because someone wants to hurt the little freak… like anyone would want him." Elizabeth closed her book then went to sit next to Danielle. "Honey, there is a woman not much older than you who is missing. Sam's best friend was murdered. I don't know if you realize this or not, but you having to stay home is not the biggest worry right now," Elizabeth said with an even tone.

Danielle got up from the couch then said, "Fine. I'll be in my room doing anything I can to pass the time." Michael walked in the room just as his daughter passed him in a huff. "Problems with Princess?" Michael said with a touch of humor. Elizabeth shook her head, "She wants to be in school. More importantly she wants to be with her friends. Where is Sam at?"

Michael sat down on the couch next to his wife then turned on a baseball game, "He's up in the attic. I think he just wants to be alone some." Before Elizabeth could respond, the doorbell rang. "Who could that be?" Elizabeth asked. Michael switched off the television, "Stay here, I'll find out."

Michael walked to the door and then unlocked the deadbolt. He opened the door slowly while peering through the widening gap to find Detective Norris with a man and women he didn't know. "Mister White, may we come in?" George asked. Michael shook his head then unlocked the screen door, "Please, come in to the living room."

"Mister and Misses White, this is Karen Brady our district attorney and Professor James Martin," George said with ease, "We've come to talk with you two first and with your permission, speak with Sam." Michael looked to Elizabeth who said, "Okay… what would you like to talk with us about?"

George looked to the furniture, "Please, everyone sit down. Professor Martin studies parapsychology at the college." Michael chuckled a bit, "You mean like ghosts and goblins?" Elizabeth gave her husband a stern look while the professor said, "On the surface yes. But I more focus on the phenomena that cannot be easily explained by known science. Detective Norris spoke with me about Sam…" Michael interrupted sharply, "Who are you to speak with anyone about my son?"

Karen did her best to calm the father, "Mister White, Sam seems to have a gift that we hope will help us find Summer Graham." Michael looked to the woman and said with anger, "A gift? Are you kidding me? He's a boy with an imagination."

George looked to Michael then said, "Yesterday we unearthed another body… right where your son said it would be. We are waiting on the dental record identification, but I can guarantee it is Beverly Larsen. Just like your son said. Now, I have a missing woman who I do not want to become the next murder victim, but I have no clues as to who took her or where she is." Karen looked to George, "Calm down, please. Mister White, the professor feels he has a way that may help Sam… and us find her."

Michael stood up from the couch, "I'll show all of you to the door." Sam walked into the room, "No! I want to help find Summer." Michael was turning red, "Go up to your room, this is none of your concern." Sam walked into the room undeterred, "Yes, it is… all of this is my fault and I need to make it right." Michael walked over to Sam only to realize his son will soon be as tall as him, "The more you help, the deeper this family slips in a deep hole. We cannot leave our home because of you… I may not have a job much longer because of you… Think about that for a bit before you open your mouth to help more."

George looked to Karen while doing his best to keep his temper under control. "Sam, do you dream of them every night?" James asked. Before Sam could answer Michael said bluntly, "He's a minor and I am his father, he is not speaking with you." Elizabeth piped up, "And I am his mother and if Sam wants to help, he will help." Michael looked

228

at his wife then exhaled, "Fine, you want to make him into the town freak, go ahead. You have babied him his whole life, you might as well keep going. All of you have fun; I need to get out of here."

Michael stormed out of the room then slammed the front door as he passed through it. "I am sorry for my husband," Elizabeth said with a somber tone, "Sam please sit down." Sam did as he was told then looked to the professor, "I don't dream of them all the time." James smiled, "Okay, what is going on when you dream of them? Do you have the radio on or is it raining, um, maybe you had a large or spicy dinner… maybe just watched a scary movie on TV." Sam thought for a second, "Sometimes it was storming, sometimes it wasn't. Sometimes I had the radio on, sometimes I didn't."

James smiled, "Okay. The detective told me that you saw a ghost on the trail… you were fully awake coming home. Is this correct?" Sam shook his head in agreement. George looked to the professor, "I have told you all of this already." Karen placed her hand on George's leg, "Let him do what he needs to."

James looked to Sam and Elizabeth, "Sam, with your mother's permission I would like to try something. Have you heard of hypnosis before?" Sam shook his head, "Yeah like in the movies with a gold watch or something." James laughed, "Yes just like that. It may be possible for you to actually see where Summer is. It's a term called remote viewing.

229

Some people are more in tune with others, people who are alive while also in tune with people who are no longer alive. I believe you are one of those people."

Elizabeth looked to Sam, "I guess it's okay… Sam, what do you think?" Sam looked to the detective who he knew wanted to find Summer just as much as he did, "It won't hurt?" The professor shook his head, "No, it won't hurt. We will need a very quiet room to do this in." Elizabeth thought than said, "Sam's room should do fine." James stood up, "Misses White I would prefer to take Sam under alone, but if you or he would like you there, you can come. George and Karen, I'll call down to you when we are ready for you." Sam looked to his mom, "Its fine, I'll be okay." Elizabeth remained quiet while she looked on as her son and the older gentleman walked up the stairs.

"We're sorry to cause problems between you and your husband," Karen said, "But we really have no other choice." Elizabeth chose her words carefully, "When it comes to Sam, Michael feels he needs to be… well more like he was at that age. Michael was an athlete whereas Sam is a dreamer, literally. Sam likes to work on things, see how they work. He likes to read, hang out with his friends. Michael has been pushing him so hard to be who he isn't…"

Sam took the professor to his room then closed the door. "My sister is in her room next door.

If you want to throw her out, you can." James laughed, "No that will not be necessary, why don't you lay back on your bed and get comfortable." Sam took his shoes off then sat on the bed. He pushed the pillows back then laid his head on them, "Okay, now what?"

James took a locket out of his breast pocket, "You mention the gold watch; I use a locket that has a picture of my daughter. There's nothing magical about this, it's just a device that you can focus on. So what I want you to do is relax and try to clear your mind of every thought." Sam looked up, "I don't know if I can."

"You can... relax and look at the white ceiling. There is nothing there but whiteness. There is no pain or fear, no sadness or happiness... just the white ceiling," James said then held the locket over Sam' head, "I want you to look at the locket and as I move it, follow it with your eyes." James moved the locket slowly in a back and forth motion over Sam's face. Sam followed the locket faithfully as it moved.

"You're doing very good Sam," James said in a soft tone, "This is making you very relaxed. Your mind is relaxed; your body is also relaxed. Now Sam, I would like for you to close your eyes. Close them and continue to be relaxed." James placed the locket back into his pocket then carefully opened the door to the bedroom. He walked to the top of the stairs then said, "Everyone, we are ready."

He returned to the room and stood next to Sam across from the door. Elizabeth, Karen and George walked in then stood at the foot of the bed. "Sam, first take me to the night you were on the trail. You are coming close to the railroad tracks. Tell me what you saw," James said softly. Sam was so relaxed it was as if he was sleeping but then he spoke, "There is something glowing on the trail. It's a woman... she's floating above the trail."

"Does she speak to you?" James asked. "No," Sam said. "What is she doing as you look at her?" James asked. Sam took a frightened tone, "She's coming toward me... I want to get away but I can't. Her eyes are just black holes... I got to get away... she is raising her hand to me; her fingers are just bones." James looked up to Elizabeth to see there are tears streaming down her face. "Okay Sam, you are doing well, you're now away from the trail, away from the ghost. You are relaxed again," James said calmly.

"Sam, please tell me about the dream with all of the women. What were they doing?" James asked. "They are standing on the lawn... they are holding signs with numbers. The numbers seem to glow in the flashes of lightning," Sam said. James looked to George, "This is like he told you?" George shook his head, "He told us more, but yes that part is the same." Elizabeth shook her head, "Yes it is."

"Sam, I would like for you to clear your head once more. Relax and keep your mind clear. When you're ready, I want you to think of Summer Graham. Can you see her in your mind?" James asked. Sam spoke with a half smile, "Yes." James noticed Sam was smiling, "Sam, tell me what you think about Summer."

"She's beautiful, she smells so good," Sam said with that same smile. George was trying his best not to laugh like a schoolboy. "Keep quiet," Karen said then lightly elbowed George in the gut. James looked up to Elizabeth, "Misses White. Perhaps you should leave the room for a minute. I want to know how strong of bond he has with this woman and… well, perhaps it's something he would not like his mother to hear."

Elizabeth looked down to Sam, "Well… Okay, I guess…" She left the room only to find Danielle peering in the door. "Get out in that hallway," Elizabeth said then softly closed the door. "What are they doing to the little freak? Finally fixing him?" Danielle asked bluntly. Elizabeth tried to control her temper, "He's not a freak. Go to your room and do your homework."

James looked to Karen and George, "It's important for this to work that he has a strong bond with the subject. If it is not strong enough, this might not work at all. Sam, tell me more about what

233

you like about Summer." Sam stayed quiet then said, "I like her eyes, they are very pretty." James started to pace slightly at the side of the bed, "Is that all you like about Summer? Is there more?"

"She has nice boobs," Sam said which caused George to cough a bit trying not to laugh. "Detective, please…," James said, "Sam think to the first moment you saw Summer. Tell me the thought you had when you saw her." Sam took a deep breath, "She walked in a way I have never seen before. I do not know why, but I was hard." Karen quickly looked to George who was trying to keep his lips tightly pressed together.

"There is nothing wrong with that Sam; that is natural. Sam, do you think you love Summer?" James asked. "I think so," Sam said softly. "Sam, have you thought of Summer while masturbating?" James asked. Sam was quiet then said, "Yes." George looked to Karen, "Time for you to go too." Karen looked back with a blank expression.

"I think he is sufficiently bonded to her," James said. "If he was anymore, they would be married," George stated plainly. James chuckled a bit, "His mother can come back in if she likes." Karen walked to the door, pulled it open then said to the anxious mother, "You can come back in if you like."

"Okay Sam, I want you to think of Summer… think very hard. You had the dream where she was kidnapped. I want you to step beyond the dream. Forget about everything before this point and only concentrate on Summer. Open your eyes and see what her eyes are seeing. What do you see?" James asked.

Sam opened his eyes widely staring directly at the ceiling, "It's an old building. The paint is peeling from the walls. Trees are growing out of the floor." Elizabeth looked to George who was thinking hard of where this could be. "Sam, can you tell me more about the building?" James asked. "Rusty metal," Sam said. "There is rusty metal? Like cars or trucks?" James asked. "No," Sam said softly.

"Sam, is it machinery?" George asked. "I think so," Sam said. "Next Sam I want you to use your ears. Tell me what Summer is hearing," James said. "Bugs… crickets… flys… bees also I think," Sam said.

"You are doing really good Sam. Now use your nose to tell me what Summer is smelling," James said. "Coffee," Sam said. "Coffee? Do you smell anything else?" James asked. Sam took a deep breath in through his nose, "It smells bad… musty, moldy… very bad." James looked to George and asked softly, "Any idea?" George shook his head, "No…"

"Sam, now I want you to feel what Summer is feeling. Does she fear this? Does she feel okay?" James asked. Sam started to move his left leg, "My leg hurts… my head hurts… I'm scared." Elizabeth once again had tears streaming down her face. "This isn't helping," George whispered to Karen.

"Sam there is one last thing I want you to do. This will take great concentration. I want you to step back from Summer. You are now yourself… walk back from Summer then turn to look at her… tell me what you see," James said. Sam closed his eyes then said, "She is lying on a mattress wearing the shirt from when she was taken." James looked to Sam to see his eyes were moving under his eyelids, "Sam, what else do you see?"

"Chain… she has a chain on her leg. It's tied to a pipe. She's crying… why is she crying?" Sam asked softly. "Before you get him out, he needs to find something that will tell me where he is," George said bluntly. James held his hand out, "Sam you are free to walk wherever you like. I want you to walk around the building and tell me if you see anything that will tell you where you are. I want you to listen, I want you to smell."

Sam was quiet for a few seconds while George waited with anticipation. "I am walking toward the windows. They are broken… ouch! I think I just walked on broken glass… I only see green leaves… vines," Sam said. "Try finding a door," James said. Sam was again quiet. The group of people watched the young boy lying in bed waiting for his response. "There is a dark hallway. It's so dark that I cannot see well. I am feeling along the wall for a door... I can feel the paint peeling off of the walls... I think I feel a doorknob," Sam said.

"With all your strength, turn the knob and open the door!" James said with excitement. Sam made a grunting noise, "I'm trying it's hard to move... I have it open." George was looking at the boy with excitement, "What do you see?" Sam exhaled quickly, "Oh... It's Red! He's there... I think he sees me!"

"Don't worry Sam, he cannot see you. You are perfectly safe... who is Red?" James asked. "He works for the railroad... he's the one who yelled at us the day we watch them dig up the girl," Sam said. "Sam you have to see if you recognize the building," George said with a harsh tone. Sam was breathing hard, "I'm trying... I'm trying. Paper... paper... the building says paper."

"Paper?" Karen asked George. She could see he was thinking hard of where Summer could be. "There was a paper mill outside of town when I was a kid... but they tore that down years ago. Shit! Sam, is there anything else you can see?" George asked with haste.

Sam was quiet yet breathing hard. "Any ideas?" George asked the professor. "Sam look around... I need to you concentrate on the building, what does it look like?" James asked. "Bricks... lots of bricks... Oh Red is coming... Please stop him! He's going to hurt Summer! Help!" Sam yelled then popped out of the trance. He was gasping for air and starting to sweat profusely. "Oh my God, his foot is bleeding!" Karen exclaimed.

James placed his hands on Sam's chest, "Sam relax… you are here in your room… no one will hurt you. Try to take a deep breath… good, now relax and calm your breathing." Elizabeth pulled the sock off of his foot that was bleeding. "Did he rip out a stitch?" George asked. "That was the other foot," Elizabeth said, "He didn't hurt this foot… until now."

"There cannot be that many abandoned buildings in the area," Karen said to George. "No… a few that I can think of… we'll check them out," George said, "Sam, who is Red?" Sam was trying to get out of bed. "Stay until I get that foot cleaned up," Elizabeth said.

"He works for the railroad… he always yells at the kids to stay off the tracks," Sam said, "He even hit Tim once… hit him in the head with a wrench… a wrench." George looked at Sam, "Whose Tim?" Sam exclaimed, "Trailer Tim! He walks along the tracks with a model train engine."

George slightly shook his head in agreement, "I know who you are talking about. He said that Red hit him in the head?" Sam shook his head, "Yes, but Red isn't his real name… I don't remember it. Tommy and me were on the tracks and a guy working told us Red's real name. He told us to stay away from Red because he wasn't right in the head." George's eyes grew large, "Why do you call him red if that isn't his name." Sam tried to wiggle out of bed but Elizabeth held him tight while trying to apply a bandage, "He has short red hair."

"Well we might not be closer to where she is, but we might just know who took her," George said to Karen. "Can I use your telephone?" George asked Elizabeth. "Yes there is one in our bedroom across the hall." George walked swiftly to the phone then picked it and dial zero, "Get me the CNW railroad in Greenly... it's a police emergency."

While George waited for a response, Karen walked in the room and sat on the bed next to him. "I don't know what to think," Karen said, "I believe heavily in science and this is like science fiction." George looked over then slightly shook his head, "Yes, dial it for me please... Hello, I need to talk with personnel. I'm a detective with the Richland County Sheriff's Department... Fuck, they put me on hold!"

"Why is his foot bleeding?" Karen asked out loud. "Because he was so connected to Summer," James said from the hallway, "That he was actually injured by the glass where she is located." George shook his head in disbelief, "If I wasn't here right now... Yes, I need to find the name of an employee of yours. He has short red hair and works on the line that goes through Riley... Hold? Oh come on! They put me on hold again!" Karen looked up to George, "I need you to calm down too. I don't want you to have a stroke over this."

"I do not know his name… that is why I am calling you!" George exclaimed to the man on the phone, "He works on the line that passes through Riley and has short red hair… What? Hold on. Karen, get Sam." Karen was walked out of the room only to return with Sam who was having a hard time walking from his cut feet. "Sam, what exactly does Red do on the railroad?" George asked.

Sam thought hard to what the signalman told him and Tommy, "He works on the tracks… a foreman I think." George smiled, "Yes a track foreman… Wallace Smith… What is his address?" George waited with little patience, "Okay I got it. Thank you." George placed the phone down, "I have it, I'll call the office to get a team ready."

Michael walked into the bedroom, "I think you might have to wait on that." George looked to the father to see his hands were raised up to his side. Karen gasped as Cletus Jones stepped out from behind Michael with a large hunting knife. "Jones, what the hell are you up to?" George asked with a sharp tone.

Chapter 17

Summer finished her donuts and coffee allowing her stomach to slowly right itself. Her stomach felt filled yet her mind, while no longer spinning, was still lethargic. She carefully studied her surroundings looking for any way to quickly get out once she was free. Now she only needed to figure out how to get free. Other than the bugs and the occasional flapping of birds' wings, there was no noise. The silence surrounding the building was more frightening than the building itself.

She tried to stand once again and found she could now do it with little problem. Her bare feet could feel the dampness in the old concrete as she walked as far as the chain would allow her. There were windows on the wall behind her, but they were about five feet above her head. Through them she could see the blue sky, but little else. She walked to the sprinkler pipe to see if she could climb it to get a look outside.

Summer wrapped her arms around the pipe firmly while also placing her arms around a sticky mess of cobwebs. As she pulled herself up with her arms, she gripped the rusting pipe with her bare feet trying to push herself up. The chain added a great amount of weight to her leg and was almost pulling her back down. She dug her foot into the pipe as much as the pain would allow. Slowly she made her way up the pipe; each inch more painful than the first.

Finally, Summer could get her eyes just above the wooden frame of the window. It looked out onto the roof of a lower section of the building. The roof looked like Swiss cheese with holes dotting all around. The gravel on the roof was blown about by years of storms exposing black tar below. She held onto the pipe as hard as she could trying to see beyond the roofline when she felt her feet starting to slip. She tried her best to focus but all she could see were trees. She could not see anything past them; she had no clue of where she was. The sight caused her to feel like she wanted to panic.

She slowly climbed down the pipe to greet a patch of moss with her bare feet. She looked along the wall for anything that would help her break her shackle off, but nothing was found. She picked the mattress up to find a mass of ants coming out of a crack in the floor. She swiftly placed the mattress back down in hopes it would stem the flow of the creatures.

Summer had given up hope of getting free when she heard the door opening in the hallway. She stayed standing up ready to fight whomever was about to approach her. Her heart was starting to beat faster as she waited. Out of the darkness, the masked man reappeared like a bad nightmare. In his left hand was a brown paper bag. Now that she could see him clearly, she could see that he was an imposing figure that looked to be a foot taller than her.

He came to within twenty feet of her then whipped the bag at her, "Place them on... it's only fair." Summer picked up the bag then opened it to find a pair of beat up shoes "What are these for?" Summer asked. "What shoes are normally for... I believe they will fit you," the man said with a harsh tone, "Put them on then move back to the wall."

Summer pulled the worn shoes out of the bag to see a tag for a resale shop. She placed them on to find that they did fit her feet with little extra room. "Move to the wall," the man stated. She did as was demanded of her as she placed her back to the cool wall. The man walked forward then knelt down before her. He grabbed her right leg then lifted it off of the floor as she allowed her knee to bend.

The man sniffed the shoe then ran his tongue up Summer's leg. "Of fuck... don't hurt me, please," Summer pleaded. He allowed her leg to go back down then pulled a key out of his pants pocket. He placed the key in the lock then twisted it. The clasps popped open. "Stay still," the man said. He removed the lock then opened the shackle. Summer now saw her opportunity.

As the man started to stand back up, Summer kneed him in his face as hard as she could with her right knee. The hardness of his head was far more than she anticipated, but she did her best to run from the angered man. Instead of running toward the hallway he entered in, she ran the opposite way. "It's no use!" the man yelled, "All of the doors are chained. There is only one way in or out! It's your destiny to become number forty-two."

Summer ran past the rotting equipment only to see there were deep pits in the floor filled with water and debris. Many of them smelled of death or worse. She was trying not to gag as she ran past them. The man slowly walked toward the fleeing woman as if he had no fear of her getting free. As she came around a large press, she saw a staircase in the corner of the building. She had a choice to go up or go down. Summer looked back to not see the man anywhere in her sight.

Summer looked down the staircase to see sunlight streaming in. As softly as she could, she walked down steel stairs trying not to make a sound. The stairs were covered with pieces of paper, beer cans and the occasional skeletal remains of some unfortunate creature that became lost in the rotting building. As she came to the last step, she saw a long hallway that had pipes along the ceiling with an occasional window along one wall. She ran to the first window to find a chain linked panel covering the cracked glass. She pulled at the steel frame, but it was firmly attached to the wall.

In the background, she could hear the sound of boots on the stairs. She took off running down the hallway only to see each window was protected firmly as she swiftly passed them. "Keep running... I love the hunt!" the man yelled down the hallway, "So many of you try to run, but I know this building... you don't." Summer found a large boiler room at the end of the hallway. The steel boilers dwarfed the young woman with their rusting steel and rotting asbestos coverings. To her left was a wooden desk that had a dust covered beige telephone sitting on it.

Summer quickly ran to the phone then picked up the receiver to find it dead. "Of course," she whispered to herself. She carefully opened the drawers hoping to find something she could use as a weapon. The first drawers held faded papers. She pulled the large one on the bottom open to find a nest of rats. She held her mouth so she could not scream out loud.

The sounds of boots were becoming louder from the hallway. Summer looked around for a place to get out or a place to hide. She saw a pair of double steel doors behind one of the boilers. She ran to them only to find the handles tied together with a steel chain and rusted padlock. "I know you're in here... I can smell you... you're ready for me," the man yelled. Summer was starting to feel like there truly was no way out.

She peered around one of the boilers to see that the man was looking for her near the desk. As she quietly came around the boiler she found a trough that had an auger in it. The end of the auger started near a conveyor belt that went up a sloping shaft through the side wall. Summer knew this might be her only way to freedom. She quietly stepped over the edge of the trough then started to climb the conveyor belt. She could feel the grittiness of the coal that used to come down the belt and a firm coating of dried animal feces.

Summer was climbing up but where this went she did not know. Occasionally there was a pin hole in the steel that would allow sunlight to stream in. When she would come to one, she tried to look out, but nothing could be seen past the pale blue sky. She could tell she was nearing the top when there was a giant popping noise and she felt the belt fall out from under her a bit. She rapidly climbed as fast as she could to the top of the belt to find herself looking at the end of another rusty auger. Summer looked as best she could in the dark, but knew she couldn't make it between the auger and the housing.

Summer was trying not to panic, but at the moment it seemed like the only option. She tried to gather her wits as there was the sound of metal snapping below her. She pushed against the face of the auger to be surprised that it moved a good six inches back. "Come on you bastard!" Summer exclaimed as she pushed with all of her strength. The auger moved more but then became stuck. She stuffed herself into the trough then using the power of her legs pushed her back against the sheet metal cover popping it free. She pushed it away like opening a tin can from the inside.

She could see she was inside a sheet metal building with metal grating for a walkway. She stepped out onto the grating quickly noticing that she could see down to the ground maybe twenty feet below. At the end of the catwalk was a wooden door with a dirty window near the top. Summer looked down to see if the masked man was around, but she did not see him.

As Summer walked along the catwalk, the steel would creak and pop loudly. When she got to the door she wiped the dirt off the window with her hand. Looking out she saw nothing but forest. She still did not know where she was and more importantly how to get to freedom.

She looked back down to the ground making sure the man wasn't around. She carefully opened the door only to find that stepping outside would be her last. The catwalk or stairs that used to be there were long gone. The only way out would be to go down back down the belt. Summer looked around for another way out to discover above her was a giant silo used for holding coal. Next to the doorway was a ladder that lead to the roof of the silo and a long pipe that angled down toward the ground.

"I know you're up there!" came a reverberated voice up from the boiler room, "You are one of the better ones. I loved when they made me hunt for them." Summer was growing angry with the masked man, "You've never met someone

like me… you don't know who you're against."
With that last statement a merciless laugh came
from below.

Summer looked back out to the ladder but
knew she would be exposed the whole way. She
needed to be hidden so as not to be seen by her
subjugator. Summer knew she was in a game that
was stacked heavily against her. She was trying to
think of where to go, what to do. She looked back
down the conveyor belt to be relieved knowing he
would be too big to climb up it.

A strong wind picked up causing the
building to shutter. Summer was not a metallurgist
but could tell the steel supports looked to be well
worn from age and neglect. "I have to get out of
here…," Summer whispered to herself. She looked
around to the other wall that were nothing but
corrugated steel sheet. The sun shone through some
of the seams. One was particularly bright meaning
the opening was wide. Summer jumped on top of
the auger trough to get to the open seam. She
pushed on the metal to find that many of the rivets
were rusted away.

With a strong push, Summer was able to
break enough of the skin away to see the roof of the
building was within a simple jump; a six-foot jump
she judged. She knew the only other ways were to
climb the silo or go back down the belt. These were
her only choices and she needed to decide quickly.

"I want that boy... he needs to pay for what he did," Cletus said with slightly slurred speech. "You're drunk and you're not touching that boy," George said then placed his left hand on Karen pulling her up from the bed, "Stay behind me... Mister White, come back over here so I can speak with Cletus."

Elizabeth tried to quietly sneak Sam and Danielle downstairs, but was quickly stopped by Cletus. He grabbed Elizabeth by the hair, "Where the hell do you think you goin'? All of you get in this room." He threw Elizabeth into the arms of her husband who was ready to rip Cletus' head from his neck. "I'm gonna use this knife to make you feel as bad as my boy did when he was drowning in that dirty water," Cletus said while looking directly at Sam, "You will drown on your own blood as I slit your throat."

"You're not going to do a thing to that boy," George said with a powerful tone. "You need to pass that heater over here detective," Cletus said, "You may have a gun, but I'm damn fast with a knife." Sam looked at Cletus, "How are Donnie and Johnnie?" The question quickly disarmed Cletus. "Why do you want to know? Have you even come to see them since you killed my boy? They told me all about you, your dreams and seeing spooks. I've heard about people like you... seeing spooks and such. You made a deal with devil or your parents did. That's how people see spooks," Cletus said with anger and sadness.

"Listen to the town hood trying to beat down a teenage boy just because he is different. Just because he has a gift that doesn't involve theft or intoxication," Michael said with pride. "You talk down to me once more and I gonna gut you first... let your wife and family see just kind of man you are," Cletus said as he pointed the knife at Michaels face.

"You are not gutting anyone," George said as he pointed his gun right at Cletus's head. Cletus quickly grabbed Sam and held him tightly in front of his body. "Son, you are in enough trouble right now. Let that kid go and we'll finish this like men," George said smoothly.

Cletus kept hold of Sam as he walked backward into the hallway. "Think about Donnie and Johnnie right now," Sam said, "You'll never see them again." James thought quickly on how to defuse this situation, "Sam can talk with Tommy... if we let him." George looked to the professor, "This is not the time for that." James used a calming tone when he said. "He can, if you let him." Cletus looked at the professor, "I don't know who you are... but stay out of my business. I'm taking the boy here so you all best stay right where you are... or I'll rip his head off right in front of you."

Michael started to move, but was quickly stopped by Sam, "Dad, no. He won't hurt me."

Cletus smiled and as his hot, smelly breath hit Sam he said, "Don't be so sure of that boy… I have nothing to lose." Sam did his best to turn his head, "What about Donnie and Johnnie. Or your wife?" Cletus held Sam so tight he started to have a hard time breathing. "Stop," Sam gasped out, "Tommy said to stop."

Cletus loosened his grip, "Don't be lying to me boy. I know when someone's shuckin' and jivin'." Sam looked toward George, "He's standing over there near the detective. He said you need to stop!" Cletus lost control of himself and threw Sam into the doorframe as hard as he could. With his back turned in rage, Michael leaped onto the man causing both to fall over Sam into the hallway.

Cletus fought with all of his strength but Michael had more weight and height. Cletus quickly got his right hand and the knife free from beneath his body. He tried to stab backward toward Michael but George quickly grabbed his wrist. "Let go of the fucking knife," George yelled. "No you son of a bitch. You'll have to take me out once and for all. I ain't leaving here alive," Cletus yelled.

As George held the man's wrist as tight as he could, Michael used his free hand to peal Cletus' fingers off of the knife. It was as if Cletus found the strength of five men as he started to lift himself and Michael off of the floor. Michael let go of his fingers then kidney punched Cletus causing him to lay flat once more. Michael went back to working on Cletus' fingers finally freeing the knife from his grip.

George pushed Cletus' arm down on to his back. "Try to get his left arm," George pleaded to Michael. He pulled at the man's filthy arm getting it out from under his body. "Reach for my handcuffs on my belt," George said, "Get one link on his right wrist." Michael did what was asked of him then pushed Cletus' left arm toward his right as the man screamed in pain. Finally George got the other link securely around Cletus' left wrist.

"Sam," Elizabeth pleaded, "Sam can you hear me?" Sam was lying on the floor out cold. The professor reached down then placed his right hand of Sam's neck, "His pulse is fine. I think he just knocked him out. Let's get him back to his bed." Michael picked Sam up then carried him across the hallway to his bed. He placed Sam down, "Sam, can you hear me?" There was no response. "Should we take him to the hospital?" Elizabeth asked the professor. "Let's give him a few minutes to come out of it," the professor stated calmly.

Chapter 18

The sound of creaking steel was heard as another gusty breeze hit the coal tower. Summer looked down through the grating to see her captor was still not present outside. She was afraid to jump but being even higher on an unsound structure was beyond thought at the moment. She looked at her options and knew she truly did not want to go back down to the boiler room. As another strong breeze rocked the structure she knew jumping was her only solution.

Summer looked at the six-foot gap between the structure and the roof of the building. She also looked at the holes in the roof praying she could make the jump while missing one of the many holes. She looked around for anything that would help, but other than flimsy sheet metal, there was nothing. She stood on top of the trough; her heart racing and her body sweating. She braced her hands at each side of the opening in the wall.

She tried not to look down to the pile of debris at the base of the structure. Just short and she knew she would land broken on top of it. She scrunched down to use her leg muscles as assistance to make the jump. She closed her eyes then said a small, silent prayer. After a deep breath, she used all her strength to make the leap to the roof of the factory. As she hit the old decking, she could feel the rocks scraping her legs and arms. She landed with her head right above one of the many holes.

Summer looked down into the boiler room as some of the gravel fell to the floor below, to see that the masked man missing.

She carefully stood up then picked the small pebbles out of her legs and arms. After regaining her breath, she did her best to run across the roof toward the handles of a ladder sticking up from a side wall. As she ran the roof creaked even under her light frame. She came to the ladder to see it went down to the ground near clumps of bushes. Summer looked around to see the man was missing and knowing she could not lose any time, she climbed down the ladder. Once her feet touched the earth, she had to fight her way through the underbrush to an old parking lot.

The asphalt was broken into tiny pieces that grass freely grew between. In the distance was a green car that seemed so familiar to Summer. She just could not place it, but there was something about that car. She did not see nor hear anyone around so she decided to run to the car in hopes the key was inside. As she ran across the pavement, she kept an eye out for the masked man. Once she got to the car she was relieved to find the door was unlocked. She sat inside looking all around for the ignition key; the glove box, behind the visor, under the seat. There was no key to be found.

"For once I wish Cletus was here, he knows how to hot wire anything," Summer said out loud. She slipped back out of the car and decided the best thing to do would be to run for freedom. She looked again for the masked man, but oddly he was nowhere to be found. She took off running down the weed filled road where she felt she was no longer in the rich farmland of southern Wisconsin but in the thick forests of northern Wisconsin. The growth of the trees and the underbrush crowded the road making it just wide enough for a single car to pass.

Summer ran like she never did before. Her shirt was starting to ride up her body from the breeze of her sprinting toward an unknown freedom. Never did she feel like running so fast, so fast that the trees became nothing but green walls on either side of the abandoned road. She thought she could see a crossroad coming with cars passing by in the far distance. Her heart was racing; her breathing was like that of a wild horse at full gallop. Suddenly something hit her in the back near her right shoulder blade that caused Summer to spin around then hit the pavement in dire pain. She was having a hard time breathing and was starting to cough. Her face was lying against the broken asphalt as she coughed again causing a stream of blood to spray out.

Summer was feeling weak. She tried to move but it was as if her limbs refused to move. Her eyelids felt heavy as she struggled to keep them open. As her gasping for air became more desperate she heard the sound of someone walking toward her slowly with heavy work boots. She looked up with as little strength she had to see the masked man looking back down at her. In his right hand was a bow, "I told you I like to hunt." Her vision was going black as the life drained from her body.

Suddenly Summer felt herself gasping for air and choking as she woke up in an old storeroom. It was all a dream. It was a nightmare. Summer started to cry knowing she was still captive somewhere. She looked down to her ankle to see the shackle was gone and she was free to move about the dimly lit room. Shelves of dusty parts surrounded her as did the voice of a man speaking to someone. Though her legs were wobbly, she managed to stand up and walked carefully toward the voices.

She came to a chain linked fence through which she could see that nasty, decaying factory she first woke in. Sitting on an old couch was an older man with short red hair. He was looking at a smut magazine while sitting on a stool with his back to Summer, was a man with sandy colored hair.

"I'm sick and tired of having to clean up after you," the man with his back to Summer said, "Ever since I was a kid I had to clean up your messes. Well this is the biggest mess you have ever made." The red-haired man looked up from the magazine, "It was all under control under those fucking kids put their noses in everything."

"Wallace I am sick of this. I know you have desires and so do I, but you need to keep this under

256

control better. Then… you took that girls damn body without telling me," the man said while rocking on the stool. "Don't call me Wallace, I hate that name; call me Wally or something, but not Wallace!" Wallace said then looked past his brother to see Summer staring at them, "Looks like our guest is awake."

The sandy haired man turned around on the stool to see Summer looking at them through the locked gate, "Did you enjoy your trip?" Summer remained quiet. "Can I have her now, Peter?" Wallace asked. Peter looked back to his brother, "Not until we have the kid." Summer was trying hard to not show her fear, "Kid? What kid?"

Peter stood up from the stool then walked to Summer, "Your boyfriend, Sam." Summer shook her head, "Leave him alone, he's just a kid. Who are you two?" Peter said with sick amusement, "Parents tell their child about the boogeyman to give them a fright before bed. Well compared to us… the boogeyman is an angel. We are your worst nightmare, darlin'."

Summer stepped back from the gate, "You killed them, didn't you?" Peter snickered, "Them? Who are you speaking of?" Wallace threw his magazine on the couch, "Leave her alone. We need to get that kid so I can have her." Summer shook her head, "Have me? What do you mean have me?"

Peter turned to his older brother, "Listen to her, so innocent. She has no idea what will be

257

happening to her. Well Summer, when we get Sam here, both of your fates will be sealed." Wallace stood up then walked to the gate, "The first time I laid eyes on you. I knew I needed to have you. So young, so fresh... look at that little body of hers." Summer felt like she was a piece of meat hanging in a freezer, "You pigs killed those women... the body the boys talked about..."

Wallace looked to his brother, "She was Peters... he likes them younger than I do. That kid knew where she was buried... he knows where they all are buried." Peter's face was turning red, "He will pay for what he did. He destroyed our family and I will make him pay." A tear ran down Summer's face, "He's just a child. How could you hurt... Tommy. You fucking killed Tommy, didn't you?!" Peter laughed, "Whoa she is a smart one when she wants to be, isn't she!"

"He was trespassing on the railroad tracks. I don't allow trespassing," Wallace said bluntly. Summer started to cry, "He did nothing to you!" Wallace shook his head, "He trespassed." Peter looked to his brother, "Wallace here is very into obedience. Should someone violate his rules, he reacts. Thomas broke the rules, he paid the price. Sam broke the rules and he will pay also... but we'll have some fun with him first."

Summer kept slowly stepping backward until she hit a shelving unit. "We have to go get him. When we return... you're going to make him a man," Peter said with a cold tone. "A man, what are you talking about?" Summer asked. Peter shook his head, "You are being a dumb bitch again. The kid is in love with you… I bet he pops off every night just thinking of you. No man should die a virgin." She looked back to the men with a somber face, "Don't hurt him. Please, he's just a boy." Wallace piped up, "He knows too much, he must die. You will make it pleasurable for him. I can't wait to watch…"

"Come on, let's get going," Peter said. Before he could turn, Summer asked, "What was in the coffee?" Peter smiled, "Oh a little this and a little that. I wanted to keep you quiet while we worked on getting the kid. So you be a good girl and wait patiently for us, okay?" Summer stood in horror as the men walked away. "Oh, if you try to get away… we'll know and we'll make your death more painful that we are already planning," Peter said as they disappeared into the darkness.

As Cletus struggled, George led him down the stairs. "I thought you had men watching the house?" Michael asked with a raised tone. "I do and they will be getting a foot in each of their asses," George said, "Quit your bullshit already!" Cletus went to spit at George but missed. "Okay, I think we need to do this the hard way," George said as he threw Cletus face first into the wood floor.

"I can't be seeing this," Karen said as she followed the men, "Mister White, I believe Sam is waking up." Michael stayed quiet as he ran up the stairs then proceeded to his boys' room. "Are you feeling okay?" James asked as he looked into Sam's eyes with a small flashlight. "I guess so, just a little tired," Sam said, "Hey! Where's the detective? Did he find Summer?" Michael looked to his wife then back to Sam, "He's still dealing with Cletus Jones. Everyone, can you leave so I can talk with Sam alone."

"I think that might be a good idea," James said, "Sam, if you ever need anyone to talk with, I'll give your mother my card. You can call anytime." Michael looked to the professor with less than enthusiasm. "Come on Danielle," Elizabeth said, "They need to have a talk... about something." Danielle for once decided to remain quiet and obey her mother. As they passed through the door, Michael closed it behind them.

"What do you want to speak with me about?" Sam asked. "The boys Aunt Summer... Sam I was your age once and at some point, every teenage boy falls for an older woman. However I think you are going beyond the typical attraction," Michael said carefully. "Did you?" Sam asked. "We're talking about you right now," Michael said, "What ever happened to Cindy Stewart?" Sam looked at his father dead in the eye and said, "She likes jocks. I'm no jock nor will I ever be."

Michael could feel the direct hit but would not let his son get the satisfaction of seeing him getting angry, "Well Summer Graham is too old for you. She is a woman and you are a boy." Sam was not about to hear this from his father, "Summer is a woman, yes. She is great woman. She is also missing right now. I want to go help find her." Michael shook his head, "No. The detective is under the impression you are in danger. You will be staying here with the rest of us."

Sam was so angry he wanted to cry like a child, "I gave them some help. Perhaps Professor Martin can work with me more. Maybe I can find more clues to where she is." Michael was starting to tap his foot on the floor and his blood pressure was creeping up, "Sam, listen to me. Forget about Summer, forget about ghosts, forget about dreaming and forget about that quack that just came in here. You are keeping your ass in this room and that's final!"

Michael opened the bedroom door before Sam could speak any further. As he swiftly closed the door behind himself he found Elizabeth waiting. "What?" Michael asked with a cross tone. "The detective wanted you to know Cletus will be in jail for a long time and the officers outside said they didn't stop him because you were with him." Michael exhaled then said, "I was with him because he had a knife in my back... those idiots have put this family in more danger than anything. Sam is not

261

to leave his room, so when it comes to dinner, he can wait until I bring it to him."

Elizabeth remained quiet as her husband stomped down the stairs like a bratty child. She lightly knocked on Sam's door and waited silently for a response that never came. She turned the knob and slowly opened the door to find Sam laying on his side sobbing. "Are you okay?" Elizabeth asked with a soft tone. "I'm never going to be like him. I don't want to be like him," Sam said as he wiped the tears from his face.

"No one ever said you have to be like your father," Elizabeth said, "Why do you feel like he wants you to?" Sam looked at her, "Because everything has to be his way. I have to do what he did when he was young. I am nothing like him and I am happy that way."

"If you are happy, why are you crying?" Elizabeth asked as she sat on the bed. "He told me to forget about Summer! She was kidnapped and I want to help find her," Sam said bluntly, "He wants me to stay in my room like a prisoner." Elizabeth looked around her son's room to see it was no longer that of a little boy. "You are growing up and that makes both your father and me feel old. Every generation wants the next to be better and I guess that is how your father wants you to be; better," Elizabeth said.

"How does telling me to forget about Summer make me better?" Sam replied. Elizabeth exhaled slightly, "Well she is a little old for you, but there is more than that I am sure. We married right out of high school and that really kept your father from having the dreams he wanted. I think he doesn't want you to be tied down to someone so young." Sam looked at his mother but he really did not understand what she meant. "Summer is so nice," Sam said.

"I am sure she is. She is also pretty too, but that does not make someone right for you. There is much more to love and Sam, if you were nineteen and she was twenty-five, we wouldn't care. As long as she didn't break your heart, neither of us wouldn't care." Sam rolled his eyes, "What is so different? Because I am fourteen?" Elizabeth shook her head, "Yes. She is a young woman who is going to college. You don't start high school until next year. You two have nothing in common and well… ugh… your choices don't have anything in common other than hormones."

Elizabeth stood up from the bed then turned back to Sam, "I need to get dinner started and try to get this house back into shape. I don't know if I will be able to sleep for days… You know Sam, you were very brave standing up like you did to Cletus. But remember bravery doesn't always work out like in the movies."

Sam watched as his mother walked out of the bedroom. He got up from the bed then walked to the door. He could hear the baseball game on the

TV downstairs and Danielle listening to music in her room. He closed his door softly then locked it. Though his mind was fuzzy, he remembered enough of the hypnosis that Summer was in an old factory. Where it was, he didn't know. He looked out his window to see there was a car parked on the street not far away. "That must be one of the cops," Sam said softly.

He knew he couldn't go out the front door without being seen by his father or the police stationed outside. Going down the back steps through the kitchen would mean being seen by his mother. He thought hard about getting out, then a small plan hatched. "The laundry chute!" Sam said out loud. It's been years since he took a ride down it and the beating his father gave him kept him from doing it again, but that was the only easy way out.

Sam opened his door then peered up and down the hallway to see no one was around. He walked down the hallway, past his sister's room whose door was cracked open, to a small closet next to the bathroom. He opened the wooden door with a long-drawn howl. He quickly got inside then closed the door behind him. In the corner of the closet was a small wooden door that opened to a sheet metal chute that went straight down to the basement. Sam opened the door then looked down to see that there was a small pile of clothes waiting for his mother.

The last time he took a ride it was head first, but he decided feet first may be a better solution this time. He placed one foot in then held to the opening so he could get the other foot in. The chute was little tighter then it was when Sam was five, but he knew he could make it. He held tightly to the opening as he let his butt slide into the opening. Before he could react, gravity took over and he fell to the basement. The pile of clothes did little to cushion the drop, but Summer is worth a little pain.

He picked himself up from the floor while hearing his parents talking in the kitchen. Sam could not make out what was being said, but he knew it had to be about him. As he started to walk, both of his feet started to ache from the wounds. The basement stairs would take him right to the kitchen, but the old coal door in the foundation wall would be easy to slip through. He went to the door to find it covered with cobwebs. Years ago, when a burglar was terrorizing the area, his father bolted it shut with a single lag bolt. Sam grabbed a wrench from an old crate of his grandfather's tools and went to work loosening the bolt.

The wrench grabbed into the head of the bolt as Sam pulled with all of his might to loosen it. With a violent tug, Sam could feel it breaking free. He kept working at the bolt all while hoping no one would come to check on him in his bedroom. Finally, the bolt was loose enough he could unscrew it with his fingers. He placed the crate of tools under the door then stepped on it so to be able to slide through the door. He pushed the cast iron door open then slid out into his mother's flowerbed.

As fast as he could, he ran to the garage and opened the side door. He grabbed his bicycle then rolled it to the gate in the fence along the alleyway. He started to feel bad about running like he did, but he knew Summer needed to be saved. Once in the alley, he jumped on his bike and peddled as hard as he could toward the factories on the outskirts of town.

Chapter 19

"That's where he lives?" Karen asked, "Looks like a nice, normal home." George looked over to her then said bluntly, "That's what they said about Gacy. You know how that story came out. How long do we have to wait on that judge?" Karen looked to her watch, "George, it's only been twenty minutes. His assistant was going to call the club and look for him." George exhaled, "Who knows what this guy is doing to that woman while the good judge is on the back nine... life it too short for golf!" Karen looked out toward the street, "I like to play golf you know... it never bothers you when I wear my golfing outfit." George looked over only to glare at her.

A squad car pulled up and parked on the curb behind the detective. Officer Stanton Smith stepped out then walked to the detectives open window. "We're waiting on the search warrant, officer," George said. "Why did you personally call for me to come here?" Stanton asked. "Well it comes full circle. This may be the man who buried the bodies along the tracks. But I also want to ask you if you have any relatives who live in town," George said

Stanton looked to the detective, "My parents do... why do you ask?" Karen was looking to George with as much curiosity as Stanton is. "I know Smith is a common name. I was wonder if you were related to a Wallace Smith." George said.

"Wallace? No, there is no Wallace in my family," Stanton said then asked, "Whose Wallace Smith?" George looked up to the officer, "The murderer." Stanton gave a queer look, "Detective, I have no murders in my family and I find it very offensive that you thought I might."

"What were you thinking?" Karen asked with disbelief. "Listen you two; this is not a sprawling metropolis. Smith is a common name, but it's also conceivable that in a town this small, people with the same last name may be related," George stated, "Damn, I wish they would radio already!" Stanton looked to the group of small homes, "Which one is it?"

George pointed to a small yellow house with brown shutters, "Two thirty-five." George looked back at his watch, "Okay this has been long enough. I don't see any vehicles here; let's just take a look around and peer in the windows." Karen placed her hand on George's arm, "You know the law. You can't be there without probable cause or a search warrant. Just wait for the judge to issue the warrant." George looked back to his girlfriend, "I know, I know... but you have to understand that a woman's life is at stake. We'll look around; we won't go inside... promise."

George opened his door, "Stay here. We'll be right back." Karen was not happy but also knew there was no way to stop George when he had a full head of steam. "You wait here out of sight. I'll knock on the door to see if anyone is home," George said to the officer. Stanton stood just at the corner of the house while George walked up onto a little covered porch then pushed the doorbell. He waited for a second then knocked on the door, "Hello is anyone home?"

George was startled when he heard the deadbolt being unlocked. The door slowly opened to show a small woman with snow white hair. "Ma'am, I'm Detective George Norris with the Richland County Sheriff's Department. I was wondering if Wallace Smith was home?" George asked with a gentle tone. "Oh no… Wallace is at work right now," the woman said in a frail tone. "Are you related to Mister Smith?" George asked. The woman smiled, "Yes, he is my older boy."

Stanton stayed at the corner of the house listening to the conversation. "You have many children?" George asked. "Oh yes… Wallace and Peter… and I had a daughter too, but she passed away when she was young," the woman said softly. Stanton looked around the corner to see George was slowly picking away at the elderly woman. "I'm very sorry to hear that," George said, "How old was she?" The woman looked up to the imposing detective, "Nine. There was an accident… My children were always so good."

George found the last statement as odd, "There were?" The woman smiled, "Oh yes… I'm very proud of the boys. Wallace and Peter have always been joined at the hip. Peter even worked with Wallace for a while, but he's never been one for hard work. So he quit the railroad." George was trying to find a way to ask about the daughter finding the direct route the best, "Ma'am, my I asked what happened to your daughter?"

The lady looked back into the house, "Oh dear, I think I hear my tea pot. Perhaps we could speak another time?" George was trying not to lose his cool, but his will was breaking, "Ma'am perhaps I can come in with you while you attend to the tea pot." The woman looked at George, "No. My boys always tell me not to let anyone in the house! Now you go and play somewhere else." George looked to the woman with a raise eyebrow, "Play? Ma'am who am I?" The old woman showed her short temper, "How should I know, just another one of the neighborhood bullies who pick on my boys. Now go before I call your father!"

"Ma'am, I am not a boy. I am a police detective. Now, where is Wallace?" George asked with a gritty tone. "Wallace? Oh, he's at work right now," the woman said pleasantly. Stanton stepped out from behind the corner of the house then shook his head at George. "Tell me about your daughter… the accident?" George asked with as much pleasantness that he could muster. "April. She was nine when it happened," the woman said. "Yes, the accident," George said. "It was an accident… Wallace didn't mean it," the woman said while trying to hold back tears, "He was just trying to help her!"

George placed his hands on the woman's shoulders, "Please Misses Smith, calm down. Let's go inside so you can relax and tell me about the accident." As he led the woman in the door, he waved at Stanton to come up onto the porch. The house was small and smelled of mothballs with the furniture clean and well kept. The woman sat in a wooden rocking chair as George remained standing near the open door. "Now, please tell me about the accident." George said.

The elderly woman rocked in her chair slowly while she hummed an unknown tune. George was trying to remain calm, "Ma'am, the story." The woman stopped humming then looked to the detective then stated bluntly, "He liked to touch her." Stanton leaned against the siding listening to the conversation. "Wallace?" George asked. The old woman turned away toward a wall of framed pictures, most of which were faded with time. "Did Wallace like to touch your daughter?" George asked with a stern tone. The woman remained looking at the photographs when she said, "No."

George walked over to the wall then looked to see pictures of happier times, "If not Wallace, then who?" The woman slowly raised her then with a frail finger pointed to a wedding photograph, "He did." George looked closely at the photograph to realize the bride was the old woman now before him. "Your husband?" George asked. "Yes," the woman said then started to hum the tune again.

"What was the accident?" George asked with a mellow tone. "Wallace was just trying to save her. That's all," the woman said with an angry attitude. "How did he try to save her?" George asked. "I was at church, it was Sunday morning… he would keep the children home so they wouldn't cause problems," the woman said while looking down toward the floor. George waved to Stanton then pointed to the wedding photograph.

Stanton walked in as the elderly woman continued the story. "He was asleep on the bed… with April. Wallace just wanted it to stop…," the woman said then started to sob. "Look at that man, he looks so familiar but I can't place him." George whispered to Stanton. "Wallace took a book of matches… he lit… he lit the mattress on fire," the woman said as she tried to hold back on crying. Stanton looked at the photograph then turned to the woman, "Ma'am, is your husband named Tim?"

The woman looked up with red, tear filled eyes, "Yes… how did you know?" George looked closer at the photograph, "Where is your husband now?" The woman shook her head, "He ran off years ago… he knew what he did… he knew he caused her to die." Stanton leaned into George and whispered, "She has no idea he lives less than a mile from here." George slightly nodded his head in agreement.

"The fire killed her?" George asked. "Yes," the woman said, "He woke from the heat and smoke… then ran out the door as the house went up around her. The boys had already ran out to the yard… I came home to find the house almost burned to the ground."

"Ma'am, I need to know where Wallace is," George stated with urgency. "Wallace? Do you know him?" the woman asked. "Why yes, of course… can you tell me where he is?" Stanton asked with a mellow tone. "At work like always," the woman said with a feisty streak reappearing. "How about your other son?" George asked.

"Peter? I don't know… he does odd jobs," the woman said. George looked back when he heard someone walking up the steps. "They just called you on the radio," Karen said slightly winded. "I'll be right back ma'am," George said then walked out the door only to stop next to Karen, "Try talking with her…please."

Karen looked at the woman with a pleasant smile, "Hello, I'm Karen. What is your name?" The woman looked up to see Karen, "My boys would like you. You're so very pretty. They like the pretty girls." Karen tried to smile, "Do your boys live here?" The woman slightly shook her head, "Wallace does every day, but Peter doesn't always come home." Stanton piped up, "Does Peter have his own house?"

"I don't know… sometimes he comes… sometimes he goes. Such a free spirit, but they love the pretty women," the woman said just as George

273

returned. "Was it important?" Karen asked. "Two fold, the judge approved the warrant... a clerk is on her way here with it," George said slightly winded, "The other can be a complication... Sam ran away. His mother thinks he's going to find Summer."

"Ma'am, no more games. I am here to search the premises in connection with the disappearance of a local woman. Your son Wallace is a person on interest. Where the hell is he?" George asked with a raised tone. "At work, damnit!" the woman fired back, "He's a good boy!" Karen looked to George then said, "How about Peter? Is he a good boy too?" The woman slightly shook her head then said softly, "Yes but he reminds me of his father." Karen asked gently, "His father?" George interrupted, "It's a long story. We need to start looking. The clerk will be here any minute."

"You get out of my home. All of you!" the woman shouted, "Little hooligans who pick on my boys! Get out!" George looked to Stanton, "Take her to your car." Karen's eyes grew large, "That's not necessary. I'll stay here with her; you two do what you need to do... Ma'am, tell me about the pretty girls your boys like." Before the woman could speak, George interrupted, "Where do your boys sleep?" The woman looked to George, "Screw off... the pretty girl is talking to me now."

"Tear this place apart if you need to," George said bluntly to Stanton. "Now, please tell me about the girls," Karen said. "Oh, ever since they were in school they always brought home pretty girls… They would listen to their rock and roll records… always the pretty girls. My boys, they knew how to find them," the woman said. "Ma'am, what is your name?" Karen asked. "It's Ester, what is yours?" the woman asked. Karen smiled, "I'm Karen, remember?" The woman smiled, "Oh yes, Karen. Do you go to school with my boys?"

George and Stanton walked through the small house looking for clues of where Summer was. "This house looks like a museum," Stanton said. "I know, it almost seems to be too clean, too well kept," George said. He opened a door into a small bedroom that was clearly that of the woman. "Her room is just as sterile as the rest of the house. Where the hell do the men sleep? There is only one bedroom." George asked.

Stanton found a door off the hallway with a small combination lock on it. "Do you want to take a bet this is where they sleep," Stanton said. "Do you have something in the car we can break it with?" George asked. "I think so, I'll be right back," Stanton said. He walked through the hallway then out into the living room to see Karen chatting with the elderly mother.

"Do the boys still bring home pretty girls?" Karen asked with a naive tone. "Oh no… I always hoped they would find nice girls to marry, but they never did." Ester said. "Does Wallace or Peter drink; do they have many friends?" Karen asked.

"Drink, oh heavens no. This is a dry house. I do not allow liquor," Ester said with a raised tone. "Friends?" Karen asked. "Well I don't know. No one ever comes by… I see them riding their bikes or playing ball… but not with my boys," Ester said with a somber tone.

Stanton reappeared with a small crowbar. "What are you doing young man?!" Ester said with wide eyes. "I'm here to help your boys… work on the house," Stanton said calmly. "Work on the house? Oh… I see," Ester said then calmed down. Stanton walked swiftly toward the door. "Quick thinking… you might just be a detective yet," George said, "See if you can pop the lock off." Stanton placed the flat end of the bar behind the clasp then pushed the bar against the trim. With a grunt, Stanton popped the lock free.

"I hope this was worth the effort," George said then opened the door that led to the basement steps. George flipped the light switch causing a small bulb at the bottom of the steps to light. The men walked down the stairs remaining quiet listening for anything that didn't sound normal. George stepped onto the tile floor then found a switch that turned all of the lights on in the finished basement. "Very sixties," Stanton said, "Complete with a broken lava lamp."

George looked around the beat-up furniture for anything of importance. "Fuck, she's not here!" George exclaimed out of exhaustion and frustration.

"Look at the windows," Stanton said, "they are all blacked out." George walked over to one of the windows then felt the glass with his fingers, "Black paint. They didn't want anyone to know what they were doing here."

Stanton went into a closet built under the staircase. "I found a bunch of movies," Stanton said, "You aren't going to believe this." George walked over to Stanton who was holding a strip of film up to the light. "Snuff films it looks like," Stanton said. George looked in the closet to find piles of pornographic magazines. He pulled a few out to show Stanton, "Looks like they are really into the lifestyle."

As Stanton dug in a box filled with film canisters, he found a binder buried at the bottom. He took the box to the couch then poured the contents out onto the cushions. The binder was caught in the box, but Stanton easily ripped the box freeing its contents. "What did you find?" George asked. "Some binder," Stanton said as he flipped the cover open, "son of a bitch."

"What is it?" George asked as he threw the smut magazines back on their pile. "Photographs, names… dates," Stanton said, "They kept track of everyone they killed." George took the binder from Stanton then flipped through the pages, "My God… what they did to them; then had the gall to photograph them while they did it."

"Shit, this still doesn't tell us where the woman is!" Stanton said. George exhaled, "You're starting to sound like me. Take a look at the background behind the women. Through all these years it looks to be the same." Stanton took the book back to closely examine the pictures, "It looks like some kind of factory." George shook his head, "Yes, just like Sam said where Summer is. Can you think of any abandoned factories?"

Stanton thought hard, "Not really, not in town at least. There might be some out in the country."

"Sam said something about paper. Like there was a sign that said paper. When I was a kid there was a paper mill outside of town, but I swear it was torn down. At least my father told me it was going to be torn down after he tarred me for playing hooky to go explore it with my friends," George said thinking out loud. "Do you remember where it is?" Stanton asked. "Yes, out in the woods not far from the river. Maybe a good four miles outside of town... I think there was a rail spur that ran there. Yeah, there was. That's how we got out there, we walked the tracks."

"Let's get out there. I can put this stuff in my car," Stanton said. As he picked the binder up, they heard Karen scream. George took off up the stairs as fast as his knees would allow him. He came into the living room to find Karen on the floor with the elderly woman out cold. "What happened?"

George asked. Karen's face was red, "She tried to strangle me! The old bitch thought she could strangle me."

George tried not to smile, "So you knocked her out?" Karen shook her head, "Yes I did and I'll do it again if she wakes back up. She is off her rocker. No wonder her son may be a killer." Stanton came with the box of movies and the binder lying on top of them, "There is no may be, he and is brother both are killers."

"Did you find something?" Karen asked. Stanton took the binder out of the box then handed it to Karen. She opened the cover then gasped, "They did this?" George shook his head, "Yes and it looks like they enjoyed themselves. All forty-one victims are in there." Stanton piped up, "Now we know who they all are."

"Call the ambulance then have her placed under a committal review," George said to Karen, "We're going to find where Summer is once and for all. You can take my car once they take the old loon away." Karen looked to George, "You are having more officers going with you? Right?" George shook his head in agreement, "Of course."

Chapter 20

Sam rode his bike like he never had before. His feet were burning from the pain of the cuts, but he paid them little attention. The industrial area of Riley was located north of the town center and surrounded the rail line. Sam knew wherever Summer was, it was old and no longer used, however the businesses in town all looked to be open and operating. This included the mill his father worked at.

He was going so fast his bike went airborne as he hit the rail crossing. He landed on the other side of the tracks then turned quickly paying little attention to traffic. He entered the parking lot of the old station doing his best to avoid potholes and broken beer bottles. Just beyond the station was the start of the industrial section. He slowed his bike looking for anything that resembled what he remembered from the hypnosis.

The area was filled with the sights and sounds of industry; smoke stakes belching smoke, power lines buzzing with current and the occasional profanity as workers sat on the open docks getting fresh air or having a smoke. Sam hoped no one from the mill would recognize him as he rode around looking for that brick building with a sign that said paper. Sam stopped his bike between two cars so he could slip his shoe off. The pain in his right foot was becoming worse. He took his shoe off to find his white sock was now stained pink.

He slipped his shoe back on just in time to see a squad car coming slowly down the street. He walked his bike to the opposite side of the cars then scrunched down until the police passed. He could hear the car slowly rumble by and much to his relief it kept going. Sam stood up only to see a man walking toward him "Hey kid! What are you up to?" the man asked.

Sam tried to think of an excuse but his mind just wasn't working right. "You are looking for open cars, are you?" the man asked. "No mister. I'm down here to see my father… he works over in the wire mill," Sam said. The man raised his eyebrow, "Really? What is your old man's name?" Sam used his most pleasant tone, "Michael White." The man smiled, "Mike is your old man? You must be Sam then. Shit, he talks about you all the time. Said you going to be the next star quarterback."

Sam smiled, "Yes sir, he always hoped I would be…" The guy hit Sam on the shoulder just hard enough to hurt, "Tell your old man Leroy Wilson says hi!" Sam shook his head, "Yes Sir I will… Hey, maybe you could help me so I do not have to bother my father at work." Leroy thought for a moment then asked with a suspicious tone, "What do you need?" Sam quickly thought of how to ask what he needed, "I'm doing a report for school on the industry of Riley. I saw an old picture of a factory, but all I could tell is that it is a brick building and a sign that said paper. I would like to use it on the section of past businesses of Riley."

Leroy looked to the side then said, "I bet you that was the old paper mill. My grandfather first worked there when he moved from Mississippi. Sadly, it closed not long after. Its south of here about three or four miles... you can get to it off of County T not far from the river, but I think it was torn down though. I used to play there when I was a kid; creepy old building for sure." Sam was about to thank the man when a whistle blew. "Say hi to your old man, I have to get back to work!" Leroy yelled as he jogged back to the building. As Leroy disappeared through a garage style door, Sam yelled, "Thanks!"

Sam jumped on his bike and with all of the strength, determination and love he had, he took off to find the old paper mill. He cut across the front of the train station then rode onto the ties of the railroad tracks off of the crossing. The quickest way out to County T was the trail through the woods. As he came close to the forty-one mile marker, he hopped off his bike then carried it over the rail and down the embankment. He jumped back on the bike then rode the trail as fast as he could through puddles, mud holes and branches that would assault his face as he passed.

The trees blocked much of the sunlight from the trail. As Sam rode he heard a voice say, "Help me!" Sam knew it was Summer calling out to him for help. This caused him to push even harder. He was going so fast he flew uphill on the trail to County T and landed in the middle of the road right in front of truck hauling grain. The driver laid on both the horn and brakes, swerving to just miss Sam.

As the man yelled in anger, Sam took off down the road toward the river bridge. Sam looked over to the Jones farm as he passed wondering if he would ever be able to talk with Johnnie and Donnie again. Far behind Sam a green car was coming up the road. Sam didn't know it was back behind him and he truly didn't know he should be worried.

"Do you see who that is up there?" Wallace asked. "Damn sure I do, I'm gonna hold back a bit so we don't spook him," Peter said. "Do you think he knows about the building?" Wallace asked as he pulled a revolver out of the glove box. "He knew where the women are, so he probably knows about the building," Peter said with an angered tone, "I can't wait to rip that little fuck apart." Wallace laughed, "You keep thinking about the boy... I got my mind on that little filly."

Sam slowed his bike to a stop on top of the river bridge. He looked around for anything that resembled the factory, but it was mostly forest. He started to pedal again slowly when he noticed muddy tire tracks coming onto the road just down from the bridge. He rode his bike over there to find a small road that led into the woods. Without hesitation he took off down the broken path.

Peter stopped the car just short of the trail. "What are you waiting for?" Wallace asked. "I want him to get inside the building. If he's outside we have more chances of losing him," Peter said, "he should be there in a few minutes. We'll wait then pull the car in just past the tree line. We can go in on foot from there so as to not scare him." Peter looked at his watch, "Two minutes."

Sam was riding briskly down the old roadway. The trees were flying by so fast it was as if it was a green wall on either side. As he rounded a curve he came to the parking lot and with that it was as if he was shocked back into his trance. It was just as he pictured it. A brink factory that was decaying away and near the top was the faded word, 'PAPER'.

Sam looked for Red or any cars, but he did not see anything that didn't look rotting, broken or lost in time. He rode to within a few feet of the door then jumped off of his bike allowing it to coast to soft crash in a bush. The handle of the door had a length of chain through it that ran around an old standpipe. Sam unlooped the chain then pulled it out of the handle. He pushed the door finding it surprisingly easy to open. As he walked in he saw nothing but complete darkness.

He turned his head to see light coming from the end of the hallway. As he walked, he heard voices calling to him in varying tone and volume, "Save her... save her." It was not a singular voice but many of them, all women. The voices were all around him yet they did not scare him one bit. As

Sam walked into the production area, he knew this was the place. "Summer!" Sam yelled so loud it reverberated through the building, "Summer!" He listened, but all he heard were insects buzzing and the occasion dripping of water.

As he walked, he kept an eye out for Red. Suddenly Sam recognized the area where Summer was chained. He ran there only to find the mattress and the shackle. His mind started to swirl with worry that Summer was already dead. "Summer! Where are you?!" Sam yelled again. Sam listened for her voice, but he did not hear anything. As he continued to walk he saw a staircase that went down. He was about to pass it when a voice whispered, "Downstairs…"

Sam quickly obeyed the hint and then carefully went down the stairs. As he came below the floor line he looked for any signs of Red, any sign of anyone. Yet he only saw debris and rotting pipes. "Summer!" Sam yelled. He listened to his heart beating in his ears then from the distance he heard, "Help me!" Sam ran as fast as he could toward the voice jumping over anything in his path.

"I told he would walk right in, didn't I," Peter said with a smug attitude, "Come on as quietly as we can." Wallace held the revolver in his right hand as he walked into the darkness. "What should we do when we find him?" Wallace asked. "Grab him… idiot," Peter replied bluntly.

As they entered the production area they could hear Sam. "Summer, talk so I can find you!" Sam yelled at the top of his lungs. "Here! I'm in a storeroom or something," Summer cried. Sam followed her voice like a roadmap through the debris. He came into a large room where some old furniture made a makeshift sitting room and a floor to ceiling chain linked fence surrounded a bank of shelving. Standing there with her fingers gripping the gate was Summer.

Sam ran toward her like a lovesick child. "Sam!" Summer yelled, "How did you find me?" Sam smiled, "It wasn't easy, but I did it. Now I have to get you out of here." Sam looked for something he could use to cut the fencing. "Sam, they are trying to find you... You have to be careful!" Summer whispered. Sam went to dig through the rotting boxes when he heard something. He looked to Summer then held his index finger to his lips. She shook her head in agreement then went to hide behind some of the racking.

Wallace and Peter walked into the room. "Where are you, boy?" We know you're here!" Wallace announced. Peter remained quiet as he looked for the boy around piles of boxes and debris. Wallace looked toward the storeroom but didn't see Summer. "Fuck! She's gone!" Wallace yelled like a bear. "She's there you idiot, she's just hiding," Peter said bluntly, "Don't worry, she's waiting for you... She's your just reward."

Sam knelt down behind a rusting metal cabinet while looking for anything to use as a weapon. He could hear footsteps coming toward him. In the corner of the room was a bathroom and in the broken mirror he could see Peter slowly creeping toward him. Sam's heart was racing and his adrenaline was pumping. Just as Peter came in front of the cabinet, Sam stood up and using all his strength pushed the cabinet onto the man.

The sound of the cabinet crashing caused Wallace to come running to see what had happened. Sam ran to find shelter but there was none. Wallace quickly saw him then fired a shot in his direction. It narrowly missed Sam who now ran toward a dark staircase. Wallace placed the gun into his pocket then pulled the cabinet off of his brother who laid there a broken man. "Are you okay?" Wallace asked. Peter moved his right fingers, "I can't breathe easily. I think he broke my ribs."

Wallace looked around, "Where are you? I promised I won't hurt you or the girl." Summer was peering out from behind the shelf to see Peter lying on the floor. Summer let out a laugh hoping it would give Sam time to run for help. "Quit laughing!" Wallace yelled. "Your brother was flattened like the cockroach he is," Summer said then laughed again. "I said to quit!" Wallace yelled fiercely.

"What wrong? Don't like to hear women laugh? Is it because anytime you were with a woman she would laugh at your tiny dick?" Summer said with a humorous tone. Sam was quietly moving behind the angered man. "Shut up!" Wallace yelled, "I can't wait to rip you apart!"

Sam came to a large crate that he could hide behind. On the floor were pieces of concrete that had long since fallen out of the wall. He looked up to see Wallace staring toward the storeroom. Sam took one of the chunks and threw it toward the stairs as hard as he could. The sound caused Wallace to spin around and run toward the stairs. Sam watched the hulking man run pass him then slowly climbed the stairs. Sam then ran to the fence looking for a way to get it apart.

He tried to twist the nuts with his bare hands, but they were heavily rusted. He looked to the fence to see if it could be folded up, but there was a base rail that it was firmly wired to. "Summer," Sam whispered as quietly as he could, "Can you find any tools in there?" She peeked her head out from behind the racking, "No, these boxes are nothing but old parts." Sam looked back toward the stairs when he heard a noise. He turned back to Summer, "Look for anything that I can cut the wire with."

Summer started to quietly search the shelves as Sam carefully crept toward Peter. The man was laying in his a small, yet growing pool of blood. Sam placed his shoe on the side of Peter's head then asked, "Do you have tools here?" Peter made a gurgling noise as he tried to talk, "You will be dead soon." Sam could feel pure evil and hatred coming over him. He took his shoe off of the man's head and with all his weight, stood on the man's neck. With a large popping noise, Peter was now silent for good.

He stepped away from Peter in time to hear boots coming down the steps. "Hide!" Sam whispered to Summer as he ran into the far darkness of the room. Wallace walked out into the light then proceeded to check his brother. He quickly saw the bloody shoe print on Peter's neck. "Peter!" Wallace yelled. He reached down and placed his right hand on his brother's neck but he could not feel a pulse.

"Come out and fight me like a man!" Wallace yelled. Sam stayed in the darkness hoping he could find a way to take the much larger brother out just as easy. "Cat have your tongue?" Wallace asked, "I know what will bring you out." He reached into Peter's pocket to pull out a small key ring. He quickly found a small brass key that he then inserted it into the lock on the gate. Sam couldn't believe the key was right there in reach the whole time.

Wallace slid the gate open and walked in going right behind the racking and out of the sight of Sam. Suddenly he could hear Summer screaming. He went to run for her when he saw Wallace walking out from the racking with his arm around Summer's waist. He was carrying her with no problem as she flailed about trying to break free of his tight grip. "Come out here! Come here or I'll break her in half!" Wallace yelled.

Sam found the courage to start walking out into the light when a voice came from the stairs, "Put, put, put her back! N, n, n, now!" Sam knew the only person who spoke like that was Tim and what he thought might mean they were saved was quickly dowsed. "Take ca, ca, care of thhh, thhh, the boy first," Tim stuttered out, "Where… where are you boy?! I, I, I told you to stay, stay, stay away. Yooo, you didn't listen!"

From the darkness Sam appeared with no worries or fear. "We found your pictures. We knew you were sick but I guess we didn't know how sick you were," Sam said. Tim smiled with his dirty teeth, "You th, th, think yo, yo, you can take us on?" Sam shook his head, "I do. I'm young and quick on my feet. You two are old."

Wallace threw Summer to the concrete floor like a sack of potatoes then slammed the gate shut. "I'll take care of him Pa," Wallace said. "He's your son?" Sam asked in horror, "I thought your family died in a fire?" Tim looked to the boy with blank eyes, "My daughter died in a fire Wallace set. Sadly he didn't know he was just like his father. The same cravings, the same desires. My other boy was just like us. I took off so the law couldn't get me but I kept in touch with them."

"You're not stuttering!" Sam exclaimed. Tim smiled, "It's nothing but an act. No one wants to mess with the crazy old man from the woods." Wallace started to shuffle his feet to take off after Sam however he was already in the position to run. He took off toward the stairs with speed even he didn't know he had, "Come get me, lard ass!"

Wallace was more than happy to do as the boy asked however his large, clunky feet were no match for the boy. Sam ran up the stairs then darted toward the equipment. He stood behind a large press while waiting for Wallace to come up the stairs. The man appeared then stopped to look around for the boy. "I'm over here!" Sam yelled, "You think you can get me? I'll take you out just like your brother!"

"Keep talking kid, I know right where you are," Wallace said as he took off running toward the press. Sam ran behind another piece of equipment waiting for Wallace to appear. "Did you find me yet?" Sam said humorously. The man was growing more angered by the second. As he walked around the equipment, Sam walked down the other side then came around to see Wallace's back. He picked up a glass jar then with the best aim he had, hit Wallace squarely in the back of his head.

Much to Sam's surprise, the jar bounced off his thick skull then hit the floor and shattered. Wallace spun around like a top and was ready to charge the boy. Sam took off running this time knowing he had unleashed more that he could handle. As he came around another rusting piece of equipment, he almost fell into a deep pit. He stopped right at the edge then carefully walked around it as a scream came from the lower level.

Sam ran toward the stairs as fast as he could with Wallace coming close behind. Sam flew down the stairs then ran toward the stockroom where Summer was held. As he came close he found Tim trying to push her down to the floor. Sam ran in the open gate, grabbed a small crate then hit Tim squarely in the back. The elderly man went down to his knees.

"Come on!" Sam yelled as he grabbed Summers' left hand. She tried to do her best to run in her bare feet. Instead of running toward the stairs, he pulled her into the darkness. "Stay here," Sam whispered. As Sam came back into the light, Wallace was near the bottom of the stairs. "You're not very smart," Wallace said, "There is no way out of here. All the doors are chained."

"You may know this building better than me," Sam said defiant, "but I have age on my side. I'm ready for more and you can barely catch your breath." Tim was stumbling to get back to his feet, "She's loose, find her you idiot." Tim stumbled then fell back onto the floor smacking his head hard. Wallace couldn't decide who he should take care of first, but Sam made the decision for him. He ran right toward the man with as much speed as he could muster slamming right into his large gut.

292

Wallace fell backward but caught himself on the railing for the stairs. Sam bounced down onto his right side hurting his arm, but still managed to get to his feet. He stumbled past Wallace then ran back up the stairs, but stopped short of the top to look down. As Wallace looked up to him, Sam stood his ground. Wallace slowly reached into his pocket to retrieve his revolver. Sam stepped backward up one step now standing firmly on the floor. "It's over kid, you can keep running all you like, but you're not making it out of here alive. I'm going to bury you right next to her," Wallace said as he pulled the revolver into view, "You run and I'm going to find her and put a bullet between her eyes. Maybe if you cooperate, she can live."

Sam shook his head franticly to show disbelief, "You just said you will kill both of us. Make up your mind!" Wallace swiftly raised the gun then shot toward Sam, but he was still too fast for the man. "Come get me, asshole!" Sam yelled. He ran behind a group of electrical panels where he could watch the stairs through a gap between the panels.

Wallace came up the stairs with the gun firmly out in front of himself. "This isn't like the movies kid, you're no hero," Wallace yelled into the void. Sam watched him as he came toward him, but totally unaware he was behind the panels. He was trying to plan another move, but his arm was starting to throb horribly.

Summer came out of the darkness then slowly walked toward the cage where Tim was lying on the floor. She pulled the gate slowly hoping Wallace would not hear it. It made a grinding noise as the rusted wheels slowly turned. She had about a three-foot opening she needed to close before she could lock it. As the gate slid, Tim started to move his head and moan a bit. He turned his head when the gate made a high pitch screech.

"You think you're going to get free of me? I have a lot of determination." Tim said with a slight moan. Summer slammed the gate shut, then picked the lock up from the floor and used it to lock the gate. She picked the key up from the floor and threw it into the darkness. "I am free," Summer said. She walked over to Peter's body and searched his pockets. She pulled out his wallet, a pocketknife and a gold lighter. Tim tried his best to lean himself up against one of the racks.

Summer looked at the elderly man with a smile, "I'm going to make you feel like all of those women and girls felt." She flicked the lighter using it to light a pile of rubbish on fire near the fence then pushed a pile of old boxes into the flames. Quickly the flames reached the ceiling as Summer found more things that would burn to throw into the fire. The heat was becoming immense as other items in the room started to catch fire. "I hope you enjoy the flames. You best get used to them," Summer said.

As she came up the stairs, the smoke came closely behind her. Sam was behind the electrical panels watching Wallace carefully look behind the equipment debris. As he saw Summer come up the stairs he yelled, "Over here! Come find me, asshole!" Wallace quickly ran toward the voice not even noticing Summer or the smoke billowing up through the hole in the floor. Sam's heart was racing again and with every beat, he could feel further pain in his arm.

As Wallace came close, Sam took off running as fast as he could toward the pit in the floor. Wallace took aim, but Sam made it to behind the press before he would get the shot off. Sam stood behind the press, "Come on! You can do better than that!" Summer stood behind a steel column trying to stay out of sight of the angered beast. Wallace carefully walked around the press listening for any sound of movement.

As he came closer to the corner of the machine, Sam waited. He tried not to breathe knowing that Wallace would pick out any sound. Just was Wallace came to the corner of the press, Sam jumped out and with all the strength he could muster pushed the large man backward into the pit. Sam cried out in pain as there was a large snap in his arm. As Wallace landed in the pit, a splash of stagnant water flew up out of the pit.

As the pain overtook him, Sam carefully walked to the edge to see Wallace lying in the water;

his face just above the waterline. "I guess I won," Sam said to the man. Wallace looked to the boy with his eyes then stated coldly, "Those voices you hear… we all heard them. Those voices will haunt you until the day you die… I hope you can handle it…" Wallace tried to move but he was stuck to debris under the water. Sam watched the man soaking in the pit but remained silent. Wallace's face grimaced in pain then said, "Those voices… they caused us to do what we did. If you hear them, they already have you."

Summer came running up to Sam, "Are you hurt bad?" Sam looked to the woman he wanted to love more than anything, "Naw, just a scratch or two." There was the sound of cracking and popping coming from the stairs. "We better get out of here," Summer said, "I made sure the old man could get a taste of hell." As they started to walk away from the pit, Wallace let out a terrific laugh. "You think you made it out?" Wallace yelled, "You haven't yet! It already has you. It won't let you go…"

Sam looked back toward the pit. "Pay him no attention, he's nuts," Summer said. As they walked toward the hallway that lead to the door, Summer asked, "Why did you come to find me?" Sam started to blush as his awkward fourteen-year-old self took over. Summer remained quiet waiting for an answer. She stopped walking and grabbed his hand, "Please tell me."

He looked to the floor trying to find the courage. "I like you," Sam said softly. Summer smiled then wrapped her arms around his neck and gave him a tight hug. "You're not a boy anymore, today you became a man," Summer whispered into his ear. He slowly wrapped his good arm around her waist and held her tight. "I think we better get out of here," Summer said softly. Sam didn't want it to end but slowly loosened his grip.

They walked to the door and as Sam went to pull the door open, it wouldn't budge. "What the hell, I opened it with no problem when I came in," Sam said out loud. He reached around the frame in the dark feeling for anything that would keep the door to move. Summer looked back down the dark hallway to see flames shooting up from the stairs. She grabbed the handle and pulled with all of her strength, "It won't budge!"

"Stay here," Sam said, "I'll be right back." He took off running back toward the pit. As he came to the edge he peered in to see Wallace lying where they left him. "What's wrong boy? Can't get out?" Wallace laughed. "Why won't the door open?" Sam pleaded. Wallace smiled, "My old man must have chained it from the outside." Sam was growing angry, "If he chained it, how did he get in?"

Wallace gave a small chuckle then coughed as the smoke was starting to collect in the pit, "I don't know. He knew far more about this building then we did. This was his personal playground."

Sam went to go back to Summer but Wallace's voice stopped him. "That smell… that smell she has, it draws you in, doesn't it?" Wallace asked in a grim voice, "You want to taste her… you've never tasted a woman before, have you?"

Sam remained silent not giving in to the mad man. "You know you want to… this is your chance to take her, do what you want with her," Wallace said then started to choke on the smoke. Sam went back to the edge, "I'm not a monster like you or your family." The dark thick smoke was filling the pit but under it all Wallace said with his last breath, "We weren't monsters, we were chosen. You have been chosen too."

As Sam started to choke on the smoke that was swirling around him like a vortex, a hand grabbed his arm and pulled him out. He was having a hard time seeing until bright sunlight shone through the smoke. He was led to an open door that went outside. "How did you find this Summer?" Sam asked as he walked out into the tall weeds. He turned toward the hand, but no one was there. The door quickly slammed in his face as smoke started pouring out of the broken windows far about his head.

"Summer!" Sam yelled as he pushed on the door with his good arm. It wouldn't budge at all. He ran through the weeds to find the door he had entered. On the ground the chain laid, nothing was holding the door closed. He tried to push on the door but it wouldn't budge. "Summer!" Sam cried. From behind the door he could hear her crying, "It's hard to breath."

Sam yelled into the door as loud as he could, "Pull on the handle as I push." Summer grasped the handle and pulled as hard as she could. Outside Sam pushed with the door starting to open slightly then slamming shut on its own. A brisk wind picked up and as it swirled through the broken windows Sam swore he heard the building say, "No." He was crying as he pushed on the door as hard has he could. Behind him the sound of sirens could be heard.

Sam turned around in time to see squad cars coming into the parking lot. "Here!" Sam yelled, "Help me!" Detective Norris and Officer Smith where the first to run to the boy. "Summer is behind the door, it won't budge!" Sam exclaimed. The men ran to the door and both pushed as hard as they could as the building groaned, "NO!" Stanton looked over to George, "Did you hear that?" George shook his head then yelled to the other officers, "Come here and help!"

Sam moved out of the way as four more men ran to help push the door open. "Summer, move back from the door!" George yelled, "Okay men, all push on my word… now!" The six men pushed against the stubborn door and as it finally yielded to the men, Summer was able to crawl out through their legs. Sam grabbed her then hugged her tight. Suddenly the door pushed back at the men with enough force to push all of them back onto one another.

The sound of screams and cries could be heard emulating from the building. "I swore I heard the building say no," Stanton said as he was trying to catch his breath. "It did," Summer said, "Then it told me I was his… I swore I heard women screaming inside… crying in pain." Sam looked to Summer, "They were all dead. The whole family was dead." Summer shook her head in agreement, "But whoever he was… he wasn't dead." They stood there watching the building fall into itself and with every burst of flame or shower of sparks, they would hear cries.

"Let's get away from this thing," George said, "before it falls on us." The small group retreated to his car as the building groaned and screamed like a trapped animal. Sam looked to an upper window where the face of a young woman looked down upon them. He slowly raised his hand to wave to her just as the window blew out from the force of a small explosion. "Did you just see that?" Stanton asked George. "A woman's face…" George stated coldly, "No… no I did not see a thing."

Sam sat on the hood of the detective's car with Summer right next to him. With his good hand, he slowly reached over and grabbed her hand. She did not say a thing but squeezed his hand tight and slightly leaned into him placing her head against his as tears streamed down her face.

Stanton was watching the flames with awe when George touched him on the arm. When Stanton looked to him, he nodded toward Sam and whispered, "The kid has the touch, doesn't he?" Stanton rolled his eyes and shook his head in disbelief.

- The end -